Dog Team

Dog Team

Zari

www.urbanbooks.net

Urban Books, LLC
300 Farmingdale Road, N.Y.-Route 109
Farmingdale, NY 11735

ISBN 13: 978-1-64556-587-1
EBOOK ISBN: 978-1-64556-668-7

First Trade Paperback Printing July 2024
Printed in the United States of America

10 9 8 7 6 5 4 3 2 1

Distributed by Kensington Publishing Corp.
Submit Orders to:
Customer Service
400 Hahn Road
Westminster, MD 21157-4627
Phone: 1-800-733-3000
Fax: 1-800-659-2436

Chapter One

Dressed in black Dickies women's long-sleeve coveralls and Adidas women's Ultraboost 22 running shoes, Elontra Montgomery and Shemika Frazier exited the Twenty-third Street subway station, located at the intersection of East Twenty-third Street and Eighth Avenue in Chelsea. This Manhattan art district was packed with trendy shops, galleries, and restaurants.

"Remind me when we're done with this that I need to stop at the store," Shemika said as they walked down Broadway.

"What kind of store do you need to go to?" Elontra asked as they passed Zona Sul Coffee.

"A grocery store," Shemika said as they waited for the light at Broadway to change before they crossed and then continued walking down East Twenty-first Street.

"You just went to the grocery store yesterday. What did you forget?" Elontra asked.

"I need to pick up some cooking spray."

"What you gonna cook?"

"I was thinking about making a lemon garlic pork tenderloin in the Ninja Foodi Grill."

"Hmm. That sounds good. What you gonna fix with it?" she asked as the light changed and they crossed the street and continued down Fifth Avenue.

"I was thinking about cooking red skin mashed potatoes and roasted brussels sprouts with bacon and Dijon mustard sauce," Shemika said, glancing at Elontra and waiting for her big smile to turn into a frown. It didn't take long.

"Mika?"

"What?" she giggled.

"You know I hate brussels sprouts."

"I know you hate brussels sprouts." She paused and smiled. "That's why I'm making your favorite braised red cabbage and cucumber vinegar salad."

"You are too good to me," Elontra said to the woman who had been one of her best friends since fourth grade.

"I know. I'm great. You are so fortunate to have a friend like me."

"Yes, I am, and a friend who cooks."

It wasn't that Elontra couldn't cook, she just never felt like cooking.

Ever.

And besides, Shemika was such a great cook that she didn't need to.

"You ready?" Elontra asked as they arrived at their destination.

"When have I ever not been ready?"

"You remember that time me, you, and Dee Dee were going to hop the train at Woodhaven Boulevard, and we missed the train because your sneakers were untied?"

Shemika stopped. "Really? That's what you got?" She paused and looked at Elontra. "We were thirteen!" she protested.

"You asked."

Shemika shook her head. "Let's just go do this."

"I'm ready!" Elontra said excitedly with a big smile on her face and her gloved hands raised in the air.

Shemika pointed in her face. She was wearing gloves too. "You stupid. That's what your problem is. You stupid."

"Always have been," she said and pulled down her ski mask. "Since the day we met."

"I don't know why I keep hanging around with you," Shemika said as she pulled down her ski mask, and they both took out their guns.

Elontra grabbed the handle to open the door, and the two women rushed into the Joaillerie Earth Jewelry store.

"Everybody down!" Elontra yelled, standing with her arms spread eagle and a gun in each of her hands.

The customers and the store employees looked at the two armed, masked female bandits and, as they were told, got down on the floor. Shemika moved quickly toward the security guard and pointed her gun at his head.

"I don't want to kill you, and you don't want to die." Shemika took the gun from the security guard and quickly removed the shells from the clip. "Now get down on the floor!"

Elontra holstered one weapon and pulled out a stopwatch. "Two minutes!" she announced.

As Elontra covered the room, she kept an eye on the security guard just in case he wanted to be a hero. Shemika quickly sprayed black paint on the lenses of the security cameras in the jewelry store. Then she took out large cloth bags, went behind the counter, and approached the first case. Shemika pointed her weapon at the clerk who was lying on the floor.

"Get up!" she ordered and moved the gun to her head.

She put up her hands and got up shaking. "Please don't kill me," she pleaded, silently praying that this wasn't her day to die.

"Behave yourself and I won't have to." Shemika handed her the bag. "Fill it up. And if your hand goes anywhere near the silent alarm, I will end you, understand?" she said, pressing the barrel of the gun to her head.

"Ninety seconds!" Elontra shouted and took a few steps to where the store manager was lying on the floor. She would have use for him soon enough.

The display cases were filled with an assortment of gold and diamond-studded rings, necklaces, brooches, earrings, and bracelets. As quickly as she could, and with her hands shaking, the clerk picked up the pieces and put them in the bag.

Once the case was empty, Shemika forced the clerk toward the next case. The watches were next. The clerk quickly removed Rolexes and other expensive watches and then placed them in the bag.

"One minute!"

"Move," Shemika ordered and moved her to the display case that contained diamond rings. The clerk reached in and began to remove the rings, dropping them in the bag.

It was at that second that Shemika saw out of the corner of her eye one of the other clerks reaching into his pocket. "You've got movement on your three."

Elontra stepped up to him quickly and kicked the clerk in the face.

"Ouch!" he yelled.

She pointed her gun at him. "Do you really wanna die today?"

The clerk quickly put his hands out in front of him. Elontra raised her weapon and checked the time before moving back toward the spot where the manager was lying. Once the clerk had finished filling the bag with jewelry, diamond-studded bracelets, expensive watches, and diamond rings, Shemika snatched the bag from her hand.

"Now get back down on the floor," she ordered.

The clerk got back down onto the floor, and Shemika moved to where Elontra was standing and handed her the bag.

She looked at the stopwatch. "Thirty seconds!" Shemika shouted.

Elontra took a few steps to where the store manager was lying on the floor and kicked him. "Get up!" Once he was on his feet with his hands up, Elontra put the gun to his head. "Move."

She shoved him in the back and walked him at gunpoint to the rear of the store where the safe was located. "Open it," she ordered.

The manager got on his knees in front of the safe and opened it. The safe contained trays of unmounted and uncut diamonds. Elontra kicked the manager out of her way and then took the bag from her waist. She quickly poured the trays of diamonds into the bag.

"Time!" Shemika shouted as Elontra came out of the rear of the store.

"Let's get outta here," she said, heading for the exit, and Shemika followed her out of the jewelry store.

When they got outside the store on Fifth Avenue, they separated and went in different directions. Shemika went to her left and moved swiftly up East Twenty-first Street, and Elontra went straight down Fifth Avenue and went into the nearby Sweet Honey Bee Foods, one of the many upscale food purveyors in Chelsea. Once inside the restaurant, she kept her head down to avoid the camera and moved as quickly as she could to the ladies' room.

Elontra closed the door and exhaled before she took off the Dickies coveralls to reveal that she was wearing jeans and a knit top, and she had a backpack on her back. She put the bag of stolen jewelry in the backpack, put the coveralls in the bag on top of it, and came out of the ladies' room. Making sure that she was careful not to look at the camera or any of the customers, Elontra left the restaurant.

When Elontra came out on the street, she walked promptly up Fifth Avenue toward East Twenty-first Street. When she turned right onto East Twenty-second Street and headed toward Broadway, Shemika was coming out of the Gotham Project Café on the corner. She had ditched her Dickies and had changed into skinny jeans and a throwback New York Knicks sweatshirt.

She nodded at Elontra when she saw her and crossed the street. Shemika went into the Icon municipal parking lot, and Elontra followed her into the lot seconds later. By the time Shemika got to the Buick Enclave that Elontra's ex, Garrett, had stolen for them and parked in the lot, Elontra had caught up. She used the remote to unlock the liftgate, and they tossed the backpacks into the Enclave and got in.

When the ladies exited the parking garage, Shemika made a hard left onto Park Avenue and a right on East Twenty-third Street and got onto FDR Drive to head for the Bronx River Parkway. Once they reached the Bronx, Shemika drove them to the building where their fence, Kayla, sometimes did business. They parked the Enclave, got out, went inside, and were greeted by two men.

"She here?" Elontra asked one of the men at the door.

"She's upstairs," one of the men said as they passed.

"Hello, Elontra," the other said, smiling greedily at her and cutting his eyes in Shemika's direction. "Mika," he uttered as she started up the stairs. "How are you doing, Elontra?"

"I'm fine," Elontra said, and she started up the stairs.

"I know that's right. Your sexy muthafuckin' ass is fine as hell," he said, watching her hips swing from side to side as she went up the stairs.

"Thank you," she said and kept it moving.

Shemika waited for her to get to the second-level landing. "Why do you let him talk to you like that?"

"I don't let it bother me." They started up the stairs to the club that was located on the third floor of the building. "After a while, it all becomes background noise that I tune out. Besides, what am I supposed to do? Tell his ugly ass that he is vulgar and disgusting?"

"Yes. Because his ugly ass is vulgar and disgusting," Shemika said, and they both laughed. "Hey, I wonder if there are any men up here."

"Probably not. It's too early."

"Maybe they're practicing," Shemika commented optimistically, hoping to see some men from the male revue that the club hosted nightly.

"Dream on," Elontra said as they walked into the club.

As the employees worked, they walked around the nearly empty club, and Elontra saw Kayla sitting at a table near the back. She waved when she saw them come in and waved for them to come back.

"What you got for me today, ladies?" she asked as soon as they were close enough.

Elontra and Shemika held up the backpacks as they approached the table. "Just a little something we picked up in Chelsea," Elontra said, and Kayla stood up.

"Outstanding. Let's talk in the back."

Shemika and Elontra followed her to the rear of the club and into the storage room away from prying eyes.

"Let's see what you got."

The ladies handed her their bags, and then they stood quietly and patiently as Kayla carefully examined each piece of jewelry.

"You got some good stuff here, ladies. I'm impressed, but I always am. You two never disappoint," she said, looking at a diamond necklace through a loupe: a small magnification device used to see small details more closely. When she had finished examining the pieces, Kayla put the loupe down and looked up. "I'll give you twenty for the whole lot."

"That include the car?" Shemika asked.

"What kind of car is it?"

"It's a Buick Enclave," Elontra said.

"Is it a late model? I don't want it if it's not a later model," she asked of the crossover SUV that General Motors came out with in 2007.

"It is. And it's in good condition."

"You know her boy don't steal junk," Shemika said.

Elontra and her car-stealing friend, Garrett, had broken up years ago. In fact, he didn't even steal cars anymore. These days he worked as security for some big-time gangster. But he still came anytime Elontra called, and he always did whatever she asked of him. Her girl had it like that.

"Well, let's go see it," Kayla said, and the ladies followed her downstairs and outside to the car. Once she looked at the late-model Enclave inside and out, she said, "I'll give you a grand for it."

"A grand? That's all?" Shemika all but shouted.

"Okay, two."

"We'll take it," Elontra said and started back inside the building.

Shemika and Kayla looked at Elontra and then at each other before they followed her back into the building. Once they were back inside and she had counted off and handed them their money, Shemika sat down to make her count. When she finished her count, she nodded at Elontra, and they left the club to head for home.

"Twenty-two thousand dollars for a couple of hours' work. Not a bad day," Elontra said as they went down the steps.

"It could have been better," Shemika said as she passed the men at the door.

"Good night, Elontra," the one man said, and she passed without speaking and left the club.

"I was trying to get at least three or four for the car before you said we'd take it," Shemika pointed out as they got to her car, which they had parked there the night before.

"I know you were. But you know her next words were gonna be 'take it or leave it.' And you know we were gonna take it. Why go through all that back and forth with her?"

"I hear you."

"Now let's go home. I'm hungry," Elontra said as they got in, and Shemika started the car.

Chapter Two

Now that they had put in their work, it was time to go home. Elontra and Shemika shared a modest two-bedroom house on Corona Street that they rented in Valley Stream, a village in Nassau County on Long Island that *Money* magazine had ranked as the best place to live in New York State in the year 2017. She drove her silver BMW across the Throgs Neck Bridge and onto the Cross Island Parkway to the village that ran along the border with Queens. After dropping by the grocery store to pick up the cooking spray and a few other items that they needed, they headed for the house.

"I know you said that you were gonna cook tonight," Elontra said as Shemika pulled into the driveway and parked next to Elontra's black Corvette, "but I haven't eaten all day, and—"

"And I cooked this morning." Shemika shut off the car. "Maybe instead of hugging your pillow until noon, you should have gotten up when I came into your room and said breakfast was ready."

"I know. And it was smelling too good." Elontra opened her door and got out of the car.

Shemika hit the button for the trunk. "And you should have gotten up instead of pulling the cover over your head."

"I know. I should have," Elontra answered and grabbed the backpack with the money from the trunk along with a bag of groceries. "But I was so tired."

Shemika grabbed the rest of the groceries and followed Elontra to the house. She turned off the alarm, and they went inside. Although the house they rented was modest on the outside, the inside was nothing that would even suggest the word "modesty." It was furnished with selected pieces from Boca do Lobo, a brand well known for its expense and luxury. The absolutely beautiful pieces of furniture were handcrafted in Portugal.

"What time did you get in last night?" Shemika asked, and then she corrected herself. "I mean, this morning?"

"Five thirty. Me and DT went out last night, and he had an early shift this morning," Elontra said of her boyfriend, Derick Thomas, who worked as a driver for FedEx. She had been with him for five years.

"Where'd y'all go?" Shemika asked as they put away the few items from the store.

"We had dinner, and then he took me to a movie."

Shemika laughed. "You should have gotten plenty of sleep."

"True," Elontra agreed. "But we stayed up and . . . you know . . . so it was after two in the morning before he let me sleep."

"So what are you saying?" Shemika said. She closed the kitchen cabinets once the groceries were put away, and they came out of the kitchen. She sat down at the dining room table while Elontra went and got the backpack.

"That I'm hungry." Elontra tossed the backpack on the table and sat down across from Shemika.

"I'll start dinner as soon as we're done here. It'll be ready in about an hour." Shemika reached into the bag and took out the money. "So what are you saying?"

"I told you, I'm hungry, and I don't feel like waiting an hour for it to be ready," Elontra said, and Shemika started counting the money. "I think we should eat out tonight. You know, a little celebration for a job well executed," she said as Shemika pushed a pile of money toward her.

"Eleven thousand dollars."

"Thank you."

"Your treat?"

"Yes, Mika, it's my treat." Elontra picked up the bills and began her count. "You know, for somebody who just made eleven grand for a few minutes of work, you sure are cheap."

"I'm not cheap. I just don't believe in spending money unnecessarily. And before you call somebody cheap, you should look in the mirror."

"Granted."

"Besides, I am a much better cook than any restaurant."

"I keep telling you we should open a restaurant."

"Maybe we should." She giggled, stacked her money, and got up from the table. "But since you're treating, I agree we should go out and celebrate. What do you have a taste for?"

"I was thinking about Prime 39," she said because she really enjoyed their lollipop lamb chops.

Shemika thought about the octopus in soy sauce that she had the last time they were there. "We go there all the time," she said and started for her bedroom.

"So where do you wanna go, Mika?"

Shemika thought about pineapple jerk salmon. "Caribbean Experience!" she shouted from her room.

"Okay, I can do that," Elontra said and got up from the table with her money.

"Is it all there?" Shemika asked as Elontra passed her door on the way to her bedroom.

"It always is," she said as she went into her room and closed the door.

Once in her room, Elontra went into the closet. She sat down on the floor in front of her Honeywell fire-and-water-resistant safe with a digital lock and tapped in the combination. She opened the safe, took out the black acrylic cash box, and stood up. She took the cash box to her California king bed, sat down, and counted off $10,000 of the dollars Shemika had just handed her. She put a money band around it and put it in the box with the rest of her money.

At this point, she had a little over $30,000 in cash in that box. Elontra returned the cash box to the safe and closed it. Since she was a child, she had always been good with money. As they got older, being good with money was one of the things that she and Shemika bonded over. Based solely on how they made their money, neither Elontra nor Shemika spent a lot of money. Of course, they had everything they needed or could have possibly wanted, but they were smart about how they chose to spend their money.

The point was to keep a low profile and not attract any attention to themselves by being flashy, flamboyant, or extravagant. And to this point, it had been working for them. With that singular thought in mind, they only planned and executed jobs when their money began to get low. The house they rented was modest, and the luxury cars they drove were in mint condition, but they were older models. Although, both loved clothes and loved to look good in them and each belonged to a clothing subscription service that featured items for African American women, so they were always very well dressed in the latest designer outfits.

Once she had put away her money in her safe, Shemika went into the closet to think about what she was going to wear to dinner. She chose a pair of Dolce & Gabbana straight-leg trouser pants and a zebra-print silk and charmeuse shirt. Since she was five feet eleven inches tall, she didn't wear a lot of heels, so she selected a pair of Chloe Piia embroidered-logo denim espadrilles that matched her top.

Always being the tallest girl in the class during her early schooling years was how she and Elontra met in the back of the line when Shemika's family moved into the neighborhood when she was in the fourth grade. She was the youngest of five children, and she had four older brothers she loved to play basketball with. Therefore, Shemika was a bit of a tomboy when they first met. She was the exact opposite of girlie-girl Elontra: the middle child of three sisters and the only girl who wore a dress every day, carried a purse, and was known to wear white gloves at times in the fourth grade.

Elontra was the tallest girl in the class, so the back of the line belonged to her until Shemika came along. Her best friend since kindergarten, Demeris Dennison, or Dee Dee as everybody called her, was an only child born to a single parent who died while she was in college. She was the shortest girl in the class and always stood in the front of the line. In spite of those differences, it didn't take long before Elontra, Dee Dee, and Shemika became the very best of friends.

When high school graduation rolled around, Dee Dee, who was also the smartest person of any room she was in, got a full scholarship to the California Institute of Technology. Shemika was on the basketball team, and she landed a scholarship at Hudson Valley Community College. Not being a genius or a three-year starting point forward, there was no scholarship for Elontra. Never having been the best student, or having much interest in school, she got a job in customer service and attended City College for a couple of semesters. However, her college career ended when Elontra quit because her work hours conflicted with her class schedule.

When Shemika was dressed and ready to leave, she came out of her room. Elontra was sitting in the living room. She had changed and was dressed in a Milly Noah ruffled button-down minidress. She was five nine, but unlike her bestie Shemika, Elontra loved wearing dresses and loved wearing her slingbacks and pumps with them, so she complemented her outfit with a pair of Andrea Waze sunset crystal ankle-strap pumps that made her legs look amazing.

"I like that top on you," Elontra commented.

"Thank you. You ready to go?"

Elontra stood up. "Ready."

They were on their way to the door when Shemika's cell phone rang. She took the phone from her purse and glanced at the display. "Hello."

"Hey, babe," her boyfriend, Elijah Larson, said.

"Hey, Elijah."

Elontra rolled her eyes, turned around, and sat down on the couch in the living room. Shemika shook her head and held up one finger to let Elontra know that she wouldn't be on the call for long. "How are you?"

"I'm good. What are you doing?"

"Me and Elontra were about to go to dinner," she said, and Elontra's eyes got big. She began frantically shaking her head.

"Where y'all going?"

"Caribbean Experience."

"Hmm. I haven't had no good Caribbean food in more than a minute."

"You're welcome to join us."

Elontra threw up her hands and frowned. "No," she mouthed, still frantically shaking her head. She bounced up from the couch and walked away.

"I'd loved to, but you know my money ain't right."

"I know it's not, and I didn't ask you about money, did I?"

"No, you didn't."

"We'll be by to pick you up in a half hour."

"I'll be ready," he said, and Shemika hung up. She looked around for Elontra. "Where are you?"

"I'm in my room!"

Shemika went and stood in the doorway. "Come on, let's go."

Elontra frowned. "Why did you have to invite him?" she asked as she got up and went toward the door.

"I know you don't like him, but—"

"It's not that I don't like him, Mika. He's a nice guy. He really is. I just know that he is not good enough for you."

"Why, because he doesn't have a job?"

"Duh. Yes," Elontra said as they got to the door. "And when he finally does get one, he never seems to keep it for very long, and it's never his fault that he got himself fired."

"I know, but the last one really wasn't his fault."

"Whatever. You're driving," she said when they got outside.

"You could call Derick and have him meet us." Shemika unlocked the BMW, and they got in.

"Unlike some people, he has a job, and Mondays are always busy for him, so there's no telling what time he'll make his last delivery."

"Elijah said that he got a job, but the people haven't called him and told him when to start."

"Until then, he has no job," Elontra said as Shemika shook her head and started the car.

"Just be nice, okay? Can you do that?"

Elontra smiled. "Aren't I always?" Although some would say it was her legs, her smile was her best feature.

"No, you're not always nice." She backed out of their driveway and headed for Caribbean Experience. "You may be smiling that big Kool-Aid smile, but what comes out of that mouth ain't always nice."

"I promise to be good and not call him a sorry ass, or a deadbeat, or a good-for-nothing parasite, and I definitely won't call him a freeloader even if I am paying for him to freeload."

"I got him."

"No, I said I was treating. I got him."

When they arrived at the house that Elijah shared with five other men, Shemika got out and went to ring the bell. Since there were only three bedrooms and somebody had already claimed the couch, Elijah had made a pallet for himself on the dining room floor. Therefore, he tried to sleep at Shemika's house as much as possible, because, after all, she did have a very comfortable Michael Amini Villa Cherie upholstered California king bed, and the floor was hard. Shemika drove them to the Caribbean Experience for Trench Town shrimp, jerk salmon, and lemon butter crab legs.

"Why does your boy always gotta order the most expensive thing on the menu?" Elontra asked after Elijah had excused himself to go to the men's room.

"I told you I would pay for his food."

"And I told you I got it. I was just making an observation," she said as he came back to the table.

"What's that?" he asked.

"Nothing. Elontra is just being her usual silly self, that's all," Shemika said, but she knew that Elontra was right. It was as if Elijah chose his meal by picking up the menu and running his finger down the prices until he found the most expensive thing. Although she really did like Elijah, she was getting tired of his excuses for not trying harder and her always having to pay for everything everywhere they went.

Chapter Three

While they were eating, Derrick called and said that he was done with work and wanted to do something, so after they finished their meal and left Caribbean Experience, he met them at Mi Amor's in Brooklyn, and he bought several rounds of drinks. Everybody had a good time, and Elontra ended her evening of celebration for a job she flawlessly planned and executed in bed with her man at his house.

He slammed his hips into her, and it made her respond by throwing her hips back at him. Elontra started throwing her ass back to him as hard as she could so she could feel it all inside her. He held her hips, plunging deep in and out of her. Her body shook, and her wetness clenched around his length.

Since he had to go to work early, he dropped Elontra off at her house at a little after six in the morning. When she got home, she changed into her Norma Kamali rectangle plunging kimono-sleeve jogger jumpsuit and went for her daily five-mile run. That was something else that separated her from Shemika. Shemika could eat everything in sight and not gain a single ounce. She'd grown up an athlete running behind her older brothers and used to play basketball with them. Those days they wouldn't let her shoot, so she became a great passer.

Nowadays, Shemika was able to maintain her voluptuous shape without doing much, if any, exercise at all, whereas everything that Elontra ate went straight to her hips and ass if she didn't work out daily. She had just returned from her run and had gone into the kitchen to make some coffee when somebody started ringing the doorbell and banging on the door at the same time.

"Okay, okay, I'm coming," Elontra said, moving toward the door as quickly as she could, thinking that whoever was at the house had lost their mind banging on the door at that hour of the morning. Elontra looked through the peephole and didn't see anybody.

"Who is it?" she asked.

But what she got was more bell ringing followed by more door banging in response. She jerked open the door and was prepared to tell whoever it was off when she got the shock of her life.

"Dee Dee."

"Somebody needs to tell me what the fuck are you bitches doing living on Long Island?" Dee Dee said, and Elontra threw her arms open and hugged her. "How you doing, Elontra?"

"I'm fine, Dee Dee," Elontra said, but she refused to let go of her oldest friend. They hadn't seen each other in more than ten years. "Come in," she finally let Dee Dee go long enough to say. "Mika! Mika!"

"Get out here, Mika!" Dee Dee shouted.

"How are you, Dee Dee?" she asked on her way to Shemika's room. "The better question is, where the fuck have you been?"

"Believe me, Elontra, it's a long story," Dee Dee said, following Elontra down the hall to Shemika's room. "Where is she? Mika!" she yelled as they got to the door. Dee Dee was about to reach for the doorknob and go in the room, but Elontra stopped her.

"She might not be alone," Elontra said as Shemika's door cracked open.

"What's all this noise?"

"Look who's here."

"Oh, my God, Dee Dee!" Shemika rushed out the door in her robe and gave her a big hug. "Where have you been?"

"It's a long story," she said to Shemika, who was holding on tight. "Okay, okay." Dee Dee freed herself from Shemika's embrace. "All them big-ass titties all over the place. Put a bra on or something."

"Sorry, I'll be right back," she said, but she hugged her again. "It is so good to see you," Shemika said and let her go.

When Shemika went back into her room to put some clothes on, Dee Dee followed Elontra back into the living room.

"It is so good to see you. Have a seat," Elontra said, and she sat down on the couch. "Can I get you something? I was just about to make some coffee. You want some?"

"Coffee would be nice. Thank you."

While Elontra made coffee in the kitchen, Dee Dee got up and wandered around the living room looking at the pictures of her two best friends that lined the walls. It was like looking at a chronology of all the years she had missed in their lives. Although she was happy that they seemed to be good years, Dee Dee felt sad that she had missed them. It was just then that Shemika's door opened, and out came Elijah.

"Oh, hello," Dee Dee said, looking up at the tall, dark, and handsome man as he came into the living room.

"Hi. I'm Elijah, Shemika's friend," he said, walking toward Dee Dee with his hand out.

"Dee Dee. Nice to meet you, Elijah."

Shemika came out of her room. "I see you two have met," she said, coming down the hall fully dressed in jeans, Nikes, and her favorite Yankees sweatshirt.

"Yes, we have," Dee Dee said as Elontra came out of the kitchen with two cups of coffee.

"I'll be right back," Shemika said.

"I just got here and you're leaving?"

"Yeah, I gotta take Elijah home," Shemika said, grabbing her keys from the dish by the door.

"Mind if we ride?" Elontra said.

"Not at all," Shemika said, and Elontra quickly took the cup from Dee Dee.

"I wasn't finished with that."

"I'm putting it in another cup to ride with," Elontra said, and she disappeared into the kitchen.

"We'll be in the car," Shemika said, heading for the door with Elijah following her.

"Okay, we'll be right out," Dee Dee said as Elontra came out of the kitchen with the coffee cups.

"Where'd they go?"

"They're waiting for us in the car." They started walking toward the door to leave. "Elijah is fine."

"That's all he is, Dee Dee, trust me," Elontra said, shaking her head as she closed and then locked the door.

The ride to take Elijah home was a quiet one. Shemika did ask Dee Dee where she had been for the last ten years, and she repeated that it was a long story. When they dropped him at the house he shared with four other men, Elijah got out.

"I'll call you tomorrow."

Shemika rolled her eyes at him. "Whatever," she said to him without so much as glancing in his direction. Dee Dee and Elontra looked at each other.

"Nice meeting you, Dee Dee."

"Same here."

"See you, Elontra."

"Bye, Elijah," she said, smiling and waving as he got out of the car. Elontra decided that she would ask Shemika about that exchange later. "Dee Dee!" she yelled as soon as he closed the car door.

"Hey, y'all." Dee Dee hugged Elontra and then put her hand on Shemika's shoulder as she drove away. "It's so good to see you two."

"It's so good to see you too, Dee Dee, " Shemika said as she drove.

"Now." Dee Dee looked around and pointed out the window. "What the fuck are you two bitches doing living on Long Island? You know how long it took me to find you two?"

"We needed to keep a low profile. White folks on our block mind their business and don't ask us no questions."

"I guess y'all are still doing your thing?"

"Yes, we are," Elontra said.

"That's why we need to keep a low profile," Shemika added.

It all began one night when Elontra and Shemika were walking to the store. At the time, neither one of them had a job. Elontra had gotten laid off from her job at the call center, and Shemika hadn't found a job since she tore her anterior cruciate ligament and lost her basketball scholarship. The rent on their tiny Bronx apartment was way past due, and they were ducking the landlord, who had happily offered to forget about the back and future rent in exchange for a monthly threesome.

"Not ever in your wildest dreams," Elontra told him the last time he made his lewd and revolting proposal. "We'll get you your money."

While they were walking to the store, Shemika thought that she saw the streetlights reflect off something shiny near a garbage can, and thinking it might be something they could pawn for a few dollars, she reached to pick it up.

"That's a gun, Mika," Elontra said, and Shemika held it up to the light. "Is it loaded?"

"I don't know," she said, gingerly handing Elontra the gun.

Shemika's eyes got big when Elontra ejected the clip and then checked to see if there was one in the chamber.

"It's not loaded," Elontra said, put the gun in her purse, and continued walking to the store.

When they got to the store, Shemika went straight to the cooler and got a bottle of Dr. Pepper. She went down the next aisle and got some chips and was on her way to the counter when she got the shock of her life. Elontra had pulled her ribbed turtleneck sweater up to cover her face and was pointing the gun at the clerk. His hands were in the air.

"Put all the money in the bag and do it quick."

"Okay, okay, just don't shoot."

Shemika stood frozen in the aisle as she watched her best friend rob the bodega. Once the clerk had put the money from the register in a plastic bag, Elontra grabbed the bag from his hand and rushed out of the store. Shemika watched as she ran off before she came out of the aisle.

"Wow," she said as she came out of the aisle and approached the counter. "Did she just rob you?"

"Yeah. I gotta call the police," he said and picked up the phone. Shemika held up the Dr. Pepper and chips. He waved her on. "Go ahead," he chuckled. "I couldn't make change anyway."

"Thank you," she said, quickly leaving the bodega and rushing home.

When she got to their apartment, Elontra was sitting on the couch in the living room, counting the money that she had just stolen. It was $1,187. It was enough to buy some food and pay a bill or two, but not nearly enough to cover the back rent. All that meant was that they had to do it again.

Their second robbery was at a liquor store on a Friday afternoon. The store was getting ready for a big weekend, so they had plenty of cash on hand. Since this robbery was planned, they were a little better prepared, so this time they both wore masks, but they both were scared to death. Those days, Shemika didn't even want to hold the gun. They went into the liquor store, and

Elontra raised the gun. The man behind the counter put his hands up.

"Open the register and back up," Elontra said, and Shemika rushed behind the counter.

That was the second she realized that they didn't bring anything to put the money in. Elontra looked wide-eyed at Shemika. Her eyes quickly scanned the area until she found the bags. With a bag in hand, Shemika emptied the register and threw the money in the bag.

"Go," Elontra said, and once Shemika was out, she backed out of the store.

Next, the pair robbed a couple of bodegas that cashed checks and had cash on hand. Elontra's hands shook a bit as she ordered the woman behind the counter to open the register. She gripped the gun with both hands to keep them from shaking.

"Now back up."

Shemika went behind the counter and quickly emptied the register, and they made their escape on foot, walking quickly but casually as if they hadn't just robbed the store. Their next time out, a customer came into the store during the robbery, and Elontra had to react quickly. She turned quickly and pointed the gun at him.

"Keep coming."

The man put up his hands and stepped gingerly into the store.

"Now get over there where I can see you," she said, motioning with her gun. Elontra turned back to the woman behind the counter. "Hurry up."

"I got it," Shemika said, coming from behind the counter, and once she was out, Elontra backed out of the store.

Once the back rent was paid and they were out of the hole unemployment had dug for them, it was time to go shopping. They had cash to spend, and they went all out after their fourth robbery. With the proceeds from their fifth robbery, the former train-and-bus riders bought a car. That was when it started. People began questioning their new lifestyle, not to mention their new wardrobe.

"Where you two getting all this money from?" their next-door neighbor, Vickie, asked.

"Y'all ain't hit the numbers and not tell nobody?" Lolita, another nosy neighbor, asked.

And that was when they made the decision that they needed to move. But where?

At first, they rented a big apartment in a better neighborhood, but after a while the questions began again.

"Where do y'all work? I have never seen either of you going to work in the morning."

Anyplace they moved to in the Bronx, the questions about how and where Elontra and Shemika made their money persisted.

"Next time we need to find someplace where the neighbors don't ask questions," Elontra recommended.

"I know someplace we could move to, and I can practically guarantee you that nobody will ask us any questions if they speak to us at all."

"Where is that?"

"The suburbs!" Shemika said excitedly with her hands in the air, but Elontra seemed unfazed.

"The suburbs, really?"

"Really. Listen to what I'm saying. I'm not talking about renting a house in a black suburb."

"Because sisters with money are just as nosy as a broke sister. So what are you talking about?"

"I'm talking about us finding a modest house in a predominantly white neighborhood. That way, even if they had questions, they'd be too scared of the black girls to ask."

"That could work," Elontra said.

"It will work, Elontra. I know it," Shemika replied, and the decision was made.

After months of looking for just the right place, they found the house on Corona Street, and they moved out to Valley Stream. The two-bedroom, two-bathroom property they lived in was in good condition with an eat-in kitchen, triple-pane windows, a washer and dryer in the unit, a microwave, walk-in closets, a security system, and central air conditioning, and it included driveway parking spots.

It was perfect.

"How's that working out?" Dee Dee asked as Shemika pulled into the driveway.

"Great. We've been living here for six years, and the most we've gotten is waves from the neighbors when we get out of the car," Elontra said.

"There was that one woman who lived next door to the other black people on the block. She spoke to me once when I saw her at the grocery store." Shemika giggled. "But that was only because she thought I was her neighbor."

"You know all y'all colored folks look alike," Dee Dee said as the three got out of the car and went inside the house.

While Shemika went into the kitchen to cook breakfast for them, Dee Dee and Elontra sat in the living room, and the conversation continued.

"Still, we go out of our way to keep as low a profile as possible."

"What do you say if somebody does ask what y'all do for a living?"

"One of us has a job, and the other is living on an annuity from a slip-and-fall accident," Shemika said from the kitchen.

"Which one has the job, and which one of you has the annuity?" Dee Dee wanted to know.

"It depends on which one of us you ask." Elontra took a sip of her coffee. "If you ask me, Mika has the job, and I'm living off the annuity."

"And if you ask me," Shemika began, "Elontra has the job, and I sit home all day chillin', watching the baby daddy and judge shows."

"Y'all must be doing all right with it." Dee Dee looked around the room. "This place is laid. The outside looks a little run-down, but in here this place is nice."

"We try to be comfortable. But we're not greedy." She paused. "We only work when our cash runs low," Elontra informed her.

"When was the last time y'all went out?" Dee Dee asked.

"Yesterday."

"Damn, I missed it," Dee Dee said. "I would have been down to go with you. Shit, badly as I need to make some money, I'd have definitely been down." She thought about the promise that she made to herself not to go back to doing what she used to do for money.

Shemika came out of the kitchen carrying a bowl of scrambled eggs and a plate of bacon and put them on the table. "Y'all come eat."

Elontra stood up. "You know what that means?"

"No." Dee Dee followed Elontra to the dining room. "What does it mean?" Dee Dee asked as they sat down to the meal Shemika had cooked for them to eat.

Shemika returned to the dining room with a plate of hash brown potatoes. "We need to plan another job so you can have some money," Elontra said, and she got a plate.

Chapter Four

"So where have you been the last ten years? And if you say 'it's a long story' again, I'm gonna slap the shit outta you," Elontra promised.

"I've been a guest of the State of California for the last ten years," Dee Dee answered, and her girls' mouths dropped open.

"You've been in prison?" Elontra asked.

"At the California Institution for Women."

"For what?" Shemika asked.

"I was arrested, charged, and convicted of unauthorized computer access."

"What?" Shemika wanted to know.

"Girl genius is a hacker, Mika, remember?" Elontra reminded her.

"How could I have forgotten that?" Shemika said with a hint of sarcasm.

"Maybe because she'd been gone for ten years," Elontra said.

"Maybe," she giggled.

"My screen name was flydeedee, and I was part of a hacking crew. We called ourselves the get cash crew, and we used to seize computer data from internal corporate networks around the world to resell credit card and ATM numbers."

"I know you made a bunch of money with that."

"You fuckin' right we did." Dee Dee leaned back and thought about those years taking whatever she wanted.

"Let me tell you, we compromised cards from places like BJ's, DSW, OfficeMax, Boston Market, Barnes & Noble, and Sports Authority."

"Damn. Y'all was all out of control," Shemika said.

Dee Dee pointed at Shemika. "And that is exactly what got us caught."

"How so?" Elontra asked.

"Me and some friends were at a restaurant in L.A., and on a dare, I hacked into Dave & Buster's corporate network and stole about five thousand credit card numbers. But what I didn't know was that one of our crew kept going back to reintroduce the hack because it wouldn't restart after the company computers shut down. She, by herself, charged six hundred thousand dollars on six hundred and seventy-five of the cards she stole."

"Greedy!" Elontra all but shouted. "That's how people get themselves caught. Being greedy."

"That is why nothing like that will ever happen with us," Shemika said.

"'Cause we're not greedy." Elontra got up from the table and took her plate to the kitchen. "We take what we need to survive, and we leave the rest for next time."

Dee Dee laughed. "I wish somebody would have told ol' girl that. That bitch was just fuckin' greedy." Dee Dee picked up her napkins, wiped her mouth, and thought back to those days when she and her partner in crime, Yolonda, thought that they were untouchable. "I tried to tell her that the FBI would get suspicious, but she didn't listen to me, and she kept going back to the well."

"What happened to her?" Shemika wanted to know.

"She got caught by the same Feds who busted me, and she got fifteen years. As far as I know, she's still locked up."

"That's what she gets for being greedy," Elontra said.

"And she didn't have to be because there was plenty of paper out there for us to take. And believe me when I say that I was trying to get it all." Dee Dee laughed and put down her fork. "When I got arrested in the raid, Feds seized a quarter of a million in cash that I had buried in plastic bags in a three-foot drum in my backyard."

"Quarter mil," Shemika said and nodded her head. "That's real money."

"For real," Elontra concurred. "And you stole all that money with computers?" she asked on her way to the kitchen.

"I sure did."

Shemika stood up. "You finished?" she asked Dee Dee, pointing to her plate.

"No," Dee Dee said and helped herself to more bacon and eggs. "I've been eating prison food for the last ten years." She made a face and shook her head. "These are the best eggs I've had in years."

Elontra came back into the dining room and sat down. "Shemika is a great cook, so be careful, because she will get you fat."

"Look at me, Elontra. I can stand to gain some weight," Dee Dee said, and she ate some more eggs. "I remember this one time this radio station was having a contest. They were giving away a Porsche 944 to the hundred and second caller, so we hacked the radio station and took over the telephone lines to make sure that she'd win."

"Did she win?" Shemika asked.

"Of course she did."

"What happened to the car?"

"She totaled that bad boy the same day," Dee Dee laughed.

Elontra had been listening to the conversation, paying special attention to the amount of money that Dee Dee told them she was making before she went to prison.

If she could still do that, they could stop walking into places with guns.

"And y'all stole all that money with computers?" she asked again.

"I sure did."

"Can you still do it?"

"Do either of you have a computer?"

Both women shook their heads. "I have a tablet," Shemika said.

"I have a tablet too. I have an old laptop that I haven't used in years, but that's it."

"With the right hardware I could. But my skills are rusty and outdated."

"What would you need?" Shemika wanted to know.

Without saying another word, Elontra got up and went into her bedroom.

"Honestly, I have no idea." She paused. "That's not true. I know the type of hardware I'd need to get back in the game." She thought about her promise once again. Ten years in prison was more than enough to convince her that she wasn't going back to that life. "Hell, I could have brought smoke with that old laptop, but like I said, my skills are rusty and outdated."

"So is being a hacker like riding a bike? Once you know how, you know how?"

"Pretty much, like I said, but I would need to get my skill level up to date," Dee Dee said as Elontra came back into the dining room and sat at the table.

"Would this help?" she asked and held a banded stack of bills out in front of Dee Dee.

"How much is that?" Dee Dee asked as she took the stack from Elontra.

"Five thousand."

"Shit, yeah!"

"This way you can get what you need and have some money," Elontra said.

"You sure? This is a lot of money." At least it was now. Ten years ago, $5,000 was pocket change.

"Don't worry." Shemika got up and started clearing the table. "She can afford it. Take that money."

"Thank you. I'll pay you back."

"No, you won't. Consider that a welcome home present," Elontra said as she began helping Shemika clear the table. "How long have you been out?"

"Two weeks. And yes, I've been looking for you two the entire time. I could never catch up with your mother or your sisters, Elontra."

"I can't catch up with them sometimes either."

"And I forgot who told me that Miss Frazier moved back to Mississippi."

"She moved back down there four years ago. She said that her social security goes further in Cold Water than it does up here. So how did you find us?" Shemika asked.

"I ran into Michaella, your brother Kevin's old girlfriend. She said he was in jail, but she called somebody, and they told her that y'all escaped to the 'burbs."

Elontra and Shemika looked at each other curiously and wondered who Michaella called who knew where they'd moved to.

"Where are you staying?" Elontra asked.

Dee Dee said nothing for a second or two, and she dropped her head. "It took most of the money I had to get home, and I couldn't afford to keep staying in a motel." She paused and looked up. "I'm just about broke, so the last couple of nights I've been sleeping on the train."

"Oh, no," Shemika said, violently shaking her head.

"That ends today," Elontra said. "You can stay here for as long as you want."

"Thank you." She got up from the dining room table and went to sit on the couch.

"You don't have to say thank you, Dee Dee. You're home now," Shemika said.

"Where you belong," Elontra said. "So we have to celebrate."

"That's right. Our girl is back," Shemika said. "We're gonna need to get a bigger place."

"You don't have to do that. This couch is comfortable as fuck." She patted the cushion. "I'll be fine right here."

"No, Dee Dee, no, you won't be fine right there. That couch is only temporary. We're moving so you can have a room of your own."

Dee Dee laughed. "I haven't had a room to myself, much less any privacy, in years."

"Well, you will now," Elontra said.

"Besides," Shemika giggled, "you are not about to get my couch all lumpy."

"If she does, Mika, I'll buy you a new set." Elontra went and sat next to Dee Dee. "I am so glad to see you." She hugged her. "I have missed you so much all these years. You just don't know."

"I missed you guys too. I'm just glad that I found y'all."

"Tell the truth, Dee Dee. You're just tired of sleeping on the train," Shemika laughed.

"You damn right I am. But I really did miss y'all. I wrote both of you when I first got locked up, but they came back as 'addressee moved' and left no forwarding address." Dee Dee wiped a tear from her cheek. "And when I came home and couldn't find you bitches"—she shook her head—"I thought that I would never see y'all again. I felt so alone."

Shemika sat next to her on the couch and put her arm around her. "Like I said, you're home now, and you'll never have to be alone again."

"We wondered why you disappeared on us," Elontra said. "All of a sudden you weren't there. One day, your phone was going straight to voicemail, and then the number was off. We were so worried that something had happened to you!"

"Something did happen to me," Dee Dee laughed. "My ass was locked up."

"So I noticed that you didn't show up with any luggage," Elontra noted.

"That, girlfriend, is because all I have are the clothes on my back," Dee Dee admitted.

Both Elontra and Shemika bounced up from the couch. "Let's go shopping," they both said.

Their first stop was the Green Acres Mall. They spent hours shopping at Macy's, Burlington, H&M, and Old Navy, and they ate at BJ's Restaurant & Brewhouse before they left the mall. Not getting everything they were shopping for, Shemika suggested that they make the hour-and-a-half drive to Tanger Outlet in Riverhead so Dee Dee would have more choices.

With the pocketful of cash that she got from Elontra, she lost her mind shopping, and by the time the outlet closed for the evening, Dee Dee had a brand-new wardrobe. Of course, she wasn't shopping alone, so Shemika's BMW was packed with shopping bags and very little room for anything else. It made for an uncomfortable but fun ride back to Valley Stream.

Later that evening, once they got back to the house and had unloaded the car, what turned into a fashion show occurred where each tried on and modeled some of the outfits they had just bought. It was after midnight when the three got in Shemika's BMW and headed out to celebrate both Dee Dee's release from prison and her return, not only to New York but to her lifelong friends. They were just about to leave for the Midnight Rooftop Bar and Lounge when Elontra ended her call with Derick.

"That was Derick. He said to have fun and that he is looking forward to meeting you."

"Tell him that I'm looking forward to meeting him too," Dee Dee said.

"I'm surprised that he didn't want to meet us there," Shemika expressed.

"He did, but I told him that this was a girls' night, you know, to welcome our girl home," Elontra said from the back seat. "He said he understood," she said, tapping Shemika on the shoulder. "And what's up with Elijah?"

"What do you mean?"

"When you dropped him off this morning, he said, 'I'll call you,'" Elontra said, imitating Elijah's voice. "And you rolled your eyes and said, 'Whatever.'"

"Oh."

"Yeah, Mika, fuck's up with that?" Dee Dee asked.

"We had an argument. Well, it wasn't much of an argument. Mostly I talked, and he said, 'I'm trying,' or, 'I'll do better, I promise,'" Shemika said, imitating the way he talked. "Whatever!"

All three laughed.

"I told him that I am tired of his shit." She looked over at Dee Dee and gave her the backstory. "I've been seeing him for nine months now, and things aren't getting any better. He doesn't have a job, and when he does get one, he can't keep it."

"So why do you even bother to fuck with him?" Dee Dee wanted to know, and Shemika smiled but said nothing.

"If you don't tell her, I will," Elontra said, giggling from the back seat.

"Go ahead and tell her. You know you want to," Shemika said as her playful smile turned into a shy smile.

"She said that he eats pussy better than any man she'd ever met," Elontra shared, and all three busted up laughing.

"And . . ." Shemika began. "And then I taught him how to use that big dick he's packing on me."

"That right there is enough of a reason to keep him around," Dee Dee commented, laughing.

"Don't encourage her, Dee Dee," Elontra said seriously, but she was laughing too. "She needs to cut him loose and find her a real man with a real job."

"And give up those skills? No, I don't think so." Dee Dee shook her head. "Not until you have a replacement."

"See, Elontra? Dee Dee agrees with me." She giggled. "But I told him that I was tired of him never having any money and me having to cover everything all the time."

"What did he say to that?" Elontra asked.

Although she agreed that she should keep him around for his skills, Elontra still thought she needed a man who could, at the very least, take care of himself.

"I told you what he said—the same tired shit he always says. 'I'll do better, I promise.'" She stopped at the light and looked back at Elontra. "And when I asked him about the job he said they were going to call him for, he said that they called him today and said that he wasn't selected and wished him luck in the future." Shemika shook her head slowly. "And that is when I snapped."

"Uh-oh."

"That's when I told him that I was tired of his shit. I told him that he was a sorry-ass, deadbeat, good-for-nothing parasite, and if he couldn't fuck me right, I wouldn't fuck with him at all." The light changed and she drove off. "It was like he didn't hear none of the shit about being a sorry-ass deadbeat, because all he did was smile and say, 'At least I got fuckin' you right going for me.'"

"No, the fuck he didn't."

"Yes, the fuck he did, Dee Dee. He's the kind of man who knows that he got a big dick and thinks that's all he needs. His arrogant nigga ass," Elontra said.

“And I told his arrogant ass that big dick I taught him to swing just ain’t enough for me anymore. And then I told him not to call me until he has a job and has been on it for at least a week.”

“Good for you,” Elontra said, happy that Shemika finally got around to moving away from Elijah.

“Yeah, but I still say that you need to keep him around until you find somebody else to suck that pussy right,” Dee Dee said, and, although grudgingly, Elontra agreed because the simple truth was that it ain’t every man who knew what he was doing between the thighs.

Chapter Five

Now that Dee Dee was living with them and had spent a lot of the money she had left on computer hardware that filled the dining room table, they decided that they needed to move to a bigger place.

"That means we need to work," Mika said.

"Anybody got any ideas?" Elontra asked.

"I got a spot I've been eyeing." Knowing that she wasn't going to like it, Shemika looked at Elontra. "It's a little bank in—"

Elontra immediately thought about the dye pack and frowned. "A bank? No, Mika, we are not robbing a bank," she said, shaking her head.

"Hear me out," Mika said.

"Yeah, at least listen to what she got to say," Dee Dee said.

"Okay, let's hear it."

"There's this bank in Deer Park I've been looking at," Shemika began.

"Deer Park?" Elontra questioned. "What were you doing all the way out there?"

"You remember that guy who paid me to drive him around for a couple of days when his car was in the shop because I got the last loaner that day?"

"Yeah, I remember. What about him?"

"That was one of the places I took him." She paused to see if Elontra had a comment to make. When she didn't, Shemika continued, "It's a small community bank. Every time I've gone there, there are only three people working: the branch manager and two tellers."

"No security?" Elontra questioned.

"Not that I've ever seen."

"And how many times have you been there?"

"I went there once with him and three times to check things out over the past few months."

Elontra sat back and thought for a moment or two. "That might work for us."

"I think so," Shemika said confidently.

"What about escape routes? Did you check that out, too?"

Shemika nodded. "We make our escape on the Southern State Parkway. The LIE isn't far, but it's not as easy to get to."

"But neither are straight shots from the bank, are they?" Elontra asked.

"Nope."

"I think it's worth a look," Dee Dee expressed.

Elontra shook her head. "I don't know, Mika. It's a bank."

"I have a question."

"What's that, Dee Dee?" Elontra asked.

"I wanna know why you don't think robbing that bank is a good move for us," she said, and Shemika immediately started laughing. But not Elontra. Her big smile had turned into a twisted-up frown.

"The last time we robbed a bank—" Shemika began.

"The only time I let you talk me into robbing a bank, you mean," Elontra quickly clarified.

"Excuse me." Shemika nodded respectfully. "What you gotta know is that this was when we first got started. What was it?"

"Maybe the ninth or tenth place we robbed." Elontra laughed. "We even had gotten a second gun and had bullets by that time."

Dee Dee raised her hand. “Hold up. Y’all had robbed seven or eight places with an empty gun?”

Shemika and Elontra laughed. “Yes,” they said, and Dee Dee shook her head.

“But the only time Elontra let me talk her into robbing a bank,” Shemika continued, “everything went great. No problem with the guard, the teller bagged up the cash, and we were out of there.”

“And what happened?”

“We got away,” Shemika began. “We didn’t have any problems, and we made it back uptown, talking about how easy it was and taking banks was all we were going to do from then on.”

“You gotta understand, those days we had robbed a few bodegas and some liquor stores,” Elontra chuckled. “We even robbed a fancy French restaurant, but we weren’t making the kind of money we needed,” Elontra explained. “So we were always looking for someplace to rob.”

“So robbing nothing but banks seemed like the right move for us,” Shemika said. “But anyway, we get to the apartment, and we’re getting ready to count the money, and”—Shemika pointed to Elontra—“your girl there opens the bag and gets sprayed with red dye.” She laughed but Elontra didn’t. “It got all over her hands and the clothes she was wearing.” Shemika shook her head. “It wasn’t pretty.”

“And no matter what I tried, nothing got it out. Soap and water, olive oil, rubbing alcohol . . . shit, I even tried using toothpaste.”

“Toothpaste?” Dee Dee questioned, laughing.

“Yes, girl, toothpaste. I read somewhere that toothpaste could remove hair dye stains from your skin, so I tried it.” Elontra shook her head. “But I tried makeup remover, baby oil . . . nothing worked. It took more than a week for me to get that red dye off my hands.”

"Like I said, it wasn't pretty. She wore gloves the entire time," Shemika said, chuckling.

"And I told her that I will never rob another bank as long as I live." Elontra paused. "And we haven't gone near a bank talkin' about robbing it since."

"But that was years ago. We didn't know what we were doing those days. We'd just walk in and point our guns. No surveillance, nothing. Now we know better. We're better prepared to do a job like that."

"I know that."

"Shit, if she doesn't wanna do it with you, Mi, I'll go with you," Dee Dee said.

"See? Dee Dee's down."

"Okay. I'll look at it, and if it's the cakewalk pushover you say it is, we can do it," Elontra said, and Dee Dee and Shemika high-fived one another. "But you are gonna be the one to open the damn bag."

"Done," Shemika said, and the two robbers fist-bumped to their next job.

The following day, the three made the ride out to Deer Park, a small community located in northeastern Babylon in Suffolk County. Shemika parked where they could see their intended target.

"On Friday, this branch has a larger-than-usual amount of cash on hand to process payroll checks from the offices in the area. When the bank opens on Friday morning, there's a small rush, which ends at approximately ten fifteen a.m. Then there's a lull that lasts until approximately eleven thirty when the lunch rush begins. That's our window. Our target time is ten thirty."

"How many times did you say you've been here?" Elontra wanted to know.

"Three times. Well, four times: once with ol' boy when I was driving him around, and three times by myself. The first time, I talked to the manager about opening an account and just got whatever printed materials they had available and left. I went back a few weeks later and opened an account."

"Did the manager recognize you?" Dee Dee asked.

"No, she didn't."

"I was wondering, you know, being as tall as you are," Dee Dee commented.

"I was worried about that too, but no, she didn't seem to recognize me."

"I imagine she sees so many people that after a while everybody just becomes a face with a voice," Dee Dee said, and Elontra nodded.

"Go on."

"Inside the bank, there will be three people: two females and one male. Two tellers and the manager. There are teller positions and offices directly across from them. During our target window, both positions will be manned, but all positions will be stocked. The three of us go in, and Elontra will cover the room and control the operation. The timeline is two minutes. Once we're inside, I'll go behind the counter and take the cash drawers. Dee Dee, your first objective is to find the bank manager. She'll have a key to the rolling cash cart on her wrist. Secure it. We have approximately one minute to get the money in the drawers and from the rolling cart, which will be behind the counter. Dee Dee, that key will open the cart and any of the cash drawers that are locked. Take the cart first, Dee Dee, while I clear the teller positions.

"Dee Dee, once you have the cash from the cart, you give me the key, and I will give you my bag. You exit the building and prepare for our escape. I'll proceed to take any of the drawers that were locked." Shemika looked around the car. "Any questions?"

"I see you got this all planned out?" Elontra asked.

"I have, for months now."

"For months? Really, Mika, you had been planning this job for months even though you knew I wouldn't be interested?"

"I hoped you'd come around," she said, smiling. "But yeah, I planned everything but the escape."

"Why didn't you make plans for our escape?" Elontra asked.

"Because escape is your thing," Shemika said.

"That's because she's always been a sneaky bitch," Dee Dee commented. "Always had a scheme, and I usually ended up getting caught because I couldn't run as fast as you two."

"Having these long legs came in handy," Shemika laughed.

"Well, let me go have a look," Elontra said and reached for the door handle.

"Hold up," Dee Dee said.

"What?" Elontra said.

"You said you been here three times, Mika. What happened the third time you came?"

"I came back on a Friday during the lunch rush, and the line was long. It was so busy that the manager was behind the counter serving customers."

"Okay, did you notice how many cameras were in there?" Dee Dee asked, because now that she had joined the team, it went without saying that shutting down the cameras and disabling the alarms was her job.

"If I'm not mistaken, there are cameras all around the bank and at every teller position," Shemika informed her.

"You go in and check it out first, Dee Dee," Elontra said. Dee Dee got out of the car and went into the bank.

"What you think?" Shemika asked Elontra.

"I'll let you know when I come back," she said and got out too.

It was three minutes after Elontra went into the bank that Dee Dee came out and got back in the car.

"Cameras?" Shemika asked.

"Seven. Four covering the teller positions, and the other three are covering the floor with one pointing at the safe."

"We're not going to go anywhere near that safe." Shemika paused. "Can you do it?"

"I may be a little rusty, but the day that I can't take out some cameras and some cheeseball alarm system is the day I hang it up for good," Dee Dee said as Elontra came out of the bank.

"Anything else?" Shemika asked as Elontra got back in the car.

"I'll let Elontra tell you."

"What's up?"

"When was the last time you were out here?" Elontra asked as Shemika started the car and drove away.

"It's been at least four, maybe five weeks ago that I was out here. Why, has the setup changed since then?"

"It has. They have a security guard now," Elontra informed her.

"That changes everything," Dee Dee commented.

"It does," a somewhat-dejected Shemika admitted, and a somewhat-disappointed Dee Dee dropped her head. This would have been her first time out with her girls, and she was excited to be a part of the team.

"It does," Elontra agreed. "But that doesn't mean we're not doing it."

"It doesn't?" a surprised Shemika questioned.

"No, it doesn't. Everything else appears to be the same. I don't see any reason not to go through with it."

"Really? I just knew that with your issues you wouldn't want any part of it."

"Like you said, now we know better and we're much better prepared. All I need to do is a little more surveillance to make sure nothing else has changed. I get the new security guard's pattern down and plan our escape. So yeah, Mika, we're doing this."

"Good," Dee Dee said as her excitement returned. "I bet that rolling cash cow is fatter than a muthafucka."

Chapter Six

A week later, and following two more trips to the bank, Elontra had gotten the security guard's pattern down and had a plan to deal with him.

"The security is stationed outside of the bank, supposedly as a deterrent to us robbing their little bank." Elontra laughed. "His standard patrol pattern is simple. He walks back and forth outside of the bank. He goes into the bank every fifteen minutes for a period of time that never exceeds ten minutes. Before he goes into the bank, I'll disarm and secure him, and once he's secure, the word is go," Elontra informed them, so it was on.

On the day of the robbery, the ladies prepared to take the bank in Deer Park. It was Dee Dee's first time going out with them, so she was excited. However, at the same time, she was nervous because Elontra and Shemika had been doing this for years. They were pros. And this being her first time out, Dee Dee didn't want to make a mistake or do something that would place her friends in jeopardy.

"You'll do fine," Elontra assured her that morning.

"That's right, Dee Dee," Shemika concurred. "There's a first time for everything. This is just yours."

"Right, just like there was a first time for us."

"Damn," Shemika said, looking thoughtful. "I barely remember what that felt like."

"We were scared, and yes, Dee Dee, we were nervous. We had never done anything even close to that. But the difference is that you have us," Elontra said.

"All we had was each other, and we were both scared," Shemika said, and she thought back to the first time she carried a gun on a job.

Their target that night was an elegant French restaurant called Rendezvous à Minuit on East Fifty-second Street. That afternoon, Elontra went to a place called Frank's Sports Shop on East Tremont Avenue. Her intention was to finally buy some bullets for the 9 mm, and she ended up getting into a conversation with another customer who seemed very knowledgeable about guns. Once she had gotten the bullets for their 9 mm, they were walking out together when Elontra decided to ask him a question.

"What's the best gun for someone who has never used one before?"

"In my opinion, the Smith & Wesson 9 mm," he said and began excitedly telling her about the gun. "Polymer-framed, short-recoil operated, locked-breech semiautomatic pistol that uses a Browning-type locking system." And then he leaned close to her. "You in the market for one?"

"Maybe."

He smiled at Elontra. "Walk with me."

"Where are we going?"

"I have something to show you. Come on." He started walking but she didn't. When he noticed Elontra wasn't coming, he stopped and came back to her. "We're going right across the street to the Lincoln." He pointed out the window to the car.

"What you wanna show me?"

"You said that maybe you were interested in buying a gun, right?"

"Right."

"Come on then. I got something to show you in the trunk."

This time when he started walking, Elontra was a step behind him. It did occur to her that he might open the trunk and push her in, and if he did, what would she do? She stood back when he opened the trunk, which was filled with assorted weapons: rifles, shotguns, handguns, and semiautomatics. He looked around before reaching into the trunk and rummaging through the guns until he found the one he was looking for.

"Smith & Wesson 9 mm." He handed it to Elontra. "That's a good gun."

"How much you want for it?"

He leaned close. "Give me three for it."

"Deal." Elontra handed him back the gun. She reached into her Rag & Bone crossbody bag and then handed him three $100 bills.

He gave her the gun. "Pleasure doing business with you," he said and shoved the money in his pocket. Then they went their separate ways.

Shemika barely wanted to touch the gun when Elontra handed it to her. She started to say, "What I need this for? We already got a gun," but she knew that they needed it.

That night, they waited outside until Rendezvous à Minuit was getting ready to close, and then they went in.

"Nobody moves, nobody gets hurt!" Elontra shouted with her gun raised.

Shemika stood behind her with her gun in her hand, but it was shaking at her side. The few remaining restaurant customers raised their hands, and Elontra put her gun in the cashier's face.

Elontra handed her a bag. "The money in the bag, now."

The cashier opened the register and put the money in the bag.

"That's it?" she demanded to know because there was only a couple hundred dollars in small bills in the register. The cashier nodded. "Shit," Elontra said softly and put the gun to her head. "Where's the office?"

She pointed toward the rear of the restaurant.

"Cover them." Elontra gave the cashier a shove. "Go."

While Elontra quickly walked the cashier to the back, Shemika raised the gun to about waist level and pointed it at the customers. Her gun hand was shaking so badly that she had to grip the pistol with both hands, and even then she almost dropped it. That was how scared she was. Shemika was relieved when she saw Elontra come out of the office.

"Go," she said, and Shemika ran out of there. Elontra backed out of Rendezvous à Minuit, laughing at Shemika under her mask.

Of course, she had gotten more comfortable with guns in the years since, but she'd never forgotten that day, so she understood Dee Dee's apprehension.

"I get all that, but I'm still nervous," Dee Dee said. "I just don't wanna fuck up."

"I hear you." Elontra paused. "So let's go through it again."

"That would be helpful," Dee Dee expressed. "Make sure I got it down."

"When we get in the bank, what's your first objective?" Shemika asked.

"My first objective is to find the bank manager to get the key for the rolling cash cart," she said. "I get that cash while you take the drawers."

"And then?" Shemika asked.

"Once I have the cash from the cart, I give you the key, and you give me your bag. And then I get the car."

"See? You got it down," Elontra said, and then she stood up.

"Yeah, so don't you worry about a thing. Everything is gonna be fine," Shemika promised as Elontra went into her bedroom. "Watch, it's gonna go down so fast that you won't have time to think about it. You just react."

"I hear you," she said as Elontra returned to the living room carrying a brown paper shopping bag from L.L.Bean. "What's in the bag?"

Elontra reached into the bag, pulled out a bright red plaid flannel shirt, and handed it to Dee Dee. "Today's uniform," Elontra said and tossed a blue plaid flannel shirt to Shemika.

"No Dickies today?" she asked.

"No," Elontra said as Dee Dee and Shemika tried on their shirts. "We're not gonna have the same opportunity to change, so we're keeping it simple today. Jeans, Tims, and these shirts," she said, pulling out a smoky lavender plaid flannel shirt for herself.

On the Friday morning that they were set to do the job, Shemika waited for Dee Dee to leave the dining room and go to her room before she asked Elontra a question.

"Are we sure about her?"

"Who, Dee Dee?"

"Yeah. You think she's up to it?"

"Yeah," Elontra said quickly, and then she paused. "I'm sure she is. Like she said, she may be rusty, but I'm sure she can take out some cameras and a cheeseball alarm system."

"Okay," Shemika said, but she still felt a bit of trepidation about her old friend who just showed up out of the blue one day.

"Ready," Dee Dee said when she came back into the room.

"Let's go," Elontra said, looking at Shemika and hoping that she was right about Dee Dee being ready. She hoped that if she wasn't ready, it wouldn't get them caught.

It was 10:25 a.m. when Dee Dee parked the stolen Toyota Camry outside the bank. Earlier in the week she was able to access the bank's security system to be sure that she could take down the alarms and disable the cameras.

"A bitch still got it," she'd said that day.

Now it was time to put her admittedly rusty skills to work in real time. Using the tablet that she had recently gotten, Dee Dee once again accessed the security system and disabled the cameras and alarms.

"Done," she said and kept her eye on the security guard as he stood outside the bank.

Shemika took a deep breath. "We ready?" she asked, and Dee Dee nodded her head. Then the security guard turned and started for the door.

"Let's do it," Elontra said and pulled down the smoky lavender mask that she got to match her flannel shirt.

"Oh, you are so wrong for that," Shemika said and pulled down her black mask. "You couldn't get us all matching masks?"

"Sorry," she said and grabbed the door handle to get out.

Dee Dee laughed as she donned her mask. "Damn, I missed you two," she said and got out.

Elontra rushed up behind the security guard just as he reached for the door handle. She put a gun to the back of his head. "Keep moving," she said, taking his gun as the three bandits entered the bank.

Once inside the bank, Elontra pushed the security guard to the floor. "Everybody down!" she yelled and fired one shot at the ceiling. Everyone in the bank immediately hit the floor. "Two minutes!"

While Shemika went behind the counter, Dee Dee moved to get the manager out of the office and put a gun to her head. "Give me the key to the cart."

"What key?"

"Ninety seconds!" Elontra shouted.

"Don't fuck with me." Dee Dee hit her on the head with the barrel of her gun. "Give me the fuckin' key or I will fuckin' end you right fuckin' now!" she shouted in the manager's face, and she quickly dug into her pocket and handed Dee Dee the key.

"Now get down on the floor!"

While Elontra covered the room, Shemika moved behind the counter and ordered one of the tellers to get up. She handed her the bag.

"One minute!"

"Fill it up, and if you reach for the alarm or put a dye pack in there, I will kill you right away. You got that?" Shemika asked and pressed the gun a little harder into the teller's head.

"Yes, yes," she said and went to each teller position and put the money in the bag. "Please don't kill me. I have kids."

"And if you want to see them again, you'll be a good girl and do what I tell you."

"Thirty seconds!"

While the teller cleaned out the drawers, Dee Dee unlocked the cart and got the money. Now that she had emptied the cart, Dee Dee came from behind the counter and handed the key to Shemika, and then she exited the bank to prepare for their escape.

"Time!" Elontra shouted, and they quickly exited the bank and headed for the car.

Elontra jumped in the back seat, Shemika got in the front, and Dee Dee sped away down Commack Road. As quickly as they could, the three unmasked, and Elontra and Shemika took off their flannel shirts. Dee Dee had already taken hers off when she got in the car. She made a left turn onto Marcus Boulevard, and then she turned into the shopping mall parking lot.

"Do you see them?" Shemika asked about the second and third getaway cars that Elontra had arranged for their escape.

"He said they'd be in front of Kohl's," Elontra said as Dee Dee cruised the lot looking for them.

"There they are!" she shouted and sped up to get to them.

Parked side by side sat a Honda Accord and a Nissan Altima. Since the police would be looking for three female bandits, Elontra had planned for them to separate. Dee Dee parked the Camry as close to the cars as she could. Elontra grabbed the money bags, and the three jumped out. As Shemika and Dee Dee rushed to the Accord and got in, Elontra opened the trunk of the Altima and tossed in the money bags before she got in the car and started it up. She took her time exiting the parking lot with Dee Dee and Shemika following closely behind her in the Honda.

Elontra headed south toward Grand Boulevard and turned onto Commack Road. She did the speed limit as Commack Road turned into Garnet Street, and she turned left onto Deer Park Avenue. It wasn't until she got onto the Southern State Parkway ramp that Elontra relaxed a little. But it was short-lived.

"Shit!" Dee Dee shouted as she drove.

"What?" Shemika asked.

"Cops are behind us."

Shemika turned to look. "Shit!" she said. In all the years that they had been doing their thing, they never had any police intervention at all.

"Don't panic," she advised, even though she felt a little panicky.

Dee Dee's eyes got big. "We just robbed a bank, and we're driving a stolen car, Mi!" she said, glad that Elontra had the foresight to separate.

"Just drive like we didn't just rob a bank and we're not driving a stolen car," Shemika said, trying to stay calm herself.

Worst-case scenario, she and Dee Dee would just be charged with grand larceny of a vehicle, but Elontra would get away with the money. She could use the money for bail and lawyers, she was thinking as the cop car turned on its lights.

"Here they come."

"Shit!" Shemika put her gun under the seat.

"I don't wanna go back to prison!" Dee Dee shouted. She had just gotten out after doing ten years, and she didn't wanna go right back.

Grand larceny of a vehicle carried a minimum sentence of one to three years and a maximum of eight to twenty-five years in state prison. They were both thinking about going to jail when the police sped up and drove around them. Both women relaxed and breathed a sigh of relief as the police sped past Elontra and kept going. Dee Dee glanced over at Shemika.

"That was close," Dee Dee said and loosened her grip on the steering wheel.

"Too close."

Chapter Seven

It had been over a week since the ladies took the bank in Deer Park, and in that time, the money was burning a hole in Dee Dee's pocket. She was spending her money in the same way she used to. It's been said that just about every woman has a shopping vice. Some women have a closetful of clothes while others are into watches. Some are into buying jewelry while there are others who can never have enough shoes. But not Dee Dee. Even at the height of her criminal activity when she had mad cash to spend, she was never into any of those things.

No!

Unless she was going somewhere that required her to dress for the occasion, most days you could find her dressed in jeans and Nikes. What Dee Dee was into shopping for, what she spent her money on, what she couldn't get enough of was computer hardware.

That, and classic cars.

Dee Dee had a 1972 Plymouth Barracuda, and she had just gotten a 1964 Pontiac GTO at auction that she'd planned on fixing up to resell. At the time of her arrest, Dee Dee was driving a 1969 Mustang Fastback coupe that was valued at $45,000. She loved that car. It was her prized possession. She had planned on buying another one when she got out. That was, until she fell in love with the 1979 Nissan 280ZX, which was the Motor Trend Import Car of the Year.

The only problem was that after a ten-year prison sentence, she had no credit. Mindful that the law required businesses to report cash payments of more than $10,000 to the federal government, her paying cash for the vehicle that was valued at $29,000 was out of the question.

Dee Dee found a 1979 sky blue metallic V6 with a manual transmission that was for sale by a private seller. It wasn't in mint condition like the one she'd been looking at online. In fact, it had a bit of minor body damage, and it wasn't running.

"How much are you asking for it?" Dee Dee inquired when she and Elontra went to look at the car.

"Give me seven thousand," he said, and Elontra's smile turned into a frown.

"It's not even running. Let's go, Dee Dee," she said and started walking to her car.

Dee Dee reached into her pocket, pulled out a roll of bills, and started counting. "I'll give you four for it in cash, right now," she said, and the man's eyes got big as she counted.

"Make it five and we got a deal."

"Deal," she said and handed him the money. He handed her the keys, and then Dee Dee followed him inside to get the title and a receipt. "I'll send a tow truck to pick it up and have it taken to a shop."

When they got back to the house and went inside, Shemika had already cooked Italian stuffed shells with ground beef, mozzarella, and parmesan, and she had made a loaded broccoli salad with a combination of bacon, sour cream, scallions, and cheddar. She was now doing what she could to straighten up the living room.

"Hey, Mika," they both said.

Shemika's fists hit her hips, and her eyes narrowed.

"Uh-oh," Elontra said.

"What?" Dee Dee asked.

"I've seen that look before." Elontra nodded. "Somebody is in trouble."

"No," Shemika said. "Nobody is in trouble." She looked around the living room. "But look at this place."

Elontra turned to Dee Dee. "It's you who's in trouble," she said and started for her room.

"What?" Dee Dee asked, but she had a good idea what Shemika was on about.

"You're not in any trouble, but look at this place."

The coffee table and the dining room table were both covered with the computer hardware that Dee Dee had been buying. She plopped down on the couch. "Too much?" Dee Dee asked.

"That just means that we need to settle on a bigger place and move," Elontra shouted from her bedroom.

"And the sooner, the better," Shemika said. "Can't even eat at the table anymore."

"You want me to make some room at the table?" Dee Dee asked as Elontra came out of her bedroom.

"What you cook, Mika?"

"Stuffed shells and broccoli salad."

Elontra sat down on the couch next to Dee Dee. "You are going to absolutely love her stuffed shells. They are to die for."

"I used to love Italian food," Dee Dee said. "I could eat lasagna, stuffed tortellini, and ravioli every day."

"Stop trying to change the subject," Shemika said.

"I'm not," Elontra said. "Like I said, we just need to move to a bigger place so Dee Dee can have a room of her own." She paused and looked around at all the hardware. "Preferably one with a basement."

"Relegating me to the basement, huh?"

"This way you'd have room to spread out and get more shit if you wanted to," Shemika said.

"Now that that's settled, let's eat. I'm starving," Elontra said, and Dee Dee nodded in agreement.

"Me too."

At that point, finding a bigger place to rent got kicked into high gear. They'd been looking for rentals in the villages of Hempstead and Farmingdale, and although they'd looked at some nice places, they hadn't settled on anything that all three agreed on. Highly motivated by her earnest desire to reclaim her living and dining areas, not to mention getting Dee Dee off her couch, Shemika intensified her efforts.

One afternoon, she was house hunting in Massapequa, a small community on the South Shore of Long Island, when she rolled up on a house that she thought would be perfect. The best thing about it was that the owner of the house and not a property manager was renting the house. She got out and rang the doorbell.

"Can I help you, young lady?" the older man asked when he opened the door.

Shemika smiled. "I was interested in renting your house."

"Please, please, come on in," he said and stepped aside to let her in.

"Thank you," Shemika said. She stepped inside and looked around the foyer.

"You came at the right time. I usually show the place by appointment only, but I was here fixing a cabinet in the kitchen," he said and closed the door.

That was when he got a good look at the woman standing in front of him. Suddenly his smile broadened, and his eyes widened. He became focused on the deep V-neck top with cap sleeves and sultry sheer lace insets that showed off Shemika's abundant cleavage. She started to say, "I'm up here," to force him to make eye contact, but she was used to it.

"Then this is my lucky day." She held out her hand. "I'm Shemika Frazier."

"Nelson Rogers." They shook hands. "Well, let me show you the place. As you can see, it is a ranch-style house with four bedrooms, two full baths, and one half bath, and it has a fenced-in backyard," he said, pointing out the window.

Shemika stopped and looked out the window. "Nice," she said when she saw the pool.

"The house is completely renovated. New washer and dryer. The house has a large living room with a bay window overlooking the front yard with a large eat-in kitchen."

"I love this kitchen." Shemika stopped and looked around. "It has so much space."

"My wife loved it, too."

"I am going to love cooking in here," she said as they left the kitchen.

"She did, too. Anyhoo, there are hardwood floors throughout the house. Gas central heating, and the tenant pays for all utilities including landscaping. I don't allow smoking in the house, and no pets."

"That's fine. Neither of my roommates smoke, and I am scared of dogs, so no, there will be no pets."

"You have roommates?"

"Yes, two."

"They'll each have to fill out an application."

"That will not be a problem." Shemika paused. "I love this house, and I am so tempted to say that we'll take it, but I would like my roommates to see it first." Shemika took out her checkbook. "So how about I write you a check for the deposit and the first two months' rent to hold it until they see it?"

"That's fine," he said, and Shemika wrote the check. They made an appointment for the following day so Dee Dee and Elontra could see the house.

When the three returned the following day, Elontra and Dee Dee both loved the place as Shemika expected. It didn't have the basement that Elontra wanted, but it did have a fourth bedroom that Dee Dee said would be large enough to hold all of the hardware she had.

"We'll take it!"

Chapter Eight

"This place is nice," Dee Dee said to Elontra over the music.

It had been over a month since they moved into the house in Massapequa, and they had just finished unpacking and setting up the house, so it was time to get out and have some fun. Shemika had heard of a new club in Queens called Atravessa that everybody was talking about, so there they were.

"It is a nice place," Elontra said. "When was the last time you went to a club?"

"The night before I got arrested ten years ago. I got home at six, and Feds were knocking on my door at seven."

"Ten years," Derick said, squeezing Elontra's hand. "I can't even imagine how hard that must have been."

"Trust me, Derick, you don't wanna know either."

"I know that's right. I try not to do anything that has a remote possibility of getting me locked up." He sipped his drink and then chuckled. "I do my best not to take no penitentiary-type chances. But I guess that's most people."

All three women looked at each other, knowing that they weren't most people.

"I guess that's true." Elontra paused and discreetly winked at Shemika. "Most people are law-abiding citizens." Then the DJ mixed in a song Elontra liked. "I love this song."

Derick stood up and held out his hand. "May I have this dance?"

Elontra accepted his hand and stood. "You may," she said, and they hit the dance floor.

"They are a cute couple," Dee Dee commented.

"They are, and they're good together," Shemika said.

"But he doesn't know what y'all do, right?" Dee Dee leaned close to ask.

"Oh, hell no, and ruin the Angel Elontra image he has of her?" Shemika shook her head. "Not happening. He thinks she's living on an annuity."

"From a slip-and-fall accident, right?" Dee Dee shook her head. "Men will accept and believe anything a woman tells him."

"As long as there's sex involved, they sure do. They're special that way, but they do serve a purpose."

A purpose that no one in Shemika's life was fulfilling. Shemika believed that sex wasn't something to be rushed, but rather something to be savored and enjoyed. She enjoyed the actual act of giving pleasure. If you give more, you get more. She loved to kiss and caress with her partners. And she had gotten Elijah to make love and give it to her just the way she liked it. The problem was, the morning that she gave Elijah that ultimatum—"Don't call me until you have a job and have been on it for at least a week"—was the last time she'd heard from him.

"I don't know how you did it."

"How I did what?" Dee Dee asked, dancing in her chair to the music.

"How did you go ten years without dick?" She giggled. "It hasn't even been ten weeks and I'm about to lose my mind."

"You adjust to the conditions," Dee Dee said, and Shemika's head snapped around.

"And what is that supposed to mean?"

Dee Dee turned to Shemika. "It means that you have to adjust yourself to the conditions around you or you won't survive."

They looked into each other's eyes for a second or two while Shemika thought about how she was going to delicately ask what she wanted to know. "So you . . ." She paused. "Like women?"

"I do now." Dee Dee laughed and paused to take in the priceless look on her old friend's face. "I got turned out my first night in lockup."

"Do I wanna hear this? Yes, I wanna hear this."

"You sure?" Dee Dee laughed.

"Yes, I'm sure."

"Okay." Dee Dee leaned closer to Shemika. "This was my first night, and I remember I was asleep in the top bunk, and this big woman grabbed my legs and pulled me to the edge of the bed. Then she jerked off my pants, slid my panties to one side, and had me covering my mouth to keep from screaming."

Shemika leaned closer and whispered, "She raped you?"

"Yes, Mika, she raped me."

"Then why didn't you scream?"

"Because she was three times my size and told me not to."

"Did you report her?"

"No."

"Why not?" Shemika asked excitedly. And then she answered her own question. "Because she was three times your size and told you not to."

"You get it."

"Was that the only time?"

"She was back the next night." Dee Dee giggled and leaned close to Shemika. "That bitch could eat pussy better than any man I had ever been with. Shit, by the end of the week I had stopped wearing panties to bed that shit was so fuckin' good."

Once again, they looked into each other's eyes while Shemika thought about how she was going to ask her next question. "So you don't like men anymore?"

"I don't know. I guess. They're still fine as hell, so we'll see," Dee Dee said as a good-looking man came to the table. "Like him," she whispered to her girl.

"You wanna dance?" he asked, standing in front of Shemika with his hand out.

"Sure," Shemika said, and his eyes got big when she stood up. He hungrily took all of her in with his eyes as he escorted her to the dance floor.

He leaned closer to her. "What's your name?" he asked in her ear.

"Shemika," she said in his ear.

"My name is Dominic."

"Hi, Dominic," she said, swaying from side to side, and the "getting to know you" conversation began.

It was shortly after that when Elontra returned to the table and sat down next to Dee Dee.

"Where's Derick?"

"He went to the men's room and then to get us drinks. Where's Mika?"

Dee Dee pointed to the dance floor. "Dancing."

Elontra scanned the floor and spotted her girl. "Damn, he's fine."

"Ain't he?"

"And that two-step she's doing ain't dancing." She shook her head. "Not for Mika. If she were dancing, that booty would be shakin', clappin', and poppin'. They're talking and she's diggin' him," Elontra said, observing the way Shemika was looking into his eyes.

"Yeah, he's all up in her ear, and she is into what he's putting down. Good for her. She was just whining about not having no dick driving her crazy," Dee Dee said, laughing, but Elontra didn't say anything. Dee Dee glanced over at the twisted frown on her face. "You okay?"

"No, I'm not," Elontra said, staring at the bar.

"What's wrong?" Dee Dee asked, and Elontra said nothing. She looked in the direction that Elontra was looking.

They sat and watched as Derick talked to a woman at the bar.

"No, they are not exchanging numbers while I'm sitting here watching," Elontra said as she watched him hand her his phone. She angrily watched as the woman put in her number and handed Derick back his phone.

"That shit is foul," Dee Dee leaned close to say. "You want me to go over there and shank his ass?"

"No, I'll handle this," Elontra said through gritted teeth.

She and Dee Dee continued to watch as Derick called her to make sure the number was correct and saved in his phone. When she walked away, he picked up the drinks he'd ordered for them before he returned to the table. Derick saw the angry look on their faces.

"I'm ready to go," Elontra said as soon as he sat down.

"What's wrong?"

"Nothing, I'm just ready to go," she said, standing up.

"Okay," Derick said, shot his drink, and stood up. When he did, Elontra started for the exit. Derick glanced at Dee Dee. "What's wrong with her?"

"I don't know."

Derick picked up and shot the drink that he got for Elontra. "Nice meeting you, Dee Dee," he said and then rushed to catch up with her. It was a minute or two later when Shemika returned to the table.

"Where's Elontra and Derick?"

"She left," Dee Dee said and explained what happened.

"That shit is foul."

"That's what I said."

"What about you? You ready to go?"

"No."

"Good. Neither am I."

"I'm having a good time," Dee Dee said, dancing in her chair. "And I would like to dance at least once. And what's up with you and Mr. Sexy you were dancing with?"

"His name is Dominic Moore."

"And?"

"And what?"

"What's up with him?"

"I gave him my number, and he said he'd call. We'll see if he actually does."

A man came to the table and stood smiling in front of Dee Dee. "You wanna dance?"

She looked him over and rolled her eyes because he was short and skinny, and she wasn't into short, skinny men. But she wanted to dance, so why not? "Sure."

Meanwhile, the ride to Derick's apartment was an unusually quiet one, but that was not surprising under the circumstances. He did ask her a few times what was wrong. But each time, Elontra told him that she was fine, but she wasn't. Even though she didn't rush over there and confront him, even though she took a deep breath, stayed calm, and observed, she was mad as hell and felt like he had embarrassed and disrespected her. But under the circumstances, she felt that the better play was to see how Derick interacted with the woman and how the situation played out. It hurt her to watch.

"Can I get you a drink?" Derick asked on his way to the bar when they got to his house.

"No, thank you," Elontra said and sat down in the Malibu vegan leather Chesterfield chair that Derick had recently gotten himself. "But what you can do is tell me who that woman was."

"What woman?" he asked innocently as he picked up a glass.

"The woman you were talking to at the club."

Derick poured a drink. "What woman?" he asked again without looking in her direction.

Elontra leaned forward. "That's how you wanna play this? Fine." She nodded. "The woman at the bar you exchanged numbers with. You remember. You handed her your phone. She put in her number and handed you back your phone."

"Oh, that woman." Derick finally made eye contact and shot his drink. He chuckled as he poured himself another one. "I can explain that."

"Then you called her to make sure the number was right before you saved the number in your phone. And I wanna know, what was up with that, DT?"

Derick put down the drink and put his hands on the bar. "I can explain that if you give me a chance."

"Okay, here's your chance." Elontra nodded. "Go ahead and explain to me who that woman was and what was up with you two exchanging numbers."

"She's my cousin."

"Really, DT?" she asked in total disbelief. *Is that the best you can come up with?* "Your cousin, really?"

"Really, Elontra, she's my cousin for real," Derick said confidently and assuredly. "She just moved here from Chicago."

"So how come you didn't introduce me to your cousin from Chicago?"

"Because she was leaving, or I would have introduced you."

Elontra stood up. "You need to take me home."

"Why?" he asked, coming from behind the bar.

"Because I don't believe you, DT."

"I swear she's my cousin."

"And I swear I don't believe you."

He walked up to Elontra in the living room and took her hands in his. "Her name is Megan Cunningham, and I haven't seen her since she graduated from high school."

Elontra looked deeply into his eyes, wanting to believe him but having a hard time.

"And she just moved here from wherever she went to college." He chuckled. "I can't remember where she said she went to college."

"And why didn't you come back to the table and say, 'Hey, Elontra, I just met my cousin at the bar. She just moved here from wherever the fuck college she went to, and we exchanged numbers'?" She pulled her hands away from his. "If you had, I might believe you. But you didn't, did you?"

"No, but—"

"But nothing." Elontra put her hand in his face. "You need to take me home."

"Don't be like that, Elontra. She's my cousin for real."

"That's all right. Don't worry about taking me home." Elontra sat down in his chair.

"Good." Derick sat down on the couch and relaxed. "She really is my cousin, Elontra."

"I'll call an Uber," she said and took out her phone.

"Okay, okay, you don't have to call no damn Uber." Derick shot the drink he just poured and stood up. "I'll take you home."

"Thank you." She got up and started for the door.

"I wish you wouldn't be like this."

Elontra stopped at the door and faced him. "And I wish you hadn't disrespected and embarrassed me," she said and opened the door to leave.

"Is there anything I could say to make you stay so we can talk about this?"

No, nigga, you ain't getting no pussy tonight. "You could have told me the truth from the start."

"I did. I told you Megan is my cousin," he said as they got to the car and Derick unlocked it.

"And I told you that I don't believe you." Elontra got in, and once he put the directions to the new house into his navigator, Derick drove her home.

Therefore, Shemika and Dee Dee were surprised when they got home an hour or so later and saw the light on in her window.

Chapter Nine

When Shemika woke up the next morning, she was thinking about money. When she and Dee Dee were leaving Atravessa the night before, she saw security taking the money from the front door. Naturally, she couldn't tell how much money it was, but she could tell that it was a lot. Shemika sat up in bed, yawned, and got in a good stretch before she got out of bed.

After a long, hot shower, Shemika went into the kitchen. Neither Elontra nor Dee Dee were up, but there was nothing unusual about that. Since it was too late for breakfast, she began thinking about what she was going to make for lunch. She settled on chicken cucumber pitas and got started. As she was mixing the ranch dressing, mayonnaise, Italian dressing, garlic powder, and pepper in a small bowl, her mind returned to Atravessa and all that cash.

"And that was just the cash from the front door," she said aloud.

In addition to the cash from the front door, there was all the cash the club made at the bar and the kitchen that she had to take into consideration.

"Yeah," she said, pouring the mixture over the chicken and tossing it to give the chicken and cucumbers a good coating.

That was the moment that she began seriously thinking about robbing Atravessa. But then Shemika began to think about all the security she saw in the club as well as all the police she saw outside.

Maybe it isn't such a good idea.

"What's up, Mi?" Dee Dee asked when she came into the kitchen.

"Hey."

Dee Dee went into the refrigerator and got a bottle of water. "What you fixing?"

"Chicken cucumber pitas," she replied as she filled each pita.

"That sounds tasty. Let me know when they're ready," Dee Dee said and started to leave the kitchen.

"They'll be ready in a minute."

She stopped and leaned against the counter. "Okay." Dee Dee opened the bottle.

"Do you know if Elontra is up?"

"I haven't seen or heard from her."

"It was fucked up how her boy did her last night."

"That shit was foul." Dee Dee finished the water. "I'm gonna jump in the shower, and I'll be back."

"Okay," Shemika said and put the pitas in the refrigerator as Elontra came into the kitchen.

"Hey, y'all."

"Hey," Dee Dee and Shemika said.

Elontra got a Classic Cinnamon Roll coffee pod from the rack. "I was looking at all the money last night, and I was thinking—" she began, and Shemika started laughing.

"Get out of my head, Elontra," Shemika said.

"What?"

"I woke up thinking the same thing," she laughed.

"You mean while I've been upstairs playing with the purple party mix, you bitches been planning to rob the club?" Dee Dee asked.

"Playing with what?" Elontra asked.

"The purple party mix." She paused. "That's what I call the two-in-one tongue-licking vibrator." She paused and looked at their puzzled faces. "It's got nine modes and it's purple."

"Party mix." Elontra nodded. "I get it."

"Yeah." Shemika shook her head.

"Well, that's what I was doing while you two scheming-ass bitches been planning to rob the club."

"I was trying to think of a way that doesn't involve us tangling with the cops at the front door," Elontra said as she waited for her coffee to fill the cup. Since they were talking about what might be their next job, Dee Dee threw her empty bottle in the trash and sat down at the table.

"Get out my head, Elontra," Shemika said. "I was thinking the same thing."

She went and got the pitas out of the refrigerator and put them on the table with some plates. She sat down and helped herself. "There's a way to do this. We just have to figure it out."

"What are those?" Elontra asked as Dee Dee put one on her plate.

"Chicken cucumber pitas," Dee Dee said and took a bite. "And they are delicious. Get me another bottle of water before you sit down, please."

"Me too," Shemika said.

Elontra got two bottles of water from the refrigerator and handed them to her girls before she got her coffee and sat down. "I think we need to go back up there tonight and do a little surveillance," Elontra said and got a pita.

"I was watching on our way out of the club how security was there while they counted the money," Shemika said.

"Me too," Elontra said, and then she took a bite. "Those are good," she said with her mouth full.

"Mika put her foot in these," Dee Dee said and took another bite.

"Thank you." She nodded modestly.

"I was thinking that they probably do that a couple of times a night to keep from having so much cash up there at one time," Elontra said.

"That makes sense," Dee Dee said. "So we'd need to hit them at just the right time."

"I'm thinking that they'd do the same thing with the bars and the kitchen, too," Shemika added.

"I agree. Maybe not as often because it's less money than the front door." Elontra paused to think. "So here's what we'll do. We go up there tonight and tomorrow, and we watch security to see if there's a time or a pattern to when they pick up money, and we plan from there. Agreed?"

"Agreed," Dee Dee said and got another pita.

"Agreed," Shemika said, and she got another one as well.

"This is why I have to run at least five times a week. Otherwise, I'd be big as a house," Elontra said, and she got another pita too.

After they had finished eating, all three ladies left the kitchen and went to their rooms. Once Elontra had showered and was thinking about what she was going to wear for the day and what she was going to wear that night to Atravessa, her phone rang. She picked it up and looked at the display.

"Derick," she said and rolled her eyes, remembering the days when she'd be excited by his call. "Hello," she answered coldly.

"Hey, babe. How are you doing?"

"I'm all right."

"You sure? 'Cause you still sound like you're mad."

She put the phone between her shoulder and her ear and went into her closet. "I don't think that 'mad' is the right word for how I'm feeling right now."

"What would be the right word for how you're feeling?"

"Confused, skeptical maybe."

"You still don't believe me, do you? I thought we got past this last night."

"I know we talked about it on the way home and I said okay, but—"

"But you don't believe me."

"It's not that I don't . . . Let me stop lying to you and myself. No, Derick, I am just having a hard time believing that you met your long-lost cousin at the club. I'm having a hard time believing that y'all got time to chat each other up and exchange numbers but not enough time to introduce your woman for the last five years."

She came out of the closet with an Alexander McQueen slashed jersey cropped sweatshirt logo slit skirt, which she thought would look cute with her Balmain lace-up ankle boots, and laid it out on her bed.

"I told you that she had to go."

"I know you did. But this is just me thinking." Elontra took the phone away from her ear and sat on the bed. "It would have only taken you, what, five minutes? You could have brought her over, said, 'Hey, Elontra, this is my cousin, Megan. She has to go.'" Elontra got up and went back into her closet. "Or better yet, she could have said, 'Nice meeting you, Elontra, but I have to go.' If you had done that one thing, we wouldn't be here."

"I'm sorry you don't believe me."

"I am too, but until something happens to change that, I guess I will just have to accept that Megan is your cousin and learn to deal with my feelings of confusion and skepticism and get past it."

She picked a STAUD Kirsten beaded cutout minidress and a pair of Aquazzura Babe satin slingback sandals with a four-inch self-covered stiletto heel to wear that night. That night, she planned on finding a member of the security staff to pump for information, and she needed to have his undivided attention.

"I gotta go, Elontra. I'll call you tonight and we can talk about this some more."

"No need. As far as I'm concerned it's behind us," she said, but it wasn't behind them. Far from it. "Like I said, I will find a way to get past it, so we don't need to talk any more about it."

"Good."

She came out of the closet, laid her outfit on the bed, and stood back to admire her choices. "And besides, me, Dee Dee, and Mika are going out tonight."

"Where y'all going?"

"Dominoes," Elontra lied so he wouldn't have to ask why they were going back to Atravessa again that night.

"You want me to meet you there?"

"Nope. It's a girls' night." Elontra was pleased with the outfits she'd chosen and was ready to get off the phone. "I'll let you get back to work now, and I'll talk to you tomorrow," she said and ended the call before Derick could say anything else.

That night, the ladies were at Atravessa, and they used their phones to communicate and share information via text. As promised, Elontra found a chatty member of the security staff to talk to, while Dee Dee posted up at a bar where she could see the kitchen and learn what she could from the bartender. Shemika found a table as close to the front door as she could. From her vantage point, she could also see the kitchen and the bars. So she spent the night turning down the men who asked her to dance and observing the flow of security as they made their way from spot to spot.

Their surveillance yielded the information that they needed to plan the robbery. Security was more than happy to brag to Elontra that he was often the one assigned to make the pickups and in what intervals. She sent a text to Shemika, and she was able to identify the runner and confirm the pickup times. Dee Dee reported that she was able to do the same with the kitchen and the bars. It was decided that they would focus on the front door proceeds. Therefore, all that remained to be decided was when to do the job.

"Next Saturday night," Shemika said, and Elontra and Dee Dee agreed.

The following Saturday night, wearing black Vince essential turtleneck sweaters, black Jen7 slim-fit comfort skinny jeans, and black Michael Kors Rory logo-embossed espadrilles, Elontra and Shemika leaned against a car that was parked in front of Atravessa. There were two uniformed police officers at the door as well as a line that extended to the corner.

Earlier that evening, they went to a used car lot so Dee Dee could show off a little.

Shemika shut off the car. "Pick one," Dee Dee said, pointing at the cars on the lot.

"The black Impala," Shemika said, and Dee Dee tapped the screen on her tablet a few times. The car unlocked and the engine started.

"After you," Dee Dee said to her impressed friends. She and Elontra got out of the car.

"What about the cameras?" Elontra asked as she cut the chain so they could drive the car out.

"Come on now. You know I used the tablet and hacked into their security system and disabled those when we pulled up," Dee Dee said and got behind the wheel.

She drove to the club and waited for Elontra's signal.

"You're up."

With that, Dee Dee rolled down the passenger window on the Impala and yelled, "Get the fuck off me muthafucka!" as loud as she could and fired five shots from her gun at a car window. When the glass shattered, the people nearby screamed and ran for cover, and the cops in front of the club started running in that direction.

"We're a go," Shemika said, covering her face with the turtleneck as she and Elontra walked toward the door and went in with their guns drawn.

"Nobody move!" Elontra shouted, pointing her guns at the two security guards at the door.

The two employees who were working the door put up their hands as Shemika went for the booth.

"You two, get over there where I can see you," she said, motioning for them to get in front of the booth. "You, open the door," she commanded.

The woman working the booth hurriedly unlocked the door, and Shemika rushed into the small room. Shemika pointed her gun at the woman. "Back up," she ordered.

All did what they were told as Shemika cleared the money from the drawer. Elontra smiled under her turtleneck because it seemed like it was a lot of money, so they'd timed it right. She was sure when she saw the guy she pumped for information come around the corner with another member of security to get the money.

"Let's go!" she shouted, and Shemika came out of the booth and hit the door. Elontra kept the Mac pointed at security as she backed out the door.

Dee Dee had the Impala idling out front. The police were still down the street looking at the broken window, questioning witnesses, and trying to reassure others that they were safe when Elontra and Shemika came out of the club. They got in the car with Dee Dee, and she drove away.

Dee Dee drove them back to the used car lot, and once she used the tablet to hack into their security system and disable the cameras, she drove the Impala into the spot where it was parked. They exited the vehicle, got back in

Shemika's BMW, and they headed home. When they got home, they counted and split the money, and they were surprised and satisfied by that night's take.

It was just after noon when Shemika's phone rang with a call from Dominic.

"Hey, you," she answered.

"How are you doing today?"

She looked at the stack of bills on her vanity. "I am great. What about you? How are you doing today?"

"I am having a good day so far. But you could make the day even better by having dinner with me," Dominic said.

"Consider your day made, sir. I would love to have dinner with you tonight," she said, and they made plans to meet.

Chapter Ten

Shemika arrived early for dinner with Dominic at a Portuguese restaurant called Brinca Deira. She distinctly remembered asking him to please be on time because she didn't like to be kept waiting. But despite that, there she was sitting alone at the bar waiting. Naturally, there was a part of her that blamed herself for being early, but still. Seven o'clock came and went without incident. By seven thirty, she had finished her drink and was about to call for the check when she saw Dominic come into the restaurant.

He waved to her, and after a quick chat with the hostess, he made his way to the bar. "Sorry I'm late. Traffic was murder. Have you been waiting long?"

"About half an hour," Shemika said with a bit of a bite because she didn't like to be kept waiting.

"I'm sorry." Dominic picked up on her tone. "Did you get my text?"

"No, I didn't." Shemika reached into her purse and got her phone. She read the text, and what little anger she felt washed away. "'I'm running a little late. Stuck in traffic.'"

"Like I said, traffic was really bad." He smiled. "Do you forgive me?"

"It's cool, you're here now. Don't sweat it."

"You look incredible tonight."

"Thank you very much. You're looking very handsome yourself," Shemika said as the hostess joined them at the bar.

"I am sorry to interrupt you, Mr. Moore, but your table is ready. If you would follow me, please," she said and escorted them to their table. Shortly thereafter, the server arrived to take their drink order.

"Rémy Martin straight up."

"And the lady will have?"

"Cranberry mojito, please."

Once the server took their drink and dinner orders, she left the table, and Shemika took a sip of her drink. "So tell me, who are you, Dominic?"

"There's not much to tell, so I'll give you the short version of my life story. I grew up in Detroit and joined the army when I was eighteen, did two tours, and got out."

"How'd you like the army?"

"I hated being in Uncle Sam's Army. That is no place for a black man to be. But I signed up because I saw it as an opportunity to better myself."

"How so?"

"Coming from where I came from, there wasn't much opportunity," he chuckled. "I couldn't sing, couldn't rap worth a damn, and I had no game at all. So I didn't see many other ways to rise up. It didn't turn out that way." He shook his head. "Don't get me wrong. I wouldn't trade the experience for anything in the world."

"I sense a 'but' coming."

"Let's just say that it wasn't all that the recruiter promised it would be when I signed up."

"So in the long run, it really wasn't the opportunity you thought it was, was it?"

"Long run or short, the benefits never outweighed all the indignities and other things that I had to endure to get through it. But I really don't like talking about myself. I would much rather talk about you. So what's your story, Shemika?"

"I don't like talking about myself either."

"It's gonna be a quiet dinner if neither of us is talking," Dominic said as the waitress returned with their drinks.

As their meal was served, the two found that they had a lot to talk about and found themselves talking their way through dinner. They did more talking than eating, and their conversation continued until the restaurant was getting ready to close. Each found that they had a great deal more in common than just not liking to talk about themselves.

"Until we can look them in the eyes and trade greenback for greenback, we get no respect."

"We're getting pretty intense for first date dinner conversation," Shemika said, but she loved it, and she found that the conversation was stimulating her in more ways than just intellectually. "You're beginning to interest me, Dominic Moore."

He leaned forward. "That's good because you began to interest me the second that I saw you sitting there."

That was when a member of the wait staff broke out the vacuum cleaner. "I think we should take the not-so-subtle hint that it's time for us to leave."

"You think?" Shemika said, smiling, and Dominic signaled for the check.

The waitress turned off the vacuum cleaner and brought him the check. When Dominic walked Shemika to her car, she unlocked the door but didn't get in. Then they talked at the car for the next hour or so until Shemika attempted to drag herself away.

"What's wrong?" he asked.

"I'm enjoying the conversation, and I'm not ready to go yet."

"Then why are you?"

"Because it's late and I have things to do in the morning," she lied and wondered why she did.

"Well, if that's the case, I'll make it easy for you. I'll say good night," Dominic said and opened her door. Shemika got in. "I enjoyed my evening, Shemika."

"So did I," she said and started the car. "Good night."

"I'll call you tomorrow if that's all right?"

"You can," she said, closed her door, and drove home excited about Dominic and the possibilities.

There was a part of her that had wanted to say, "It doesn't have to end," and follow him to the nearest hotel. Every fiber in her being was screaming to be fucked, and she could tell by the look in his eyes that he wanted her too, but they each chose the polite option and said good night. When she got home and went upstairs to her bedroom, Shemika was surprised to find a stack of bills on her bed.

"What the fuck?"

It seemed that while she was out on her date with Dominic, Elontra and Dee Dee had been busy. They were sitting around, talking, watching TV, and snacking on the fried seafood that Shemika made for them before she left on her date, and Dee Dee was saying that her skills were improving and it wouldn't be long before they could start to plan bigger jobs with confidence.

She held up her iPad Pro 12.9-inch tablet. "With this bad boy, I could get into most systems and disable their alarms and cameras."

"Really?" Elontra said, smiling because she'd been waiting for Dee Dee to say those exact words. She was always thinking about ways to make money and had something in mind. "Well, let's test that."

"Let's."

Elontra leaned forward. "I know about this check-cashing place that can't lock the back door," she began, and Dee Dee laughed.

"Go on."

"The lock is broken, and it's not going to be repaired until Tuesday."

"So we don't have much time."

"They've been using a chain to lock the door, but the other day they had an inspection, and the fire marshal said that was a fire hazard. So they had to take the chain off the door while they're open."

"Okay, how does that work for us? I imagine that the alarm will still sound when you open the door."

"It does, but if you could disable the alarm and whatever cameras they got, I could just walk right in and take them."

Dee Dee was quiet for a second or two. "Let's do it."

It wasn't too much longer after that when Elontra and Dee Dee were dressed in jeans, Tims, and their plaid flannel shirts, and they left the house for the check-cashing place. Once they arrived and made their way around to the back door, Dee Dee was as good as her word, and she was able to shut down the alarm and camera.

"The alarm is disabled, and cameras are off."

Elontra pulled down her ski mask. "You ready?"

"Ready," Dee Dee said, pulling down her mask.

The pair of robbers readied their weapons and went in through the back door. They rushed into the store directly behind the counter.

"Everybody down!" Elontra yelled. She had a gun in each hand, and they were pointed at the employees.

The two employees were startled when they turned and saw them. Dee Dee moved quickly toward them and pointed her gun at one's head.

She put her hands up. "Don't kill me!" she cried, scared out of her mind.

"I don't want to kill you two, and you don't want to die, so get down on the floor and don't move or make a sound!"

"Okay, okay."

Once the two employees got down on the floor, Elontra covered while Dee Dee got the money from the drawers and the conveniently open safe. They were out of there in less than a minute.

The following morning when Elontra and Dee Dee dragged themselves out of bed and came downstairs for breakfast, they found scrambled eggs with cheese, homemade croissants, bacon, and hash browns. Since Dee Dee liked them, Shemika had cooked grits as well. They were on the table next to the stack of bills that they had left on her bed.

Chapter Eleven

"Morning, Mika," Elontra said and sat down and grabbed a plate as if there weren't a stack of money on the table.

Shemika shook her head as Dee Dee yawned, stretched, and got a coffee cup.

"Morning, Mi," she said, grabbing an Iced Mocha Frappé Keurig pod.

"Y'all don't see that money on the table?" she finally asked.

"Yeah, I saw it," Elontra said and filled her plate with scrambled eggs and bacon. "I figured you'd get around to telling us why it's there," she said and got a croissant.

"I thought maybe it was a contest, you know: see if Elontra can eat grits without frowning up," Dee Dee laughed and got a bowl of grits.

"Not happening." Elontra shook her head. "I don't know how you eat them."

"Once you put some butter and jelly on them, them shits is the bomb," Dee Dee testified.

"Stop it!" Shemika shouted, and it got her girls' attention. "You two know damn well I ain't running no damn grits contest."

"Okay, okay," Elontra said and put some hash browns on her plate. "Why is there a stack of bills on the table?"

"Where'd the money come from?"

"Game show, maybe," Dee Dee mused, and Shemika gave her a "don't fuck with me" look.

"I don't know, Mika. Where did it come from?" Elontra asked, sensing that Shemika was serious.

"When I came home last night, I found that money on my bed, and I wanna know where it came from."

Dee Dee sat down. "That money is yours."

"Now we're getting somewhere. Where did the money come from for it to be mine?"

Dee Dee and Elontra looked at each other curiously.

"Last night, while you were out with Dominic, me and Dee Dee were sitting around talking, and she was saying that she was getting her skills up to date and how she could disable any alarm with her tablet."

"Then Elontra started telling me about this check-cashing joint that she'd been eyeing."

"Right." Elontra took a bite of bacon. "I told her that the check-cashing place can't lock the back door because the lock is broken and they've been using a chain to lock the door. But the fire marshal said that was a fire hazard and it's going to be repaired on Tuesday."

"So I said that we don't have much time."

"I said that if Dee Dee could disable the alarm, I could just walk right in and take them."

"And I said, 'Let's do it.'"

"So you did the job without me," Shemika said angrily.

A confused Elontra and Dee Dee looked at one another. "Yeah," they both said.

"You could have called me."

"We did it on the fly," Elontra said.

"Right. Elontra was talking about it, and we just went and did it."

"You could have called, and I would have met you there."

"My bad, Mika," Elontra said and kept eating because it was no big deal to her.

But not Dee Dee. "So let me get this straight. You wanted us to call you while you were out on a date with . . ." Dee Dee paused and glanced at Elontra.

"Dominic."

"Thank you." Dee Dee nodded. "You wanted us to call you while you were out on a date with Dominic? And by the way, how was your date with Dominic? You were home too early to have gotten some dick, so how'd it go?"

"Not to change the subject—"

"I thought we were through with it," Elontra said, and Shemika cut her eyes at her.

"Not to change the subject, but yes, I do want you to call me even if I'm on a date. You could have called and said, 'Hey, Mika, here's what's up, here's what we're doing,' and at least give me a chance to decide whether I'm in."

"She's right," Elontra said. "And I'm sorry, we should have called you." She got some butter for her croissant. "I promise you that will never happen again."

"I know it won't," Dee Dee added. "I doubt if Elontra finds another check-cashing place with a busted lock, but I'm sorry too. If it ever happens again, I'm calling you. Now I'm changing the subject."

"Thank you," Elontra said, and once again, Shemika cut her eyes at her. "Sorry, Mi."

It was settled, but Shemika felt left out, and she was still a little hurt because of it.

"How was your date with Dominic? You were home too early to have gotten some dick, so how'd it go?" Dee Dee asked again, and Shemika's angry expression eased into a smile.

"Come on, Mika, give it up. Something got you smiling like that," Elontra encouraged her.

"Dominic was . . ." Shemika paused. "He was . . . Let me put it this way. So far, Dominic is everything that Elijah wasn't."

"He must have a job," Elontra said quickly.

"He paid for dinner, and he has a car," Shemika said.

"Where'd he take you?" Dee Dee asked.

"Some Portuguese restaurant called Brinca Deira."

"I never heard of it," Elontra said. "Was it nice?"

"Fuck that, was it expensive?" Dee Dee wanted to know. "Paying for dinner don't mean shit if you're eating at Mickey Dee's."

"I couldn't tell you." Shemika paused for effect. "There were no prices on the menu."

"You know what they say. If you have to ask how much, you can't afford it," Dee Dee commented.

"All that's fine, and believe me, I am so glad that you found a man with money, but do you like him?" Elontra asked because that was what was truly important.

"Yes, Elontra, I like him. We had a really nice time." She looked at Dee Dee. "And if he hadn't said good night when he did, I was gonna find out if he's everything Elijah was."

"I sure hope so," Elontra said and got up from the table. "You get grumpy when you don't get no dick."

"Is that what it is?" Dee Dee questioned and helped herself to more bacon and eggs.

"Yeah, girl, she is much nicer when she gets some dick."

"Fuck you, Elontra, and look who's talking. What's going on with you and DT?"

"He invited me to dinner at his uncle's house on Sunday, and this so-called cousin is supposed to be there, so we'll see." She chuckled because she was much happier when she got some dick. "But yeah, you're right."

They both looked at Dee Dee.

"When y'all start talking about years without dick, then y'all can talk to me."

"We need to find you a man," Elontra said.

"Or a woman," Shemika said, and it caught Elontra off guard.

She looked puzzled for a second or two, but then it made sense. "Or a woman."

"Thank you, but I'll find a man—or a woman—on my own," Dee Dee said. "But I appreciate the offer," she said as Shemika's cell phone began to ring.

She looked at the display and saw that it was Dominic calling. "Excuse me," she said, bouncing up from the table and rushing toward her room.

"That must be Dominic," Elontra said.

"Gotta be," Dee Dee added.

"Hello, Dominic," they heard Shemika say before she slammed the door.

Chapter Twelve

It was Saturday afternoon, and Dominic had taken Shemika to *Beyond Van Gogh: The Immersive Experience,* and then they planned to hang out on the boardwalk at Jones Beach. As for Elontra, she wasn't home either. She was in Brooklyn at the home of Derick's uncle Vincent Thomas. That afternoon, Uncle Vinnie was hosting a family barbeque, and Derick had invited, damn near insisted, that Elontra come so he could introduce her to his cousin Megan Cunningham.

"Alleged cousin," Elontra said to Dee Dee on her way out the door. "So we'll see how this goes. You sure that you don't wanna come with?"

"I'm sure. But bring me back a plate."

"You want a burger, hot dog, or chicken?"

"All three, and get me some ribs, too, if they got any."

"Anything else?"

"Some potato salad if it's good." Dee Dee giggled. "Not everybody can make good potato salad, you know."

"I know that's right."

Elontra took one last look at her outfit in the full-length mirror by the front door. "How do I look?" she asked of the Veronica Beard Keita canvas shorts, Ferazia canvas jacket, and black leather Tom Ford ankle-strap thong sandals she had selected for the occasion.

"You look cute," Dee Dee said and got up from the couch as Elontra grabbed her Coach tabby leather shoulder bag.

"See you later," Elontra said, and Dee Dee closed and locked the door behind her.

"Alone at last," she said on her way to the kitchen.

She grabbed a bag of tropical trail mix with cashews, Brazil nuts, dried mango, coconut flakes, and banana chips, a bag of Gummy Bears, and a Mountain Dew and headed for her room. She sat down in her X-Tech Ultimate executive chair, switched on her hardware, and got on the dark web.

Using sophisticated encryption technology, the dark web, consisting of websites that couldn't be found using a normal search engine, was one of the main hacker strongholds on the web and had become synonymous with black markets and other illegal activities. However, for Dee Dee, it was home, a safe haven where hackers could meet and discuss their craft with little fear of being exposed.

She was once what they referred to as a Black Hat hacker, the sort who broke into a system and stole stuff, as opposed to a White Hat hacker. The difference was that the White Hats generally worked to legally test and improve security. White Hats implemented it. For Black Hats, it was what they worked to defeat.

Now, after her ten-year State-sponsored vacation and mindful of the promise she made to herself, Dee Dee was trying to get her skills back up to par. At this point, she was little more than a script kiddie because all she could do was use software, tools, and techniques that other people had created.

If she was going to be of any use to the team, she would need to improve her knowledge and skills and get back to being able to write scripts on the fly. The scripts she'd run on the bank and check-cashing place were ones she'd copied from other hackers.

What most people called cybersecurity hackers called infosec. It was the practice of protecting information, foreseeing risk, and putting measures in place to prevent potential attacks like encryption, firewall implementation, and antivirus development. If she were going to once again do justice to the title of hacker, she would need to defeat those measures.

In order to accomplish that, for the last month or so, Dee Dee had been chatting online with a fellow hacker who was sympathetic to her situation and was offering advice and information. He was what was known as a hacktivist or politically motivated hacker. He was the type of hacker who used his knowledge of computer security to achieve political goals like breaking into a government system in order to extract information. Before he went on the run, he famously managed to hack into ARPANET, which was a network being run by the United States Pentagon. Those days, he operated under the screen name Hellscape, and nowadays his screen name was Cloudburst. After chatting for a while, each felt comfortable enough with the other to share real names.

Dee Dee.

Makaiden Hellström.

That's a very unique name, Dee Dee typed. What does it mean?

It's Swedish. It's a type of flat rock, combined with ström, which means stream.

That's interesting. Not what I expected, but interesting.

Most of my friends call me Kaiden.

Then I'll consider myself a friend and call you Kaiden too.

Well, friend, have you been working on the backdoor scripts I gave you to use as a template so you can get into a secured system and go around the usual security measures?

Backdoors were added to a system during its development that were not published or revealed, but implemented by the legitimate owner of the system so that they always had a way in. However, when an intrepid hacker discovered one, they could infiltrate the system and do a lot of damage.

I have. However, I've been focused on infecting a network of devices with malware to compromise the system so I can control all of them.

A minute or two had passed before Kaiden typed, Hmmm.

What?

What are you planning?

Nothing, she lied, because it was definitely a skill that would come in handy in the future. Just working to improve my skills, you know, get back to the level I was on.

Hmmm.

What?

Nothing. I just think your focus should be on writing your own scripts.

Instead of stealing yours?

Yes. But you'd be better served working on brute force attacks and taking the simplest and most direct approach to breaking a security measure.

They spent the rest of the afternoon and into the evening chatting about their past conquests and how things had changed in the past decade. Dee Dee found their digital conversation stimulating to both her mind and body. However, what she was particularly interested in was ways to defeat firewalls, penetrate networks, and take out cameras and alarms.

Piggybacking on authorized connections, or you could use a man in the middle attack to take control of an authorized communications stream and insert a command, Makaiden shared.

But wouldn't they counter those attacks by encrypting any communication that can potentially be hijacked, and restrict access to critical systems?

There's a tool that records the encryption passphrase and then decrypts its contents without trouble, he responded as there was a knock at the door of her computer room.

"Come in!" Dee Dee shouted, and Elontra opened the door and came in.

"What you doing?"

"Online chatting. What's up?"

"Who are you chatting with? I'm so nosy," she giggled.

"Just somebody I met online. Why? What up?"

"You wanna go to a party?"

"Yeah, I'm down."

"Shemika called and said that Dominic has passes for Cameron Cage's album release party tonight at Eastern Parkway Estates."

"Shit yeah, I wanna go."

"Then get dressed," Elontra said and left the room but came right back in. "You can invite your new friend if you want."

Dee Dee thought for a second or two. "I just might do that."

"Either way, I wanna hear all about him . . . or her."

"It's a him, and yes, you are so nosy."

Elontra put her hands on her hips and smiled. "How long have you known me?"

"Long enough to know how damn nosy your ass is."

"So you know I wanna know everything," Elontra said and left the room, and Dee Dee turned back to her keyboard.

Are you still there?

I am.

You wanna go to a party?

In the real world?

Yes, in the real world.

There was a long pause.

Sure, why not.

Have you ever heard of Cameron Cage?

Who hasn't?

There's an album release party for her at Eastern Parkway Estates.

Wow, of course I wanna go.

Once Dee Dee went to check with Elontra, she let Kaiden know that his name was added to the guest list. He wanted to know how he'd find her.

I'll be the cute black chick in red leather.

I'll be the scared-looking white boy.

Chapter Thirteen

Later that evening, Dee Dee emerged from her room wearing a red Dries Van Noten Larma leather turtleneck top and skirt with matching Alexander McQueen peep-toe sandals. Elontra was sitting on the couch waiting for her.

"About time," she said and stood up.

"That dress looks hot on you," Dee Dee said of the purple La Danza Zadeh cutout dress by BAOBAB that Elontra was wearing with Gianvito Rossi slingback pumps.

"Thank you." They walked to the door. "You're looking pretty sexy in that red. Like a sister with a plan for the evening."

"Just trying to look good standing next to you," Dee Dee said modestly and closed the door.

On the way to Eastern Parkway Estates, Dee Dee wanted to know what happened that afternoon at the Thomas family barbeque with cousin Megan.

"And yes, I am being nosy, so give it up," Dee Dee said as Elontra drove.

"So when she gets there, just about everybody was in the backyard. His uncle Vinnie—"

"Wait, Uncle Vinnie?" Dee Dee laughed. "Are you being serious with me right now?"

"Yes, not cousin Vinnie. Uncle Vinnie." Elontra chuckled. "But anyway, Uncle Vinnie rushes up to her went she gets there and announced, 'Hey, everybody, this is our cousin Megan Cunningham. She just moved here from Chicago.' Then he walked her around and introduced her to a few people."

"Did you talk to her?"

"Just long enough to be introduced. DT wouldn't let me get away to question her ass. But here's the thing. You know I was watching her, and I noticed that it was mostly the men who talked to her. From what I could see, she stayed away from the women in the family, and they really didn't have much to do with her."

"I'm gonna go ahead and call bullshit," Dee Dee said. "That sounds like that whole thing was staged for your benefit."

"See? I'm not paranoid. I was thinking the same thing." Elontra laughed. "If you could see the way one of his aunts rolled her eyes when Uncle Vinnie introduced her, you'd have screamed bullshit right then."

"So you done with him?"

"I would be, but he was there when Shemika called, so he'll be there tonight. But after that, we'll see."

"You know what I think?" Dee Dee asked.

"What you think, Dee Dee?"

"The nigga gotta go," she said as they arrived at Eastern Parkway Estates.

When Dee Dee and Elontra made it inside the event, Shemika was already there with Dominic, and Derick was sitting at the table with them. They were all enjoying themselves, listening to the music, pointing out celebrities, and people watching, when Elontra told Derick that she was going to the ladies' room.

"I'll go with you," Dee Dee said, standing up.

"We'll be right back," Elontra said, and the ladies walked off.

When the DJ began mixing some of Cameron Cage's old hits, Shemika and Dominic hit the dance floor, leaving Derick alone at the table.

They were on their way back to the table when Dee Dee saw a white man wandering around as if he were looking for somebody. "That might be Kaiden," she said.

"Where?" Elontra asked, and Dee Dee pointed him out. "He's cute."

"He is," Dee Dee said, looking at Kaiden and looking surprised. She didn't know what she was expecting him to look like. *Yes, I do. I expected him to be some nerdy white boy with zits.*

"I'll be right back."

"I'll be right here," Elontra said and watched Dee Dee until she reached the man.

When Dee Dee gave her the signal that it was indeed Kaiden, Elontra nodded and was about to head back to the table when she felt someone tap her lightly on the shoulder.

"Excuse me."

"Yes?" Elontra turned and came face-to-face with a dark-skinned man with the most intense brown eyes she'd ever seen.

"Can I talk to you for a second?" he said in her ear, and his deep voice shook Elontra to her core.

"We don't have time for that, Pee," the man with him said.

"Shut up, CK," he shouted without looking away from Elontra. "Like the man said, I don't really have time right now, but I would very much like to get to know you. Would it be all right if I called you sometime?"

"Yes." She glanced at the table. Derick was breaking his neck to watch a woman walking by the table. "I think it would be all right," Elontra said in his ear and reached into her GiGi New York leather clutch and took out her phone. "My name is Elontra. Elontra Montgomery."

"Pearson Alexander."

Elontra unlocked and then handed him her phone, and they exchanged numbers the same way she'd seen Derick do it the week before. He quickly tapped in his number and handed the phone back to her.

"Come on, Pee, we gotta go," his friend said impatiently.

She called his phone, and when it rang, he saved the number. "I got it," he said and leaned close to her. "Elontra." He leaned in closer and spoke in her ear. "That's a very pretty name for a very pretty lady."

"Thank you."

"I'll call you soon," Pearson promised and went off with CK as Dee Dee walked up with Kaiden.

"Elontra Montgomery, this is my friend Kaiden Hellström."

"It's nice to meet you, Kaiden," Elontra said, and the three headed for the table where Derick was waiting alone but getting his eyes full watching all of the fashionably dressed women in the house that night.

Elontra had just introduced Derick to Kaiden when Shemika and Dominic returned to the table, and Dee Dee introduced them.

"It's nice to meet you, Kaiden," Shemika said as Dominic shook his hand and then signaled for a waitress. When one did finally arrive, he ordered drinks for everybody, and that was when the commotion began not too far from them.

Elontra looked and saw that it was her new friend Pearson and his friend CK who were in the middle of the upheaval. CK grabbed a man out of his seat, punched him in the stomach, and then pushed him toward Pearson. He punched him in the face and threw him on a table. It broke on impact. CK rushed toward the man and dragged him until he was able to struggle to his feet.

CK punched him in the stomach and then pushed the man toward Pearson. He stumbled into Pearson's arms.

He straightened him up with a knee to the face. Pearson dragged him to the exit. The man tried to get to his feet, but before he could, CK kicked him in the face. Then he pulled him up and kept punching the man, and he kept backing up until he backed into Pearson. He grabbed the man, spun him around, punched him in the face, and threw him outside.

"Wow," Dee Dee leaned close to Elontra and said. "They beat the shit outta that man."

"That shit was brutal," she agreed, watching Pearson as he exited the venue but not letting on that she had just met him.

"I wonder what he did to warrant a beating like that," Derick said.

"I don't know, but whatever it was, it must have been serious," Elontra said, rubbing her thighs together.

For the rest of the night, Elontra couldn't get out of her mind Pearson Alexander and the beating she'd witnessed. Each time she thought about it, the more she wanted him. And when she left the party, Elontra followed Derick to his house, and they had what he considered makeup sex.

But for Elontra it was something a bit different.

Therefore, when Derick took one of her nipples into his mouth and sucked it, Elontra imagined that it was Pearson. And when he kissed his way down from her nipples along her stomach and didn't stop until he found the wetness between her thighs, it was Pearson's fingers that she felt gently massaging her clit and making her squirm on top of the sheets.

And when he entered her, Derick's pace was slow and methodical, and it brought with it thoughts of Pearson pumping deep inside her. It made her so wet that Elontra felt herself quickly building toward an orgasm.

And when it was over, she got out of bed and started getting dressed to leave. When Derick asked her what was wrong and why she was leaving, Elontra assured him that it had nothing to do with cousin Megan. But she still hadn't gotten past that.

"That's all behind us. I just got a lot on my mind that I need to work out, that's all."

"You sure that's all it is?"

"Yes, I'm sure, Derick, that's all it is," Elontra said as she put on her dress. Derick got out of bed to help her with the zipper.

"Thank you," she said, grabbed her purse, and headed out of the room with Derick in pursuit.

"I had a good time with you tonight. But I always do. Thanks for inviting me, and say thank you to Dominic for me."

"I'll call you tomorrow," Elontra said with a weak hug and a kiss on the cheek.

Chapter Fourteen

Over the next week, Dominic wined and dined Shemika in some of New York City's best restaurants. He took her to the off-Broadway performance of *No Tears in the End,* and she was his guest in the green room to meet the stars after the show. And through it all, Dominic was the perfect gentleman. Since Shemika wasn't comfortable with allowing him to know where they lived yet, they'd arrange a meeting spot, and he would be on time to pick her up.

And Dominic did the little things. He opened doors for her and held out her chair to sit down, and compliments flowed from his lips like water. But it was the way that he looked into her eyes when he said her name.

"Can I see you tomorrow, Shemika?" Dominic asked as he opened her car door. They had seen a movie and then shared a late grilled fish dinner at Kind of Blue.

"You sure can." Shemika turned to Dominic. "I'll text you my address. Why don't you pick me up at seven?" she said, and he stepped closer to her. Close enough to kiss.

"What do you wanna do tomorrow?" he asked and put his arms around her.

Shemika put her arms around his neck. "I'm sure we'll think of something."

When their lips touched, the flame that had been simmering inside Shemika raged, and she had to fight to control it. She wanted him now.

Instead, she kissed him, and she allowed his hands to travel from her waist to her breasts, and he caressed them. He began to nibble on Shemika's neck, and she ground her hips into his hardness. Their lips parted, and she stepped back, and like any good temptress, Shemika got in the car.

"See you tomorrow at seven," she said and closed the door.

"Can't wait," Dominic said and stood watching as Shemika drove off.

The following evening at seven, Dominic picked Shemika up at exactly seven o'clock. And after she introduced him to Elontra and Dee Dee, they left the house, and he took her to the Four Points by Sheraton.

Once they were in the suite, Dominic started to undress her. His lips and his kiss were hot and demanding, and it caused Shemika's lips to open and take his tongue deep into her mouth. She moaned with pleasure as he ran his fingers through her hair while his other held her tightly. Shemika gasped as he lifted her onto his lap, cradled her face in his big hands, and he kissed her hard and hungrily.

Her head drifted back, and her eyes drifted closed as his lips moved across her cheek and down her throat. He kissed her neck, and his lips trailed a path down to her breasts. Dominic pressed them together and took both nipples into his warm, wet mouth.

Shemika screamed, "Yes, Dominic, yes!" as her clit swelled, and she ground her body harder against him. "That feels so good," she whispered, aching for more as desire washed over her body.

He peered deeply into her eyes. "You are so beautiful," he said and got on his knees.

"Thank you," she breathed out.

Dominic ran his tongue along the edges of the lace and down the inside of her thighs. Shemika held his head in place as he ran his tongue up the seam of her panties. She moaned in breathless anticipation as he slid them off.

The closer he got to her wetness, the more Shemika squirmed. He began sucking her lips gently, gliding his tongue slowly along her lips, up one side and down the other. Then Dominic made circles around her clit with his index finger.

"Shit!" she screamed as he gently slid one finger inside of her.

He moved it in and out of her tight wetness slowly, circling her clit, keeping pace with his other finger. The circles became shorter and shorter, and then he massaged her clit lightly.

Dominic slid his tongue around the edges of her Brazilian-waxed mound and then spread her lips. Her back arched as he penetrated her with his tongue, moving in and out slowly and gently. She rotated her hips. He spread her lips apart, and with the tip of his tongue, he flicked against her bud until her moans got louder. Shemika reached out and held his head as her body tensed and shook.

"Shit yeah!" Shemika shouted.

Shemika closed her eyes and ground her hips in a slow, almost musical motion. She leaned back slightly and swayed from side to side, rubbing her nipples. Shemika wanted him inside her, and she felt her whole body shake from its core. In one fluid motion, he was on top of her, his heart was beating hard against her chest, and his breathing was as rapid as her own. She wrapped her arms around his neck, and they shared another ravenous kiss.

Reaching between her legs, he entered her in one thrust, and once he was deep inside of her, Dominic began thrusting hard and deep. His pace was relentless, and all she could do was nod, her breath too labored to speak. He kissed her again, pumping in and out with no mercy, giving it to her the way that she hoped he would, and it wasn't long before her body started to warm from the inside out. Her womb clenched hard, and Shemika released spasms around his long, hard dick.

Shemika squeezed his ass and arched up to meet his deep thrusts. He kissed her eyelids and her lips and sucked on her neck as he continued to pump hard and deep inside of her, making her shudder from the sweet sensation.

Shemika screamed, "Dominic!"

He covered her mouth with his and then pulled her on top of him. Shemika straddled his lap and slid down his length. Dominic bit his lip, and his brow furrowed as her body swallowed him inside of her. It was feeling that damn good. His hands reached for her hips as she moved up and down on him. She moved faster and harder, following his rhythm. His hands were all over her body, grabbing her swinging titties, catching one in his mouth and sucking her nipple like it was the sweetest thing that he'd ever tasted.

Shemika felt him so deep inside of her, and that made her walls squeeze around him hard. She leaned forward and kissed him, but she didn't stop moving, rotating, rocking, and swirling her hips, slamming down on him as if her life depended on it. The feeling was much more intense than anything either of them had ever experienced.

"Come on!" she screamed for more.

Dominic began to pound away, harder and faster as if this were the last bit of wet pussy in the world. The screams of passion brought them both to powerful and all-consuming orgasms. She was wrapped in his arms, her body still twitching from the toe-curling orgasm.

"That was good," she finally managed.

Chapter Fifteen

Elontra parked the black Corvette in the driveway and turned it off. She had just come from the Bronx, and she was excited about what she was about to share with her girls. When she went inside, Shemika and Dee Dee were sitting in the living room, watching television.

"Hey, y'all," she said.

"Hey."

"What's up, Elontra?" Dee Dee said.

"Turn that off. Kayla just turned me on to a job for us to look at."

Shemika picked up the remote and turned off the television. "What you got?"

"It's a jewelry store. The job pays fifty thousand dollars. We take all the diamonds in the safe and selected pieces from a display case." Elontra paused. "And that's where it gets tricky."

"Tricky?" Shemika asked.

"How tricky?" Dee Dee wanted to know.

Elontra took her time and ran down how the job was to go and all that it entailed. When she had laid it all out for her girls, she paused and looked around the room. "What do you think, Dee Dee?"

She thought for a second or two. "I can do it."

"Mika?"

"I can handle it. So the only question is, when are we gonna do it?" Shemika asked.

"We'll do it when we're ready to do it," Elontra said and told them her plan to get them ready to execute this robbery.

It was a Monday morning a month later when Dee Dee pulled the Lincoln up in front of the jewelry store. Dee Dee turned off the car. "I got something for us," Dee Dee said and handed small boxes to Elontra and Shemika.

"What are these?" Shemika asked as she opened her box.

"These are earpieces. So we can stay in contact with each other during the job," Dee Dee said.

"Thank you, Dee Dee. We've needed these for a long time," Elontra said and put hers in. "Sound check."

"I hear you," Dee Dee confirmed.

"I can too," Shemika concurred.

"So we ready to do this?" Elontra asked.

"I'm ready." Shemika nodded.

"Let's go do it then," Dee Dee said.

Dressed in their uniform black Dickies women's long-sleeve coveralls and Adidas women's Ultraboost 22 running shoes, Elontra got out and opened the rear passenger door for Shemika. They quickly walked down the street toward the store and got into position. Dee Dee took out her tablet and went to work on the security systems. Once she had disabled the cameras and the store alarms, she moved the Lincoln into escape position and exited the vehicle.

"It's a go," Dee Dee said as she walked past Shemika and Elontra and approached the store.

When Dee Dee reached the store, she grabbed the handle and went in. Elontra and Shemika fell in behind her, pulling down their masks as they entered the jewelry store.

"Everybody down!" Elontra yelled, moving to the middle of the store and standing with her arms spread eagle and a gun in each hand.

While Shemika covered, Dee Dee immediately stepped to the security guard and pressed the barrel of her gun into his back. The guard started to reach for his gun.

"Don't do it," Dee Dee whispered in his ear. "It's not worth it."

The security guard moved his hand away from his gun, and Dee Dee took it. She quickly removed the shells from the security guard's gun.

"Now get down on the floor and don't move."

Elontra holstered one weapon and pulled out a stopwatch. "Two minutes!"

Shemika and Dee Dee immediately took out large cloth bags and headed off to complete their tasks. As Dee Dee went into the office to prepare to take the safe, Shemika moved to the first targeted case, which was filled with gold and diamond-studded bracelets. Elontra had briefed them thoroughly on which pieces Kayla was interested in obtaining.

She took a deep breath.

The display case was armed with sensor beams that were invisible to the naked eye. If the beams were broken in any way, it would set off an alarm that was separate from the store alarms that Dee Dee had already disabled. She would need to cut and remove the glass before she could get the jewels. They had bought a similar display case and extra glass and had spent weeks practicing until Shemika could do it in under a minute and without tripping the alarm.

Shemika removed a glass cutter and suction cups from her bag. She placed the suction cup on the glass and, with the glass cutter, made four even cuts.

"Ninety seconds!"

Shemika carefully lifted the glass from the case and placed it on the floor at her feet. Then she reached in cautiously and began to remove the designated pieces from the case and dropped them into the bag.

"One minute," Elontra announced.

By that time, Dee Dee had the safe open and was emptying trays and uncut diamonds into her bag. She had brought along a device to implement a brute force attack that could attempt 2.8 trillion different password combinations—all lowercase, all alphabetic, six-digit passwords and mixed-case, mixed-character, or ten-digit passwords—in a matter of seconds, but she didn't need it.

To prepare to break the store's security measures, Dee Dee had hacked into their system and gained access to the cameras. She was able to slightly reposition the ones in the office so she could see the safe's keypad. It took her a week and a half of watching the manager enter the password before Dee Dee was sure that she had it down.

"Thirty seconds."

Dee Dee placed at the feet of Elontra the bag she had filled with the uncut diamonds from the safe. Then she made her way out of the store, got in the Lincoln, and prepared for the three to make their escape.

With time remaining, as planned, Shemika quickly moved to the next case that contained diamond necklaces and bracelets. Since there was no sensor beam alarm on that case, she broke the glass with her gun, removed the designated pieces, and put them in her bag.

"Time!"

Shemika stepped to Elontra and picked up the bag at her feet.

"What's it look like?" Elontra needed to know as she and Shemika backed out of the store.

"All clear," Dee Dee informed her.

"We're coming out," Elontra said.

As Elontra and Shemika exited the jewelry store, two cops came around the corner on foot and saw the two masked bandits.

"Freeze!" one yelled.

"Drop your weapons!" screamed the other.

"Shit!" Elontra said and reached into her backpack.

As Shemika rushed toward the Lincoln, Elontra took the MAC-10 with a suppressor out of the backpack. She began shooting in the direction of the cops, firing over their heads, and they took cover behind some cars. It allowed Shemika time to get to the Lincoln. She took out her 9 mm and began firing at the cops, who were pinned down behind the cars, to allow Elontra to make it safely into the Lincoln. The sound of police sirens approached.

"Get us outta here, Dee Dee!" Elontra shouted, and Dee Dee dropped the Lincoln into drive and sped off down the street. A police car was now in pursuit.

"Where did you get that gun from?" Shemika shouted.

"Not now, Mika," Elontra replied as Dee Dee drove the Lincoln up the street and made a hard left against oncoming traffic. They were headed westbound with the police car maintaining its pursuit. She made a sharp right onto the next street with the police closing in on their vehicle.

"You need to get them off me!" Dee Dee shouted.

Elontra got up and opened the sunroof.

"What are you doing?" Shemika demanded to know.

Elontra stuck her head out the sunroof.

"What are you doing, Elontra?" she said louder.

"Not now, Mika," Dee Dee said as Elontra fired several rounds.

The police car dropped back as Dee Dee made a left and then another left. With the police momentarily out of sight, she quickly made her way to the pickup spot in a parking garage. She quickly made her way to the top level and parked next to the stairs. All three got out of the car, ran to the stairwell, and ran down the steps to the next level seconds before the police approached the Lincoln. Parked by the stairwell was an old Chrysler Pacifica.

The ladies got in and quickly began to take off their Dickies and running shoes. Each had a dress on under it: an English Factory baby doll ruffled dress for Dee Dee, a Wayf ruched mock turtleneck dress for Shemika, and an Aidan by Aidan Mattox one-shoulder fit-and-flare minidress for Elontra. Once they were changed, Shemika and Elontra exited the vehicle, and Dee Dee got behind the wheel of the Pacifica.

Shemika and Elontra took their time walking to the other escape cars: an old Toyota Corolla, and an old Nissan Altima. Shemika got in the Corolla and started it up. As Dee Dee drove away, Elontra got in the Altima and waited for Shemika to drive off before she started the car. Her jaws got tight as the police car rolled slowly past her.

When she got to the last pickup spot, Dee Dee pulled the Pacifica up next to a Lexus and got out. She had just put her bag of jewelry in the Lexus when Shemika pulled up. She got out, got her bag, and got in the Lexus as Elontra arrived. As soon as she was in the car, Dee Dee started the car and drove them to Kayla's house. When they arrived, Kayla opened the door.

"Good to see you, ladies. Come inside." They walked into the house past Kayla. "What have you got for me?" She closed and locked the door.

"We have the items we discussed," Elontra said.

"Good deal. I knew you ladies could handle it. Did you have any problems?"

"No," Elontra said quickly, believing that she didn't need to know about the cops.

"Come on," she said, and they followed her into the dining room.

Kayla sat down at the table and proceeded to meticulously examine each piece. It was an hour later when Kayla put down her loupe and looked at Elontra.

"Very impressive, ladies," she said and got up from the table. When she returned, she had a metal briefcase with her. She placed it on the table in front of Shemika. "As promised, fifty thousand dollars."

Elontra got up. "Pleasure doing business with you," she said, and she shook hands with Kayla as Shemika opened the case and began her count.

"Now that you've upgraded your level of skill," Kayla said, looking at Dee Dee, who was watching Shemika count their money. "I may have some more work for you ladies."

Dee Dee looked toward Kayla. "We appreciate it," she said and nodded.

"It's all here," Shemika said, closed the case, and got up.

Elontra started for the door, and Dee Dee stood up. "We're out," Elontra said, and they left the house.

"Now let's talk about that gun, Elontra," Shemika said as soon as they were in the car.

Dee Dee started it up. "Not now, Mika," she said and drove off.

"Give me a chance to breathe," Elontra said and got comfortable for the ride to Massapequa.

"Okay, but we are gonna talk about it when we get home."

Chapter Sixteen

Once they had crossed the Throgs Neck Bridge, they ditched the Lexus at a Bagel Club, and once they were in Shemika's BMW, she drove them home. When they got there, all three ladies sat down at the dining room table while Shemika counted and split the money.

"Sixteen thousand six hundred," she said and slid the stack of bills to Elontra, and she began her count.

Despite the fact that she carried one on every job, Shemika didn't like guns. "Where'd you get the gun?" Shemika asked as she slid Dee Dee her share.

"I got it from Kayla when I told her that we were going to do the job. She said we might need some extra firepower for this job."

"And she was right," Dee Dee said while she counted.

"Did you know about this?" Shemika asked.

Elontra and Dee Dee were already the best of friends when Shemika moved to the neighborhood, and there were times when she felt left out. It was something that she thought she had gotten past in adulthood, but maybe not.

"No, but I'm glad she had it."

"Why didn't you tell us?"

"Because I didn't want you to talk me out of bringing it," Elontra explained.

"What kind of gun is it anyway?"

"It's a MAC-10."

There was silence in the room.

"You did right." Shemika nodded. "I would have told you that we've been doing fine and that we didn't need it."

Elontra stood up. "I didn't just meet you, girlfriend," she said, picked up her money, went into her bedroom, and closed the door.

Shemika glanced over at Dee Dee. She was finished counting her money.

"What?"

"Nothing," Shemika said, and she got up from the table and sat right back down. "You think I'm wrong?"

"About what? Elontra and the MAC?"

Shemika nodded.

"No, but Elontra was right not to talk to us about it because I would have said we didn't need it too. But like I said, I'm glad she had it, and don't think I didn't see you." Dee Dee laughed. "Busting shots at the cops so Elontra could make it to the car."

"I've never been so scared in my life, Dee Dee," Shemika admitted.

"It all happened so fast that I didn't have time to think about it until we got to Kayla's. That's when it hit me," Dee Dee admitted.

"In the ten years we've been at this, this is the first time that we had to deal with the police," Shemika said, and Dee Dee got up from the table.

"If we step up to bigger jobs, it may be something that we have to get used to," Dee Dee said.

Shemika stood up. "And since we've stepped up to bigger jobs, we need to start planning for them."

Elontra slept late the following morning and was awakened by her cell phone ringing. Without opening her eyes, she felt around the nightstand until she found it. "Hello."

"Good morning, you sexy-talking devil."

"What's up, DT?"

"Just wanted to know if you had any plans for tonight."

"No," a still-groggy Elontra answered.

"Why don't I pick you up around eight-ish, we have dinner, and then we find something to get into?" Derick proposed.

"Okay," she said, mostly because she didn't feel like talking. "Talk to you later."

She put the phone down, peeked at the clock, saw that it was ten forty-five, and went back to sleep. It was after one in the afternoon when Elontra finally emerged from her room. The house was in silence. She went into the kitchen to see if Shemika had cooked that morning and saved a plate for her. Elontra opened the refrigerator. No plate.

"Damn," she said aloud because she was hungry.

Elontra left the kitchen and went back to her room to shower and get dressed, thinking about where and what she wanted to eat. Once she was dressed in a Rodarte floral silk, satin, and chiffon wide-leg jumpsuit that she thought she would look cute in and Alexandre Birman Aila leather strappy mules adorned her pretty feet, Elontra got in the black Corvette and headed out.

She had decided that she was in the mood for seafood, and since she liked the food and the view, Elontra settled on Captain Jack's so she could have lunch on the patio. When her server arrived, she ordered a Dark and Stormy cocktail that was made with dark rum, ginger beer, and a splash of lime juice to enjoy with blackened mahi-mahi, roasted potatoes, sautéed spinach, and a magnificent view of South Oyster Bay.

She had just finished eating and was seriously thinking about a slice of New York cheesecake and a scoop of ice cream for dessert when she saw the hostess seat Derick and Megan. Her first thought was to give him the benefit of the doubt. After all, it might be Derick taking his new-in-town cousin Megan out for lunch. That ended when not his cousin Megan slid her happy ass into the booth next to him.

Elontra was shocked and angry to see them there together, but she was not at all surprised. She'd known that there was something going on between them since she saw them exchange numbers at the club, and the little charade they tried to pull off at his uncle Vinnie's barbeque was unconvincing.

Since then, she had planned to move on from the situation. Her feeling about it was that if a man wanted to be with another woman, there was nothing that was going to stop him. With that thought in mind, Elontra had been giving Derick distance, making excuses not to see him. Now she saw how he had chosen to fill the void. Although she wasn't surprised, it still hurt to see them out together.

All types of things to do in response to Derick's betrayal rushed through her mind.

Should I go over there, throw a drink in Derick's face, and bitch slap Megan?

Should I go over there and curse them both the fuck out?

Should I send them a bottle of their cheapest champagne to celebrate their new relationship?

Elontra had just decided to not make a scene, walk out, and confront him about it later that night, but that was when Derick looked up, and they made eye contact.

"Shit," she could see him say, and then he leaned close to Megan and discreetly pointed to Elontra. He got up and came toward the table.

"Hello, DT," she said, and he stopped in front of the table looking mad.

"Are you following me?"

Are you kidding me? "No, I'm not following you," she said just as the server got to the table.

"Can I get these out of your way?" she asked.

Derick looked and saw the plate, silverware, and glasses on the table, so he knew that she wasn't following him.

"Yes, I'm finished," Elontra said, and the server cleared the table.

"Can I get anything else for you?"

"Just the check, thank you."

Derick glanced at Megan, and the server finished up and walked away from the table.

"It's not what you think."

"Yes, it is. It's exactly what I think it is. You're cheating on me with her. How could you do this to us?"

"I'm sorry. Elontra. I never meant to hurt you."

"Because I was never supposed to find out." Elontra shook her head in angry disgust. "So what was your plan? Wine and dine her for lunch and fuck me after dinner? And aren't you supposed to be at work?" Elontra asked as her server returned with the check. "He gets the check," she said, and the server handed it to him.

"I'll take that whenever you're ready," she said and walked away.

Elontra stood up and grabbed her Coach jacquard satchel. "Goodbye, Derick. I hope I never see you again."

As tears rolled down her cheeks, Elontra dropped her head and walked quickly out of Captain Jack's. She got in her car and drove away, but instead of going home, she got on Sunrise Highway and drove north, crying. Two hours later, Elontra found herself in East Hampton, driving by Two Mile Hollow Beach. She parked her car, got out, and walked toward the beach. Once she reached the sand, Elontra took off her sandals and walked through the water.

As she walked, Elontra thought about how she felt betrayed. The thoughts and visual images of him having sex with Megan filled her mind and were hard to escape from. The image in her mind played back over and over again until she shouted, "Stop!" at the top of her lungs. "Fuck that nigga!" Somehow, it made her feel a little better.

She didn't understand why it happened, why he didn't want her anymore, and it affected her self-worth. On some level, Elontra felt like Derick was cheating on her because she wasn't enough for him.

Am I not attractive enough?

Am I too fat or too skinny?

Am I not sexual enough to satisfy him?

Or was his plan to fuck both of us?

Then she thought maybe it was just a physical thing for him.

Is Derick fulfilling a sexual fantasy with her?

Maybe he just wanted to have sex with Megan and not ruin what he had with me.

Was he not happy in the relationship and that's why he cheated on me?

"If he were happy, he wouldn't have cheated on me. Right?" she asked herself aloud. "Wrong. He's just another thirsty man trying to get as much pussy as he can get away with."

After a while, she turned around and walked back to the spot where she parked, and she sat down on a bench. She was telling herself that it wasn't her or anything that she had done when her cell phone rang. She dug into her shoulder bag and looked at the display. It was Pearson calling, and she started not to answer.

"Hello."

"Can I speak with Elontra, please?"

"This is she speaking."

"How you doing, Elontra? This is Pearson Alexander. We met at Eastern Parkway Estates."

"I remember," Elontra said with a slight smile breaking through as she wiped away the last of her tears, deciding in that second that she was done crying over Derick's betrayal of her trust. "How are you?"

"I'm good."

"Listen, this really isn't a good time for me. But please, call me again because I do want to talk to you. Like I said, this just isn't a good time for me."

"I understand. So yeah, I will call you again, and again, until it is a good time to talk to you, because I know that I want to know you and everything about you, Elontra." He paused. "That is such a beautiful name."

"Thank you, Pearson. That was nice of you to say." It made her smile. "I'm gonna go now."

"I'll talk to you soon, Elontra," Pearson said, and he ended the call.

As afternoon turned into evening and the sun began to set, Elontra got up from her spot and went back to her car. She stopped at the Os Grilos Grill. She wasn't hungry, but she needed a drink. Elontra sat down at the bar.

"What can I get for you?"

"Surprise me. As long as it's strong."

"One Aunt Roberta cocktail coming up," he said and placed a bar napkin in front of her.

When he returned, the bartender placed a red drink in a martini glass in front of her, and she took a sip.

"That's good." She took another sip. "It's strong, but it's good. You said it's called an Aunt Roberta?"

"That's right," he said as he wiped down the bar.

"What's in it?"

"Gin, vodka, brandy, blackberry liquor, and absinthe."

It didn't take her long to drain the glass, and he brought her another. After her third Aunt Roberta cocktail, Elontra called for the check and made the drive back to Massapequa. When she arrived at the house, Shemika and Dee Dee were in the living room, and Elontra hoped that she could make it to her room without having to answer any questions.

"Good, you're home," Shemika said as soon as she closed the door.

Elontra glanced in the full-length mirror by the door to see if her eyes were still red and puffy from crying. "What's up?" she asked and sat down, glad that her eyes wouldn't tell her story.

"We were talking about the last job and the police," Dee Dee said.

"This isn't still about the gun, is it?" Elontra wanted to know because as far as she was concerned, her having the MAC-10 was a closed issue and she had no desire to talk any more about it.

"No, it's not about that," Shemika said. "We've never had to deal with the police before, and I thought that from now on, we should start planning for police intervention and come up with contingencies for dealing with them."

"I think that's a good idea." Elontra stood up and started for her room. "With us stepping up to bigger jobs it makes sense that we plan for the cops. It's something we should have been doing all along."

She didn't say anything else. Elontra simply left the living room and went into her room, closing the door behind her.

"What's wrong with her?" Dee Dee asked.

Shemika shrugged her shoulders. "I don't know what's wrong with her, but there's definitely something bothering her."

Chapter Seventeen

Since the last bank job was such a successful operation, even easy, Shemika had been busy scouting out another for her and her girls to hit. She selected a target and began surveilling it. Shemika parked her car in a spot near the bank where she would be able to see the entire parking lot and both entrances and exits to and from the bank. She spent the entire day in her car watching the bank. When she had to use the bathroom, she went to a store nearby and picked up something to eat at the same time.

She'd paid close attention to her surroundings and taken pictures of the employees as well as the customers who came to the bank on a regular basis. She paid particular attention to armored truck delivery days and times, who the driver was, and who was riding shotgun. She had even been developing a profile on the drivers. In order to break up the day, Shemika began taking short drives around the neighborhood to check streets and traffic patterns in the area for escape routes.

In order to get a feel for the layout, Shemika opened an account at the bank and deposited some money. It allowed her to observe the comings and goings in the institution. While she was in the bank conducting business, Shemika observed the layout of the bank and studied its procedures.

There was one more thing that Shemika knew that she needed to do in preparation to take this next bank. If they were going to stay in this business, they needed to be aware of police response times. But since they had never done it before, she wasn't exactly sure how she was going to do it.

Even though they were confident that Dee Dee could take out the cameras and alarm systems, the fact that the cops just happened to walk up on them had a profound effect on her. And if there was anything that she could do to keep Elontra from needing to pull out the MAC-10, that was what she was going to do.

On her way to the bank the following day, Shemika stopped at a convenience store. While she was there, she got gas and then went into the store. The night before, she had made some spinach tortellini and shrimp skewers to snack on during her surveillance operation and wanted to pick up a sugar-free electrolyte drink. On her way to the register to check out, Shemika picked up a couple of burner phones before she left the store, and then she headed for the bank.

Her research told her that, on average, the police responded to robbery calls within five minutes 32 percent of the time, and within ten minutes 38 percent of the time. Their strict two-minute limit should be sufficient to insulate them, but it was time to test that. It was a little after eleven thirty and the bank was starting to get busy. She took out the burner and dialed 911.

"911 operator. What's your emergency?"

"I'm outside the First Premier Bank, and I just saw a man go into the bank with a gun."

And then Shemika hung up the burner, took out her cell, and opened the stopwatch app. It was four minutes and twenty-eight seconds when the first cars began to arrive. The following day she made the same call, only that day Shemika directed the police to a big-box appliance store in the same plaza and found that the response times were similar.

It was getting late in the evening, and she had accomplished her task for the day. Shemika was getting bored and was thinking about calling it a day when her phone rang.

"Hey, Mika," Dominic said.

"How you doing?"

"Wondering what you're doing tonight."

"Spending the night with you. Why? What are you doing tonight?"

"Trying to find the quickest way to be deep inside you. What you doing now?"

"I was just finishing up for the day on a project I've been working on."

"Well, since you're just finishing up, why don't you meet me at my place and we'll see what develops from there?"

"Sounds like you got it all figured out."

"I do."

"Well, I need to stop at the house for a minute to holla at my girls and freshen up. But after that, I'll be on my way," Shemika said and started the car. "Think you can hold out for that long?"

"It won't be easy, but I can handle it. Just know that the longer you make me wait, the harder it's gonna be on you."

"Is that a promise or a threat?"

"Oh, it's definitely a promise, for sure."

"Harder is always good. Deeper, too, but that's just me thinking out loud. So I'll see you soon," Shemika said and ended the call.

When Shemika arrived at the house, Dee Dee and Elontra were watching *Let's Make a Deal* because they both thought that Wayne Brady was fine.

"Hey, Mika," they both said at the same time.

"Where you been all day?" Dee Dee asked.

"I've been out scouting our next job," Shemika said and sat down on the couch next to Dee Dee.

"I thought you said that with the money we made from the last job we could lie low for a while," Elontra said.

"I did say that, and we could do that." She turned off the television. "But I don't see anything wrong with planning so when we do decide that it's time to work again, we'll be ready."

"I hear you," Dee Dee said.

"Can't argue with your logic. So what you got for us?"

"We're gonna take the First Premier Bank." She stood up. "I'll be right back," Shemika said and went to her room.

"Where's she going?" Dee Dee asked.

"I don't know," Elontra said as Shemika returned to the room and called for her girls to join her in the dining room. She laid a diagram of the bank on the table.

"Impressive," Elontra said, looking over the detail Shemika had put into her diagram.

"You're serious about this one, aren't you?" Dee Dee asked.

"I am," Shemika said proudly because she had put a lot of work into this plan and was happy that her girls recognized and appreciated it.

Elontra's phone rang with a call from Derick. She glanced at the display, rolled her eyes, and ignored it. "Go ahead, Mika. What you got for us?"

"Something going on with you and Derick?"

"He decided that he wanted to be with another woman, and I decided not to be a part of it," Elontra said and sat down at the table.

"I'm sorry, Elontra," Dee Dee said and hugged her.

"Megan?" Shemika asked.

"Yup. I saw them together at Captain Jack's."

"What did you do?" Dee Dee wanted to know.

"I didn't cause a scene and make a fool of myself, if that's what you're asking. Even though I wanted to, I didn't throw a drink in Derick's face, and I didn't bitch slap the fuck outta Megan. And as bad as I wanted to, I didn't curse them both the fuck out." Elontra laughed and it felt good. "I did think about sending them a bottle of champagne, you know, to celebrate their new relationship, but I didn't do that either." Her girls laughed. "I just told him that I was done with him and I hoped that I never see him again."

"I'm sorry, Elontra," Dee Dee repeated, and Elontra nodded.

"So enough of that." Elontra bravely posted her power smile. "What you got for us, Mika?" she asked, and Shemika told them what she observed.

When she was finished laying it all out for them, Shemika asked, "What do you think?"

"Sounds good to me. I'm in," Elontra said.

"I'll have to look at their security systems, but yeah, it sounds good to me too."

But even though they said they weren't going to do any jobs for a while, it was that next Friday morning at approximately 10:15 a.m. when Dee Dee drove the stolen Dodge Charger GT sedan into the bank parking lot. She took out her tablet and easily disabled the bank's security systems.

"Alarms are down, and cameras are disabled."

Elontra pointed out the security guard as he came out of the bank and began walking around the sidewalk. "Time," she said and started the clock.

As time ticked away, all three donned masks, exited the vehicle, and quickly approached the guard just as he was about to enter the bank.

Dee Dee put a gun in his back. "Behave yourself and you won't have to die today,"

He put his hands up, and she took his gun. Dee Dee walked him into the bank as Elontra and Shemika rushed in behind them.

"Nobody move!" Elontra yelled, moving to the center of the bank with her two guns drawn. "Two minutes!"

With security disarmed and on the floor, Dee Dee cleared the offices and moved everybody to the center of the room. She ordered them to get on the floor while Elontra covered. Shemika wasted no time and quickly found the bank manager. He had the key for the cart on his waist. She put her gun to the manager's head.

"Give me the key!" she ordered, and he quickly gave it up. "Now get on the floor."

"Ninety seconds!" Elontra called as Shemika joined Dee Dee behind the counter.

As Dee Dee got the money in the drawers in each of the teller positions, Shemika took the rolling cart before she helped Dee Dee clear the cash drawers.

"One minute!"

Once Dee Dee had gotten the cash from the drawers, she gave her bag to Shemika, and she exited the bank to prepare to make their escape.

"Thirty seconds!"

Now that she had cleared all the teller positions, Shemika came from behind the counter and made her way to the exit.

"Time!" Elontra announced. "We're coming out."

"We got trouble out here," Dee Dee said as Elontra and Shemika backed out of the bank with their guns raised. "Cops just pulled in the parking lot!" she shouted, took out her gun, and fired as the police exited their vehicle with their guns out.

"Police!"

"Freeze!"

When Elontra got the MAC-10 from her backpack and opened fire, the cops dropped behind their car for cover. Not wanting to kill a cop and have every law enforcement officer in the state hunting her, she concentrated her fire on the hood and windshield.

"Aim for the tires!" Elontra shouted.

Shemika dropped to one knee, took aim, and pulled the trigger. Where Elontra made a point of going to the shooting range at least once a week, Shemika never went. Therefore, when she emptied the clip, one of her shots ricocheted off the ground and just happened to hit the tire.

"Go!" Elontra yelled and put another clip in the MAC.

Dee Dee kept firing as Shemika made it to the car and got in. Elontra tossed Dee Dee her bag and marched firing to the car. Once she was in, Dee Dee put the SUV in reverse and slammed into the police car as the officers dove to get out of the way. She put the SUV in drive, cut the wheel hard, and stepped on it. Elontra heard sirens approaching in the distance.

"Get us away from here, Dee Dee!" Shemika yelled.

She turned sharply onto the street, swerving to avoid the oncoming cars. With the police in pursuit, Dee Dee drove them away from there, dodging cars as she sped by them. The light turned yellow as they approached.

"Hold on!"

DeeDee floored it, and she made it across the intersection before the light turned red. But so did the police. It didn't take long for the squad car to close the gap as she weaved her way through traffic on the crowded street.

Just then, the cars in front of her began putting on brakes. She cut across lanes and drove on the median to avoid hitting the cars. Dee Dee slammed on her brakes and cut the wheel hard. The car turned sharply and ended up facing in the other direction. Before the cops could react to her move, Dee Dee sped away and drove to where the drop car was parked.

"What happened?" Elontra demanded to know. "I thought you took out the alarms."

"I did."

“Then what were the cops doing there?” Elontra shouted.

“I don’t know!” Dee Dee shouted back.

“It couldn’t have been the alarm!” Shemika shouted. “Response times are close to five minutes, and we were outta there early! Even if an alarm was sent, they couldn’t have gotten there that fast!”

Elontra calmed down and she looked out the back window. “I don’t see anybody.”

Believing it was safe, and the tension between them waning, Dee Dee drove to the drop car as Shemika’s and Elontra’s pounding hearts began to slow down and they got out of their Dickies.

They got out of the car, and without saying a word, they transferred the money to the drop car while Dee Dee changed. Once she was in the car, Shemika drove them to her car, and then they went home in silence. They had just had their first real close encounter with police, and they were scared more than they were angry with each other.

As they always did after a job, the three assembled in the dining room to divide the money. No one said a word while Shemika counted the money. They barely looked at each other as she gave each their share.

“I’m going to my room,” Elontra said and got up.

As the door to her room closed, Dee Dee stood up and walked away from the table. She stopped just before she reached the hallway that led to her room.

“Thanks for having my back with Elontra,” she said without turning around and then continued down the hall.

“No problem,” Shemika said, folding her arms on the table and resting her head.

Chapter Eighteen

Other than coming into the living room to open the front door for takeout food, nobody came out of their rooms much that night. Shemika got up early the next morning and cooked breakfast for everybody. Then she fixed her plate and went back to her room, leaving Elontra and Dee Dee to help themselves whenever they dragged themselves out of bed. That day, all three made a point of staying out of the house, and that continued into the next day. That afternoon, Elontra purposely planted herself in the living room and waited for Dee Dee to come home. She turned off the television when she saw the 280ZX pull into the driveway.

"Hey," she said to Elontra and started for her room.

"Wait a minute, Dee Dee."

She stopped and put her hands on her hips. "What is it?"

"I think all of us need to talk."

"I think so too." Dee Dee moved to sit down on the couch.

Elontra took a breath. "Mika!"

"What!" she shouted from her room.

"Could you come out here for a minute, please?"

"Coming!" she shouted.

Elontra and Dee Dee sat in the living room looking at one another until Shemika came out and sat down next to Dee Dee. "What's up?"

Dee Dee extended her hand toward Elontra.

"I think we need to talk about the other day."

"I agree," Dee Dee said, and it was obvious that she had a bit of an attitude about how it all went down.

"Where do we start?" Shemika asked.

Elontra turned and looked at Dee Dee. "I'm sorry, Dee. I shouldn't have yelled at you."

"No, you shouldn't have." Dee Dee nodded because that was really all she needed to hear. "But I get it. I knew I shut off the alarms, but when I saw the cops, I was questioning myself."

"I think that was everybody's first thought," Shemika said. "I knew that it couldn't have been the alarm. I clocked the police response times at close to five minutes, and we were outta there early for a change." She turned and looked at Dee Dee. "So even if they did send an alarm, there was no way that the cops could have gotten there that fast."

"Still, I overreacted, and I'm sorry," Elontra said. "In my defense, I had just been through a very traumatic experience." She smiled, and her girls both laughed.

"I think we all did," Dee Dee said.

"And that was some hella driving you did to get us outta there," Shemika said and high-fived Dee Dee.

"I knew getting all those speeding tickets in L.A. would come in handy sometime," she laughed.

"Thanks for getting us outta there," Elontra said.

"But that's the second time we've had to run from the cops," Shemika said, and then she paused. "And to me, that is two times too many."

"Like we said, Mika, we've stepped up to bigger targets," Dee Dee began. "Police involvement was inevitable."

"Yeah, but it's happening too often. Are we gonna have to fuck with them every time out?" Elontra questioned.

"Maybe," Shemika said. "And maybe it's time that we rethink how we do what we do."

"Maybe it is," Elontra said solemnly.

"I agree, and that's on me," Dee Dee said, knowing that improving her skill level hadn't been a priority. She was free, and DeeDee was more interested in enjoying that freedom than being stuck in her computer room all day and night. "If we're gonna keep doing this, I need to start looking for jobs that don't require us to walk into places with guns."

"And as your skills improve and you get better connected, I'm sure you will. Right now, we just got the jobs we get from Kayla and what we plan on our own," Elontra said and looked at Shemika. "But in the meantime, I think we need to leave these banks alone for a minute."

"You never liked messing with banks anyways," Shemika pointed out. "But I agree with you." She laughed a little. "Especially these banks out here on the island."

"Cops be rolling around protecting these white folks' money," Dee Dee mused.

"All the more reason for us to back off," Elontra said. "Or at least stop shitting where we eat."

"What do you mean, stop shitting where we eat?" Shemika asked.

"Just that we live around here, and maybe we need to think about working in New Jersey or Connecticut."

"Or Delaware even," Dee Dee added.

"We do our work out of state and come on home? I like the sound of that," Shemika said and got up.

"Anyway," Elontra said, "I'm glad we got past that. I hate it when we aren't speaking."

Shemika sat down again. "So it's agreed. We back off and chill for a while."

"Agreed," both Elontra and Dee Dee said, but despite that, when Kayla called Elontra later that same day and asked her to drop by the club, she said, "I'll see you tonight."

That night, Elontra arrived at the club where Kayla sometimes did business and was escorted to a table. "Kayla will be with you as soon as she can," the waitress said. "Until then, enjoy the show."

It was male revue night, and Elontra laughed because she knew Shemika would be envious because she didn't get to see the men dance. She had been there for an hour when Kayla sat down at the table with her.

"Sorry about keeping you waiting."

"No problem. I've been enjoying the view." She laughed. "What's up?'

"I got another job I thought you might be interested in."

"What's the job?"

"Let's talk in the back."

Kayla stood up and Elontra followed her to the storage room. She looked around at the boxes stacked against the walls of the small room. "So what's the job?" she asked when Kayla closed and locked the door.

"Another jewelry store." Kayla sat on some boxes. "Nothing you ladies haven't done before."

"True." It had been their specialty until they stepped up to banks.

"The only difference this time is that there's going to be a man with a briefcase that I need you to get for me."

"What's in the case?"

"Uncut African conflict diamonds." Kayla paused. "You interested?"

"I'm listening."

Kayla went into the details of the job, and once she had gone over the where and when, she said, "It's a simple snatch and grab. Nothing you haven't done a bunch of times. The job pays seventy-five thousand dollars. I know you need to run it by your crew, but get back to me soon."

"Will do," Elontra said, and then she left the club to run the job by her girls.

Despite their conversation earlier that same day, Shemika and Dee Dee were interested in doing the job.

"I'm in," Shemika said.

"Me too," Dee Dee said without hesitation.

Then Elontra pointed out that the job was in Manhattan and not on the island, so they were sticking to what they had agreed to: to not commit robberies so close to home. Since there were no questions, they began planning to rob the jewelry store for Kayla.

On the designated afternoon on a crowded Manhattan street, a limousine parked in front of the store, and the driver got out. Once he opened the back door and the man with the briefcase chained to his wrist got out, they walked toward the jewelry store. Elontra and Shemika fell in behind them and pulled down their masks as they approached the door of the jewelry store. The man with the briefcase handcuffed to his wrist walked to the door. Dee Dee followed the driver into the store and pulled down her mask. She pressed the barrel of her gun into the man's back. He started to reach for his gun.

"Don't do it."

Dee Dee took his gun as Shemika took out a small but sturdy set of bolt cutters and cut the handcuff chain, freeing the briefcase. She emptied the contents into her bag and dropped the briefcase. Other than that, it was like Kayla had said: "Just like any other jewelry store that you've robbed." Dee Dee took out the cameras and alarms and they went in.

"Two minutes!"

Dee Dee disarmed the security guard, and then she and Shemika took out large cloth bags and got to their tasks. She implemented a brute force attack and took the safe. Shemika removed the targeted gold and diamond pieces from the display cases. Dee Dee left the store and prepared for their escape.

That was when everything got very real.

Dee Dee saw two cars coming at them fast. As they got closer, she could see that there were two men in each car, and then she saw the guns come out the windows.

"Y'all need to get outta there now!" Both cars stopped across the street from the jewelry store, and the gunmen began getting out. "There's four of them out here, and they have guns!"

As two of the men got out of their vehicle and stood in the street, Elontra and Shemika exited the jewelry store. All four gunmen raised and pointed their weapons.

"Freeze!" one yelled, and another opened fire with AK-47s.

"Get down!" Dee Dee shouted and took out her weapon and returned their fire. As the people on the street ran and found cover wherever they could, Elontra backed into the doorway, and Shemika dove for cover behind a car.

Elontra took out the MAC-10 and got to one knee. She raised the MAC and fired several shots in the direction of the men, and they fired back. The men took cover behind some cars as Elontra kept shooting. When they returned fire, Elontra dropped for cover, and she and Shemika lay motionless as bullets flew over their heads. Dee Dee crawled behind the car.

"You okay?" Elontra asked while she waited for a chance to fire back.

"I'm all right."

"We gotta make it to the car!" Shemika shouted.

"I'm gonna make a run for it," Dee Dee replied.

Elontra readied the MAC-10. "I'll cover you!"

Dee Dee handed Shemika her gun. When there was a lull in the shooting, Shemika began shooting with both guns while Elontra fired the MAC.

"Go!" Elontra shouted, and Dee Dee stayed low and made her way toward the Rodeo.

Elontra turned and fired at one man as he came around the car. He took cover. Shemika came up firing both guns. When the men returned their fire using semi-automatic weapons, Elontra grabbed Shemika, and they hit the ground. Elontra stood up and fired from behind the car.

She ducked down. "Who are these guys?"

"I don't know!" Shemika stood up and fired a couple of shots at their attackers. The once-crowded street now seemed deserted. "We gotta get outta here!"

She took cover behind a car with Elontra. The men continued firing at them. They had them pinned down and began moving toward them. Shemika tightened her grip on her guns, rose up, and fired. She took cover as the men continued shooting at her.

As the shooters kept firing, Shemika and Elontra saw that Dee Dee had made it to the Rodeo. She got in, started it up, dropped it in reverse, and floored it. When they saw her coming, they came up firing.

Dee Dee drove the Rodeo between Shemika, Elontra, and the shooters. She got out and opened fire to cover them until they made it to the Rodeo and got in the back seat. The men kept firing as Shemika rolled down the window and covered as Dee Dee got back in the Rodeo and prepared to leave.

"Get us out of here, Dee Dee," Elontra said as she got in.

Dee Dee dropped the Rodeo in drive and drove down the street to get them out of there. All four shooters returned to their cars and went after them. With the cars closing in on their vehicle, Elontra opened the sunroof, came up with the MAC-10, and began firing at the pursuing cars. They kept coming, and it didn't take long for them to close the gap. Dee Dee weaved her way through traffic. Once their pursuers were close enough, the shooting began again. The light turned red, and traffic began to slow down in front of them. Dee Dee gripped the steering wheel tight and pulled out into oncoming traffic and kept going.

"What the fuck are you doing?" a wide-eyed Shemika shouted.

"Not now, Mika," Elontra said, holding on like her life depended on it.

She dodged a couple of cars coming at them before she made it through the intersection. But they kept coming. Shemika rolled down her window and fired a few shots blindly at them. Elontra kept shooting until she had emptied the clip.

"I'm out!" she shouted and reloaded the MAC. "I only have one clip left!"

Elontra stood up in the sunroof, opened fire, and shot out the windshield of the car. She fired a few more shots at them, and they went into a spin, and they crashed into a parked car. The other car dropped back as Dee Dee sped up, and she lost them in traffic.

"We need to ditch this car and steal another one," Elontra said since they were nowhere near where they had parked the drop car.

Chapter Nineteen

With things being quiet for the day, it gave Shemika a chance to calm down. And since she was in a better state of mind, she decided that would be the day that she would experiment with cooking Thai food. Cooking, in its own way, was therapeutic for her. Not only did it encourage creativity, but cooking had a way of engaging her senses in ways that gave her an immense sense of satisfaction.

It was also that she wanted to have a house meeting, and food always made those go better. She found some Thai recipes online, and she made Thai chicken, steamed mussels, stir-fried mushrooms with baby corn, and spring rolls with dipping sauce. Shemika also had a couple of bottles of Le Fief Noir 2018 chilling because she read that chenin blanc wines were born to pair with Thai cuisine, and wine also always made house meetings go better.

Once the magnificent meal was ready, Shemika went and knocked on Elontra's and Dee Dee's doors and asked them to join her for a house meeting.

There were a few grumbles: "What do we need to talk about now?" and "Is this about the jewelry store?"

Which it was, but she knew her girls well.

"At least she knew to have wine," Dee Dee said and got a glass once they made it into the dining room.

"I'm experimenting with Thai cooking," Shemika said as Elontra came and sat down.

Her phone rang. Elontra glanced at the display. It was Derick. She rolled her eyes, got a spring roll, and dipped it in the sauce.

"So what about the jewelry store?"

After they ditched the car that night and stole another, they made their way to the Bronx and drove to Kayla's house. As could be expected, everyone was still on edge when they arrived, so it was decided that Elontra should go in alone. Dee Dee stayed in the car and tried to calm Shemika's rattled nerves.

"What the fuck?" Elontra asked when she opened the door.

"Come inside."

Once Kayla closed the door, Elontra got in her face. "What the fuck, Kayla?" Elontra asked, handing her the briefcase.

"What happened?"

Elontra shoved the bag of jewelry into her hand. "When we came out of the jewelry store, four men with masks ambushed us," she said and gave Kayla a shot-by-shot description of the action. Then she had a question. "Who were those guys?"

"I don't know," Kayla said calmly. "I can only assume that they were the buyers coming to make the deal for the contents of this briefcase," she said, holding it up and smiling because she knew that she had chosen wisely. "But you handled them."

"Yeah, but—"

"No buts. You women handled them. Take the win." Kayla went and got a briefcase and handed it to Elontra. "Where's Shemika tonight? She doesn't wanna count the money?"

"Trust me. It's best that Mika sits where she sits for the time being."

Elontra sat down and opened the case. Not being up for all of that shooting, Shemika was livid, and that fury was directed solely at Kayla for sending them into that mess.

"Believe that," she said and began her count.

Shemika got the bottle of Le Fief, poured herself a glass, and handed the bottle to Elontra. "She cooked, so I guess she's in a better mood," Dee Dee commented.

"I am, and I'm sorry for my little temper tantrum. But the more I think about some of the things I said—"

"Which things?" Dee Dee asked.

"Like I'm tired of us getting shot at."

"Obviously," Elontra quipped.

"Me too," Dee Dee added.

"And I'm tired of us having to run from the cops."

"And whoever those guys were," Elontra added.

"Right. Them too," Shemika said. "But all this is happening for one reason."

"What's that?"

"We got greedy."

There was silence in the room.

"After we did the first job for Kayla, we agreed to lie low for a while, but what did we do? We hit another bank."

"You brought that job to us," Elontra pointed out.

"Oh, when I said we got greedy, I meant we, and I included myself in that. Because once I planned it, I pushed us to hit that bank. Both of us wanted to rob the club, and I was all in to hit the jewelry store for Kayla. We all were. We got fuckin' greedy, and that's why we keep getting shot at. That's why we keep having to run from the police and whoever the hell those guys were. Greedy!"

"So what are you saying?" Dee Dee asked.

"I'm saying that we made plenty of money these last couple of months. It's time for us to stop being so damn greedy."

"She's right." Elontra paused. "That's what we used to say is that we'd never get caught because we'd never get greedy. You remember that, Mika?"

"I do."

Dee Dee laughed. "Then I got out of prison, and you two bitches been on a tear ever since."

Elontra and Shemika looked at one another. "The girl has a point," Shemika said.

"It's all her fault." Elontra pointed at Dee Dee.

"That's right," Dee Dee giggled. "Blame the ex-con."

"But seriously, we need to take a break," Shemika said. "Stop talking about stopping and stop. 'Cause I'm tired."

"I'm with you on that," Dee Dee said.

"I am tired of getting shot at and chased too," Elontra said. Her phone rang again with a call from Derick, and once again, she ignored it and sent the call to voicemail. The second it stopped ringing, ringing began again.

"That's me," Dee Dee said and picked up her cell phone to answer it. "Hello."

"Hey, Dee Dee. It's Kaiden. How are you doing?"

Since they had met that night at Eastern Parkway Estates, they had been talking on the phone. "Hey, Kaiden."

"The white boy?" Elontra quietly questioned, and Dee Dee nodded.

"Hold on," she said and stood up.

"You don't have to go anywhere," Shemika said.

"Just pretend we're not here," Elontra said smiling, and once again, it felt good to smile.

"Bye, bitches," Dee Dee said on her way to her room.

When her door closed, Shemika stood up and started for her room.

"Where you going?" Elontra asked.

"I'm going to shower and change. I'm meeting Dominic tonight," Shemika said, and then she noticed the sad look on Elontra's face. "I don't have to go. I can stay home if you need me to."

Elontra shook her head. "No, you go on and have a good time. I'll be all right."

"You sure?"

"Yeah. Mika, I'm sure. Derick isn't the first man to cheat on me, and he's not the first man I've broken up with because he can't keep his dick out of other women. I'll be fine."

"Okay," Shemika said and headed for her room.

It was over an hour later and Elontra was still in the living room watching television when Shemika came in the room. She was wearing a Tuberose Chiara Boni La Petite Robe malva jersey strapless minidress with a voluminous flower chest that she looked amazing in with Manolo Blahnik Hangisi embellished satin pumps. Even though she was just going to get fucked well and wouldn't have the dress on for very long, Shemika thought that she was falling in love with Dominic, and she wanted to look good for him.

"You look nice," Elontra said.

"Thank you."

They heard a door open, and seconds later, Dee Dee emerged from her room.

"Wow. You look amazing," Shemika said of the Cinq à Sept Loretta embellished knit minidress that she was wearing with Dolce & Gabbana floral-print platform ankle-strap sandals.

"Thank you, Mika. You look pretty good yourself."

"Where are you going?" Elontra asked Dee Dee.

"Kaiden is taking me out for dinner at Bianchi Italian Steakhouse."

"Well, you two have a good time," Elontra said.

"You sure you don't want me to stay and hang out with you?" Shemika asked.

"Yes, Mika, I'm fine." Elontra stood up and walked to the door. "Just be sure to holla my name when you cum," she said and opened the door.

Shemika pointed at her. "You stupid."

"She always has been," Dee Dee said on her way out of the house.

"You want me to bring you anything?" Shemika asked.

"Nope, I'm fine. Now go!" she said forcefully.

"We're going," Dee Dee said on her way to her car.

Elontra stood in the doorway and waved as her girls drove away before she went back inside to spend a quiet evening alone.

At Bianchi Italian Steakhouse, Dee Dee and Kaiden agreed that they were not going to spend the entire evening talking shop. It was supposed to be about getting to know one another. After cocktails, their first course was Puglia's garlic bread and Broome Street fried calamari. They both had Bianchi's signature chopped salad. Dee Dee had the cavatelli salsiccia: sweet sausage sautéed with broccoli rabe, garlic, and extra virgin olive oil, and Kaiden had linguine and clams served in a white sauce. The pair of ex–Black Hat hackers spent the evening talking about their past conquests and talking shop. After all, it was all that they really had in common.

As for Shemika, Dominic was blown away by her in that dress, and as expected, he wasted no time at all stripping her out of it. His lips captured hers before she had a chance to say anything. He was hungry for her when she got there, and it wasn't long after that when his pants were down, and in the next breath, he was inside her. Shemika held on to his back, and her legs wrapped around his waist as he thrust inside of her. She was going to scream his name, but he covered her mouth with his to muffle her screams as he made her eyes cross. Before she knew it, her body started to warm from the inside out. Her womb clenched hard and then released in spasms around his long, hard dick, and they came together.

Meanwhile, back at the house, Elontra was having a very different evening. After a while, she got hungry, and since she never felt like cooking, *ever,* she ordered General Tso's chicken and shrimp lo mein, had it delivered, and enjoyed it along with a half bottle of chardonnay. She had grown tired and was about to call it a night when her phone rang. Thinking that it was Derick calling again, Elontra was slow to pick it up.

"Pearson!" she exclaimed and answered. "Hello," Elontra said, but it was too late. The call had gone to voicemail. She quickly called him back.

"Hey, sexy," he answered.

"How are you doing tonight, Pearson?"

"I'm doing great now that I'm talking to you. How are you?"

"To be honest with you, I'm a little down, so I'm glad you called."

"What are you down about?"

"I'd rather not get into that. It's behind me now, and I need to move away from it, not dwell on it."

"That's a good attitude to have."

"Thank you. I try my best to do intelligent things. My world seems to work out better for me when I do."

Pearson laughed. "And believe it or not, it is that easy."

There was a second or two of silence before Elontra said, "By the way, I saw you and your friend and what the two of you did that night at Eastern Parkway Estates after we met."

There were a few seconds of silence before Pearson chuckled. "You saw that, huh?"

"I did."

"And how did you feel about it?"

"It didn't bother me if that's what you're asking."

"That is what I'm asking."

"I see. I'm going to assume that isn't something that you'd really want to talk about over the phone."

"You'd be right."

"I thought so, so I'll just say that whoever that was must have done something to deserve it."

Pearson chuckled. "Oh, believe me when I say he got exactly what he deserved."

"Mind if I ask you a question?"

"Go ahead."

"Is that something that you do a lot?"

"Yes, it's what I do."

"I see."

"I wanna see you, Elontra." He paused. "That is such a beautiful name. Elontra."

"Thank you. I like the way you say it."

"How do I say it?"

"Like my name is the most beautiful thing that ever crossed your lips."

"That's because it is. It's almost as beautiful as you."

"Thank you."

"But that doesn't change the fact that I wanna see you."

"When do you want to see me?"

"I wanna see you right now, but I gotta make a run. So what are you doing tomorrow?"

"I don't have any plans."

"Cool, I'll call you tomorrow."

"It will give me something to look forward to."

"Good night, Elontra."

"Good night, Pearson. Be careful."

"Oh, I'm Mr. Careful out here in these streets," Pearson chuckled. "Talk to you tomorrow. Enjoy the rest of your night."

"I will now," Elontra said and ended the call as the front door opened, and in walked Dee Dee. "Hey, girl, how'd it go?"

"It was nice. I enjoyed myself. Kaiden was the perfect gentleman." Dee Dee giggled. "He said that he was a little nervous because he'd never been out with a black woman before."

"To tell you the truth, I wasn't expecting you back tonight. In that dress"—she shook her head—"I was sure you'd be banging your head against the headboard right about now."

"Nope." Dee Dee shook her head. "He's nice for a white boy, and he's fine . . . for a white boy, but no. I've dated white boys before, and they just don't do it for me."

"I understand. I was just thinking that a nut is a nut is a nut, white boy or not."

Dee Dee took off her platform sandals and sat down next to Elontra. She patted her thigh. "Don't worry about that. I got that covered."

Elontra's eyes got big. "You do?"

"I was at an electronics store, looking at a new tablet, when this woman came up next to me and asked about the tablet I was looking at. It wasn't until she started talking about herself and how pretty the blouse I was wearing looked on me that I realized that she was hitting on me."

"And?"

"And we went for drinks, and like I said, I got that covered."

"You go on and get yours, sister," Elontra said and high-fived Dee Dee.

"I did."

Chapter Twenty

As it always does, the morning sun found the space between the curtains and was shining into Dominic's bedroom. Shemika was sore in all the right places, and she slowly opened her eyes. She sat up in bed, and after a deep yawn and a good stretch, she inhaled deeply. The smell of food cooking had filled the air.

"And he can cook, too," she said softly, pumped her fist, and rolled out of bed.

After a quick stop in the bathroom, she put on the shirt that Dominic had worn the night before and then followed the aroma to the kitchen.

"Good morning," she said, and it caught Dominic off guard.

"Oh, hey, good morning, sleepyhead," he said and quickly began to untie the apron he had on.

Shemika leaned on the granite counter and glanced at the clock. It was eleven thirty, which meant the sleepy-head title was appropriate but so out of character for her. She was always the first one up, cooking breakfast and cleaning her house, and it was Elontra who was the pillow hugger, and Dee Dee wasn't too much better.

"What's all this?" she asked, motioning toward the covered dishes on the counter.

He put the apron down and took her in his arms. "This, beautiful lady, is brunch."

"Oh, really?"

"Yes. I woke up hungry, and so I cooked. This is quiche Lorraine that I made with caramelized onions, spinach, mushrooms, bacon, and Gruyère cheese. That's roasted bacon, and those are hash browns that I made in the waffle maker," he said, pointing out each item. Dominic turned toward the pan on the stove. "And these are breasts of chicken that I'm sautéing in butter and marsala wine with a mushroom wine sauce." He paused and proudly saw the impressed look in Shemika's eyes. "So I hope you're hungry."

"I am. Very hungry."

"Oh, yeah, and I have a pitcher of mimosas chilling in the refrigerator."

"Great."

"Everything is just about ready. Why don't you have a seat in the dining room, and I'll bring the food out?"

"I can help you bring the food out."

"No, you can't." He took her hand in his. "You're my guest. Come on," Dominic said and led her out of the kitchen to the dining room. He pulled out her chair and she sat down. "I'll be right back."

"I'll be right here."

"I hope so," Dominic said, smiling, and returned to the kitchen.

He broke out the champagne flutes and got the candelabra from the cabinet. Dominic grabbed the mimosas and went back into the dining room. Once he poured her a glass, he lit the candles and dimmed the lights in the room, giving it a romantic ambiance.

Seeing the gleam in her eyes made Dominic feel amazing, and as she sipped mimosa, he happily returned to the kitchen, plated the quiche Lorraine, roasted bacon, hash browns, and breasts of chicken to serve. Like a waiter in a five-star restaurant, Dominic carried out the dishes with a towel draped over his arm.

"Look at you," she said with her smile growing.

Everything was delicious, and Shemika ate until she was full and couldn't touch another bite. Although she offered, Dominic wouldn't allow her to help him clean the table once the meal was complete. Instead, he escorted her to the living room, and after a passionate kiss, he went back to the kitchen to straighten up before joining her.

Dominic took Shemika's hand in his and brought it to his lips. "There's something that I need to tell you."

"You have another woman," Shemika said jokingly, but she was serious. She'd been in this place before, finding an amazing new man who seemed so perfect in every way, and then she'd find out she was the side piece.

"No," he said, and his face contorted into something unrecognizable. "I'm in love with you."

Silence.

"That's funny," she finally said.

A little confused by her response, Dominic asked, "Why is that funny?" After all, he had just told this woman that he was in love with her, and she thought that was funny.

"Because I'm in love with you."

There were a few seconds of silence. It was as if each was happy to say it aloud and get it over with.

"But that's not what I want to talk to you about."

"Okay," she said, relieved that this chat wasn't going to be about her sharing him with another woman, but she was curious about the serious look that covered his handsome face. "What do you want to talk about?"

"You never asked me what I did for a living."

"It just never came up." She giggled. "I assumed you'd tell me when you wanted me to know."

"Well, I want you to know. I want you to know everything about me."

"So what do you do?"

Dominic paused and took her hands in his. He took a deep breath and looked directly into her eyes. “I’m the type of guy you call when you need something stolen, usually something expensive or hard to get,” he said and paused to await her reaction.

Shemika smiled. “That’s funny.”

“Why is that funny?”

“It’s funny because you never asked me what I did for a living,” Shemika said flirtatiously.

“Okay,” he said, smiling at her. Dominic put his arm around her. “What do you do for a living, gorgeous?”

“I rob banks,” Shemika said and paused to await his reaction.

“That’s interesting.” He nodded because, although it was definitely not what he was expecting her to say, it did fit into what he was about to share with her. “The reason I wanted you to know what I do is because I have an appointment to see a new client about a job. I was going to ask you to wait here until I get back, but now, you being a bank robber and all, I’m wondering if you want to come with me.”

Shemika touched his face and then leaned in to kiss him. “I would love to come with you.”

Later that afternoon, once again dressed in the mini-dress she wore the night before, Shemika was being seated at a table at an upscale French restaurant called the Embassy.

“Good afternoon,” the woman at the table said. “Milica Ibrahimovic.”

“Dominic Moore.” He glanced in her direction. “My associate, Shemika Frazier.”

“My pleasure,” Shemika said.

“Thank you for coming,” she said to Dominic without looking in Shemika’s direction. “I won’t waste any of your time, Mr. Moore. There’s an item that I need you to obtain.”

"What's the item?"

"It's a prototype artificial intelligence system."

Dominic sat back. "The particulars?"

"The item is currently housed in a secure warehouse in the Port Morris area of the Bronx. In order to obtain it, you'll need to bypass perimeter cameras and an electronic security system that consists of a control panel connected to various wired or wireless sensors that are designed to detect the presence of an intruder."

"What happens if the system detects the presence of an intruder?"

"Upon detection of an intruder, the control panel sends a signal to the central station to verify the alarm. If the proper password cannot be supplied, the system locks down the building and dispatches the police."

"I understand."

"The entire complex is sensitive to environmental changes like fire and temperature. Even changes in the humidity in the building will trigger an alarm," Milica informed him.

"So cutting the power in the building is out of the question."

"That's correct."

"Okay, I'm inside. What's next?"

"Once you've gained access to the system and shut down all the security protocols, you'll have to make your way to the vault. When you get to the vault, there are a series of biometric security protocols that will have to be defeated."

"And those would be?"

"Fingerprint recognition, iris and retinal scans, and a voice recognition system that tracks and measures vocal modulation."

Dominic nodded. "Go on."

"Inside the vault, there are other secure projects stored in addition to the AI prototype. Each has its own separate security protocols. You will only have access to the vault where the AI prototype I want is secured. There are pressure plates on the floor. Therefore, if you divert from the path, it will set off alarms and lock down the entire building."

"Anything else?"

"That's it. Can you do it?"

"Yes, I can," Dominic answered confidently.

Shemika was totally blown away by what the job entailed and impressed by what Dominic said he could do because it was far beyond anything that she and her girls had ever done or could imagine themselves doing.

And we thought we were big time.

"Excellent. Your contact specified that you require half of your fee in advance."

"That's correct."

Milica held up one finger, and a man quickly approached the table with a metal briefcase. He placed it on the floor at Dominic's feet.

"Half of your fee, in advance as specified, as well as everything you'll need to complete the job." She stood up. "I expect results, Mr. Moore, and I have no tolerance for failure."

"I am well aware. Your reputation precedes you."

"Excellent, so there will be no misunderstandings between us?"

"None whatsoever," Dominic assured her. He stood up and they shook hands. "I'll be in touch within the week."

Without speaking another word, Milica Ibrahimovic walked away from the table and left the restaurant. Dominic sat down. "What did you think?"

"I'm impressed."

"Good, because I've been doing my damn level best to impress you."

Shemika gave him a thumbs-up. "So far, so good, Mr. Moore."

"You ready to go?"

Shemika looked around the upscale restaurant. "Is there any rush?"

"Not at all."

"Buy a lady a drink."

Dominic signaled for a server, and they had a drink to celebrate his new job. "And to us," Shemika added, and they left the Embassy.

Shemika didn't see Dominic over the next week as he assembled his usual team and they prepared to do the job. One night after a mission briefing, she came over, and he introduced her to them.

"My wheelman, KR Keys," Dominic began, and he nodded. "That's Brianna Quinn, my head of security. And this is Jack Gomes, the best computer guy in the world."

"I have a friend who might give you a run for your money, but it's nice to meet you, Jack," Shemika said, shaking his hand.

She made herself comfortable as Dominic laid out the job for them, and they asked questions and reviewed the planned operation over and over until there were no more questions and each knew what his responsibilities were.

Chapter Twenty-one

When they left Dominic's home that night, they were confident that the task ahead would be just another day at the office for them. However, you are familiar with the old saying about the best-laid plans of mice and men?

They often go awry.

No matter how carefully a project is planned, something may still go wrong, and two days prior to execution, it all went terribly wrong.

"What's up, Dom, it's Jack."

"What's up?"

"We've got a serious problem."

"What's that?"

"KR and Brianna are out."

"Fuck you mean, they're out?"

"Stupid. For God knows what reason, the two of them were drunk—"

"Oh, shit," Dominic shouted, and an angry look washed across his face.

It caught Shemika by surprise because she'd never heard him raise his voice or be mad about anything.

"Nothing good ever comes after those words. What did they do?"

"They robbed a liquor store—"

"On a dare, I'm guessing."

"You know them. Brianna dared KR, and they do the robbery, KR grabs a bottle of Clase Azul Tequila on the way out, and they get in the car, drunk, swerving all over the place. Cops show up, chase them, and KR crashes the car."

Dominic shook his head. "Of course he does."

"The cops take the two of them to jail. And since they both have open warrants—"

"They're not going anywhere anytime soon. Fuck!" Dominic shouted.

"What do you wanna do?"

"I'll call you back," he said and ended the call. "Fuck!" he shouted again and threw his phone.

"What's wrong?" Shemika asked.

"I'm two men down for the job."

"That's not good."

Dominic got up and went to the spot where he threw his phone and picked it up. For the next two hours, he tried in vain to get people to replace his team, but all declined, some because of the short notice and others because they each thought it was too dangerous.

"Okay, thanks anyway."

"If it were anything else, you know you could count on me, Dom, but there's too much risk involved in what you're talking about doing."

"I understand," Dominic said and once again tossed his phone. This time the screen cracked, and the back came off when it hit the wall. "Fuck!"

"No takers, huh?"

"It was either not enough notice or it's too dangerous," he said and dropped his head in the palms of his hands. "I can't back out now, but I might have to."

"So what are you gonna do?"

"I don't know." Dominic thought for a second or two, and then he looked up at Shemika and smiled. "What about your crew?"

"My crew?"

"Yeah, your crew. The ones you rob banks with."

"What about them?"

"You think you could recruit them to do this job?"

"You mean recruit them to do the job that all of your people say is too dangerous?"

"Yes." He nodded and paused. He took her hands in his. "I know it's a big ask, but I don't have a choice. I need men, good men, to pull this off."

"My crew is all female."

"As long as they're good, I could use them." He thought for a moment. "A female bank-robbing crew. I love it."

"We do jewelry stores, too," Shemika boasted.

"Wait a second. You're talking about Dee Dee and Elontra?"

Shemika smiled proudly. "That's my crew."

"Wow." Dominic shook his head. "You think they'll do it?"

"All I can do is ask them, see what they say."

"Thank you, Shemika," Dominic said, and after they made love, he took her home.

When Shemika got there, neither Elontra nor Dee Dee were home, so she would try to convince them to help with Dominic's robbery plan over breakfast the following morning. She cooked an egg casserole with shredded cheddar cheese and mushrooms and a small pan of sausage enchiladas. She found a recipe for halloumi cheese and zucchini frittata specifically for Dee Dee because she liked zucchini. She even baked Elontra's favorite, raspberry pain au chocolate, a French patisserie to satisfy her sweet tooth.

"What's all this?" Elontra asked when she came dragging into the kitchen.

Shemika spread her arms wide. "It's breakfast! I got up early this morning and felt like cooking, so here it is," she said as Elontra got a cup of coffee and sat down. "And there's something I want to ask you two."

"So this is a bribe, huh?" Dee Dee stated when she came into the kitchen. "A bribe to get us to do what you want us to do?"

"That's what she always does." Elontra got a plate and began filling it because she liked to eat and loved Shemika's cooking. "And it usually works. Is this what I think it is?"

Shemika nodded. "Raspberry pain au chocolate."

"Yeah, Dee Dee, it's a bribe." Elontra sat down with her plate.

"I knew that when I smelled the zucchini," Dee Dee commented as she helped herself to some of the halloumi cheese and zucchini frittatas. "She knows that I love me some zucchini."

Once Shemika got her food and sat down, she told her girls about the job that Dominic had contracted and what he had offered to pay them, and they were interested.

"Really?" Shemika said excitedly, and she then took out the paper that Dominic gave her. It contained all of the relevant information that they needed to know. Elontra and Dee Dee sat and listened as they ate the fabulous meal that Shemika had prepared to bribe them with. And once she had finished explaining the details of the job, Elontra frowned and shook her head.

"I pass, Mika."

"Me too."

"Why?" Shemika needed to know.

"That shit you're talking about doing is too dangerous," Dee Dee said, and Elontra nodded in agreement.

"That is way, way, way beyond anything we've ever done," Elontra said. "And on a day's notice." She shook her head. "I'm sorry, Mika, but I can't do it."

"Maybe if we had more time—" Dee Dee began.

"And more money," Elontra said quickly.

"And more money to make it worth the risk, but otherwise, I think we should stay in our lane."

"I hear y'all," a disappointed Shemika said. "But I understand."

"You're not mad, are you?" Elontra asked.

"No, not at all." She paused. "To tell you the truth, I thought the same thing when I first heard about all the security protocols that needed to be defeated."

"You sure, Mi?" Dee Dee asked.

"Yeah, I told him I'd ask."

"I agree with Dee Dee. We are doing fine in our lane, and we need to stay in it," Elontra said, and that ended any further discussion.

Chapter Twenty-two

"Hello."

"Can I speak with Elontra, please?"

"This is she speaking. Hello, Pearson."

"How you doing?"

"I'm fine. What about you?"

"I'm cool. You're not still feeling down, are you?"

"No. I'm actually in a great mood tonight."

"Then maybe you'd consider hanging out with me for a few hours."

"You're right, I might consider that as a possibility for the evening," she flirted.

"Well, then, check this out. Do you like Salomé Warner?"

"Yes, she's got a beautiful voice."

"She's performing at a club called Boom on East Forty-eighth. You wanna go?"

"I'd like that."

"Cool. I'm in the Bronx handling some business, but we about to wrap this thing up."

"Business, huh? You and CK kinda business?"

"Yeah."

"Well, Mr. Careful, you be cautious about how you handle your business in the Bronx and call me when you're done."

"I will," Pearson said and ended the call.

"You really into this one, ain't you?" CK asked.

"Shit, you seen her. Hell yeah, I'm into her. And I'm gonna try to get deep into her as soon as we end this."

"Good, 'cause here comes that nigga now." CK pointed to a man coming toward the building and then walking through the breezeway. "So let's go end this."

His name was Davis Brown. They were there to kill him and Richie Jackson for not paying what they owed. Pearson checked his gun before they got out and went toward the building. While Pearson watched the front, CK went around to the side of the building and looked in the window of the first-floor apartment.

"You see Jackson in there?" Pearson asked when CK returned.

"Yeah, he's in there. With two or three other niggas."

"Let's go end this."

CK laughed. "You in a hurry to get at that pussy, ain't you, nigga?"

"I am. So come on and let's get this done."

When they reached the apartment, CK steadied himself, and then he kicked in the door. Pearson opened fire and shot the first one in the chest. Then CK turned on the other. He had his gun out and took a shot. CK fired back and ducked behind the wall while he fired away. When he stopped shooting, CK came out from behind the wall and hit him with three shots to the chest.

CK reloaded his gun and went after Davis. When he turned around, there was Richie. He fired and missed every shot. The recoil knocked him on his ass. CK walked up, stood over him, and shot him in the head.

Pearson moved through the apartment slowly with his gun raised. He saw that Richie was dead and looked around for CK, but he didn't see him, so he checked the first room he got to. When he found that nobody was in there, he closed the door and moved on to the second room. There was a man with his hands up. When Pearson relaxed and lowered his weapon a little, the man reached for a gun. Pearson dove onto the floor as the man started shooting at him. When he hit the floor, Pearson got off a shot. When he got up from the floor and looked at the man, Pearson saw that he'd hit him with a shot to the head.

CK heard the shot and came running into the room. He saw the body on the floor.

"Davis?"

"I don't know who that nigga is. I know he can't shoot," Pearson said, and they left the room.

As soon as Pearson and CK walked out into the hallway, Davis came out of a room and started shooting. He fired shots wildly at them until he emptied the clip. Then he ducked back into the room and quickly reloaded his weapon. He pointed it at the door and waited.

As soon as Pearson touched the doorknob, Davis fired through the door. Pearson and CK stood on either side of the door until the shooting stopped. Pearson and CK came into the room just as Davis went out a window.

"I got him," Pearson said. "Go out the front and cut him off."

CK ran out of the room. Pearson put another clip in his gun and went out the window after him. He walked along the side of the building with his gun raised. Then he saw Davis run out of the shadows and went after him. When he got to the street, Davis turned and fired. Pearson returned his fire and hit Davis with two shots: one to the chest and the other in his head.

CK came running up and saw the body on the ground. He lowered his gun, and they went back inside the apartment to search for the money Davis owed. Although they knew that the police took their time responding to reports of shots fired in that area, they still searched the unit as quickly as they could and got out of there. Once they made it back to their car and CK sped away, Pearson took out his phone and called Elontra.

"Hello."

"Hello, Elontra."

"I guess you're done handling your business with CK," Elontra said. She had the phone on speaker while she did her makeup.

"Just now."

"I hope everything went the way you wanted it to."

"It did. It wasn't totally successful." Because he didn't find the money that Davis owed. "But it went the way it had to go." He paused. "So you still wanna get together?"

"I do."

"Great. I was thinking that since I'm in the Bronx and you're way out there on 'Strong Island,' you could meet me there instead of me rolling all the way out there and then going back to Manhattan. What you think?"

"I think I can meet you there."

"Great! I'm on my way there now. Why don't you call me when you get there and I'll come out and get you. Cool?"

"Cool."

"I'll see you later then."

"Right," Elontra said, and she swiped end.

Now that her hair and makeup were done, she went into the closet. Elontra knew what she wanted to wear to see Pearson and knew that he'd be blown away when he saw her in it. She came out of her closet with a blush-colored Carolina Herrera Nicola silk minidress that featured her amazing legs. Sleeveless to show off her toned arms, the dress had a dramatic plunging V-neckline that teased her cleavage and a sash back that hugged her hips. She completed the look with a pair of matching Jimmy Choo Azia patent leather sandals and a Varenne quilted metallic leather clutch on a chain.

"You look cute. Where you going?" Dee Dee asked.

"I'm meeting the guy I've been telling you about, Pearson," Elontra began.

"The one you met at Eastern Parkway Estates?"

"That's him. I'm meeting him at a club called Boom on East Forty-eighth. Salomé Warner is performing there tonight."

"I like her."

"You wanna go?"

"Nah, I'm not in the mood to be the third wheel tonight."

"You could call that cutie white boy and ask him to meet you there."

"I could, but no. You have fun."

"Okay. I'm out," Elontra said and headed for the door.

When Elontra reached Boom on East Forty-eighth, she parked in the first space she could find, and then she called Pearson.

"You here?" he answered.

"I am."

"Where you at?"

"Sitting in my car. I'm parked on Forty-ninth Street and Third Avenue."

"I don't want you walking these streets alone. Stay there. I'll come get you."

"I'll be all right walking down the street."

"Maybe, but I'm still coming for you. What kind of car you drive?"

"Black Corvette."

"Okay, I'll be there in a few."

A few minutes later, Pearson got to the car and opened her door. Elontra got out, and as she had hoped, he was totally blown away by the sight of her in that dress.

"Would it be all right if I held your hand while we walk?"

"It would be all right," Elontra said. She eased her hand in his and they walked hand in hand to the club. They bypassed the long line and security let them in.

"Welcome back to Boom on Forty-eighth, Mr. Alexander," the security guard said and opened the velvet rope to allow them into the club.

Once they were inside, another security guard escorted them to the VIP room where a bottle of Bollinger Brut Special Cuvée champagne awaited them. When the show was getting ready to start, another member of the security team escorted them to a table close to the stage.

"It's good to have connections," Pearson whispered in Elontra's ear when she asked about the VIP treatment they were receiving. "I grew up with the AR guy at Salomé Warner's record company. He hooked me up with all this."

Salomé Warner put on an amazing show. They enjoyed the performance and each other and danced to a few of her hits before Pearson suggested that they go somewhere they could relax, get comfortable, and get to know each other better.

"What did you have in mind?"

"I have a room reserved at the Berimbau at Fifth."

"That was kind of presumptive of you, wasn't it?"

"No, not really. I'm not driving. CK dropped me off, and it just made sense to get someplace nearby to sleep instead of trying to make it back to Brooklyn," he said as they walked hand in hand out of the club.

Once they got to the room and went inside, Elontra tossed her purse on the bed and was all over Pearson. She kissed him a few times and began fumbling with his belt. She wanted him. It was almost a need. He lifted her skirt a little and began massaging Elontra's clit through her panties. She moaned from the pleasure he was giving her. Pearson took off his shirt and looked at Elontra and then began to undress her slowly. Her body was beautiful. Elontra threw her arms around Pearson and kissed him before turning and leaning over the bed to get her purse. She pulled out a three-pack of condoms. Pearson stepped out of his pants, and Elontra dropped to her knees. While staring into his eyes, she put one on him, and then she stood up and knelt on the bed.

Pearson ran his hands over her ass and then up and down her back. Elontra's body shook a little when Pearson ran one finger down from her ass, along her lips, to her clit.

"What are you waiting for?" Elontra moaned.

Pearson spread her lips and pushed himself inside her. Elontra moaned louder.

"Oh, yes," she moaned softly as he slid inside.

Pearson leaned forward, grabbed Elontra by the shoulders, and began slamming himself in and out of her. When Pearson let go of her hips, Elontra began grinding back at him, furiously pounding her ass into him until her body started to tremble.

"Oh, yes!" she screamed.

Pearson grabbed one of her cheeks and squeezed it as Elontra began to buck harder and harder, and Pearson smacked her ass. He reached between her legs, fingering her clit with one hand and squeezing her breast with the other. Elontra screamed and rolled over on her back and lifted her legs.

"Come get it," she encouraged him.

When Pearson got up on the bed, Elontra began kissing him passionately and stroking his erection. Pearson closed his eyes and lost himself in the sensation of hands and lips against his chest and then back down to his throbbing erection. Then Elontra got on top of him, he grabbed her hips, and she slowly slid down on him.

With her eyes squeezed tightly shut, Elontra rode him slowly, grinding her hips until Pearson was so deep inside her that her body started to tremble.

"Yes, yes!" she screamed and rode him harder.

Elontra was a screamer, and her screams of passion excited Pearson. He arched his back and pushed himself as deep and as hard as he could into her. Pearson was hitting it so hard that it knocked Elontra forward, and she collapsed on his chest. She shoved her tongue in his mouth and kept slamming her ass down on him. Pearson kissed her until she sat straight up, and he took a nipple into his mouth.

Elontra grabbed the back of his head, and he licked and sucked her nipples and continued to hit it as hard as he could. Her head drifted back, and her eyes opened wide, and she screamed.

"You're gonna make me cum again!"

Elontra rolled on her back, and Pearson eased himself inside her again. He began a steady motion, and Elontra wrapped her legs around his waist. Elontra worked her hips and inner muscles, licking his nipples until his body began to tremble. Elontra was tossing her hips furiously, and Pearson exploded inside her. He rolled off of her, breathing hard.

"I think I love you," Pearson managed to say, and Elontra smiled a satisfied smile.

Chapter Twenty-three

The day had come. It was Saturday afternoon, and Dominic was supposed to do the job that night. However, he still hadn't found anybody willing to do the job with him and Jack. They could do the job themselves, but there would be too much risk involved. Dominic needed someone to watch his back. Each person he called was down to do it for the money, but once he told them what the job required, each turned it down. He was about to call Milica Ibrahimovic and back out of the job when there was a knock at his door. Dominic put down his phone and went to open the door.

"Hello."

"Hello yourself."

Shemika's lips immediately pressed against his as she pushed him into his apartment. She was wearing a Mackage Thalia belted coat. Shemika backed Dominic to the couch and pushed him down. She stood over him, staring into his eyes, and slowly untied the belt on her coat and opened it to reveal that the only thing that she was wearing was a pair of Gianvito Rossi ribbon PVC D'Orsay pumps. As the coat dropped to the floor, Dominic quickly unbuckled and came out of his pants.

Dominic sat beneath her, and she straddled his lap before sliding down his length. He bit his bottom lip, and his brow furrowed as her wetness swallowed him up. His hands reached for her hips as she moved up and down on him. The sounds of her pussy popping fueled her desire for him, and Shemika moved faster and harder. His hands were all over her, grabbing her thick thighs, squeezing her pretty titties, and tweaking her erect nipples.

She kissed him and could feel him so deep inside of her that it made her walls clench around him harder. He must have felt it, because his growl sounded pained, but she didn't stop rotating, from slamming down on him to rocking and swirling her hips.

"I'm coming!"

She rolled off of him, and once she caught her breath, Shemika got up and led Dominic to the bedroom. They fell back on the mattress, and he worked her slowly and thoroughly, giving her inch by delicious inch, tapping it just hard enough to make her body feel so astounding that soon Shemika was cumming all over him, but when she looked into his eyes it was as if he weren't there.

He pumped harder, his hand rubbing her nipples, grabbing her tits as they bounced and hit her chin. Her mouth opened to cry out, her womb clenched hard and then released in spasms around his hot length. They both screamed out as they came.

Shemika looked over at Dominic as they lay next to one another, trying to catch their breath. She looked at him, and he was staring at the ceiling with a blank look in his eyes.

"What's wrong?" she rolled close to him and asked.

"I gotta do that job tonight, and I still haven't found anyone to do it. I need at least one more man to watch my back."

"I'll go with you."

"No, Shemika. I can't ask you to do that."

"You're not asking. I'm telling you that I'm going with you." She pointed in his face. "And that's all there is to it."

So it was on.

***

Jack parked the van near the secure warehouse in the Port Morris area of the Bronx. Armed with AK-47s and 9 mm, Dominic and Shemika got out of the van. Once Jack deactivated the cameras and the fence, Dominic cut the wires, and they entered the far south end of the property. Dominic and Shemika made their way toward the building under the cover of night. Once they reached the building, Jack bypassed the electronic security system and shut down all the security protocols. Now that they were in the building, Dominic and Shemika made their way to the vault area without being detected. They reached the vault with the pressure plates on the floor that would set off alarms and lock down the entire building if they diverted from the path.

"How's it going, Jack?"

"I'm working on it."

"Hurry up, I need that path clear."

"Got it! You are free and clear to proceed, but remember you need to stay on the path or we're fucked."

"Got you," Dominic said.

Dominic and Shemika made their way along the path to the vault with her walking directly behind him, careful to stay on the path.

"How are you going to defeat the series of biometric security protocols?" Shemika asked.

Dominic turned around but didn't stop walking. "I have a cast to get around the fingerprint recognition," he said, walking backward along the path, "a contact lens for the iris and retinal scans, and a recording for the voice recognition system." As he was turning around, the side of his right foot accidentally deviated from the deactivated path.

Red flashing lights suddenly came on, and the alarm sounded.

"We gotta get outta here!" Dominic shouted, and they ran out of the vault and back the way they came.

"Hold it right there!" the security guard yelled with his weapon drawn.

Shemika froze and quickly put up her hands. Dominic pulled out his gun and fired a round of shots in the direction of security. The guard took cover and called for help.

Dominic grabbed Shemika's hand. "Come on!" he shouted, and they took off running in the opposite direction. At the end of the hall, they were cut off from the exit by more security.

"Hold it!"

He shot wildly at security. "This way!" he yelled as they ran down the hallway.

Dominic and Shemika got to an open area where the hall forked off in two directions. They stopped while he peeked around the corner. When he didn't see anybody, Dominic turned back to Shemika. "You go ahead. I'll cover while you make it across."

Shemika nodded her head and started to cross the open area to the hallway.

"Hold it right there!" the security guard yelled with his weapon pointed at Shemika.

Dominic stepped out and fired at the security guard, and he dove for cover. When Shemika took off running, a cop came up behind Dominic and put a gun to the back of his head.

"Move and you're dead."

Shemika looked over her shoulder as she ran and watched as Dominic slowly put down his gun and raised his hands.

"Shit," Shemika said and kept running.

She saw an exit sign at the end of the hall and ran faster toward it. She stopped suddenly and hid in a doorway as the door opened and two more police officers came running inside the building. When they ran past her, Shemika came out from hiding and ran, barely making it out the door just before it closed.

Once outside, she carefully made her way around outside of the building looking for more security or police. Not seeing any, she made a run for the fence and called for Jack.

"Jack!" Shemika called out. "Can you hear me?"

"I hear you, Shemika," Jack said, relieved to finally hear her voice. "Are you all right? I thought I heard shooting in the building."

"Security got Dominic. Cops are everywhere. I need you to meet me at the rendezvous point."

"Hold on, Shemika, I'm coming for you."

As quickly as possible, Shemika made her way to the fence and went through the opening Dominic had cut for them to enter. Shemika stayed in the shadows close to the buildings and could see a police car drive by and head toward the corner. She crouched down to avoid being seen. Once the cop car was out of sight, Shemika moved as quickly as she could down the street. Once she was far enough away from the building, Shemika called Jack, but there was no answer. When she got to the rendezvous spot, she dropped behind a car for cover when she saw the police lights.

Shemika peeked over the hood of the car and watched the police walk Jack to a squad car and put him in. She stayed as low as she could and got away from there. When she reached the corner, Shemika started running. She saw another police car coming toward her and dropped for cover again. The area was crowded with cops.

Chapter Twenty-four

Exhausted and scared, Shemika sat down on the curb, leaned against the car, and tried to catch her breath as the police lights passed.

What do I do now? she thought, and then Shemika took out her phone.

"Hey, Mika. What's up?" Elontra answered.

"I'm in trouble," she said quietly.

Elontra grabbed the remote and turned off the television. Dee Dee sat up straight.

"What's wrong?"

"I did that robbery with Dominic, and things went bad. Dominic got caught by the police, and I ran."

"Where are you?"

Shemika looked around until she saw a street sign. "I'm hiding behind a gray Jeep Wrangler on 136th Street and Locust Avenue."

"Okay." Elontra thought for a second about what to do. "You need to get under the car and stay there. We're on our way," she said and ended the call.

"What's wrong?" Dee Dee asked.

"Mika did that robbery with Dominic. Shit went south, Dominic got caught by the cops, and Mika is on the run," Elontra said and got up.

"Where is she?"

"She's hiding. She needs us to come get her."

Dee Dee got up, shaking her head. "Something told me that she was gonna go do that fuckin' job with him."

"I thought she would too. Come on. Let's go get our girl," Elontra said, but she turned around and headed toward her room.

"Where are you going?"

"To get the MAC."

"Good point," Dee Dee said and went to get her gun.

Moments later, Dee Dee was zooming the 280ZX down the Long Island Expressway heading toward the Grand Central Parkway, and she took the Triboro Bridge to the Bronx.

"I hope she's all right," Elontra said.

"You should call and check on her, make sure she's okay."

"I thought about that, but I didn't want her phone to ring while she's hiding and somebody hears it," Elontra said.

"Text her."

"Right," Elontra said and sent the text.

Shemika was lying on her back under the Jeep and was glad that the ground clearance was at least ten inches when she felt her phone vibrating in her pocket.

Are you all right?

She replied, I'm under the car. Where are you?

Dee Dee had just gotten on the Bruckner Expressway when Elontra got her reply.

"She's all right, still under the Jeep," she said as she replied to the text.

We're on the Bruckner Expressway.

Okay.

Hold on. We're coming for you.

When Dee Dee got off at the 138th Street East exit, there was still police activity in the area. She drove slowly down East 136th Street, looking for the Jeep Wrangler.

"There it is!" Elontra shouted and pointed to the Jeep. "Stop the car."

Dee Dee pulled over, and Elontra hopped out of the car. She walked down the street until she got to the Jeep Wrangler.

"Mika."

"Yeah."

"Come on out," Elontra said as she waved for Dee Dee to come, and Shemika rolled out from under the Jeep and stood up. When Dee Dee pulled up, Elontra opened the door for Shemika, and she got in the back seat. Elontra got in the front seat and closed the door. Dee Dee drove off.

"Are you okay?" Elontra asked.

"I am now," Shemika said, slumping in her seat as Dee Dee drove past a police car cruising the area. "Thanks for coming for me. I was so scared lying there, thinking that a cop would find me and pull me from under the car."

"What happened?"

"We were in—" Shemika began, but just then, a police car with its lights on came up fast behind them.

"Oh, shit," Dee Dee said, and Shemika slumped down in the seat.

They all relaxed when the cruiser zoomed past them.

"They're gone, Mika," Elontra said, and then she turned to Dee Dee. "Get us the fuck outta here."

"Fuck you think I'm doing?" Dee Dee said as she got back on the Bruckner Expressway and headed for home.

"What happened?" Elontra asked once Dee Dee picked up speed.

"Like I said, we were in the building, we'd made it inside the vault, and we were on our way to get the prototype. You remember me saying that the floor had pressure plates, so you had to stay on the path or it would set off the alarms?"

"Right," Elontra said.

"Well, don't ask me why, but Dominic decided he wanted to walk backward so he could answer my question."

"That was stupid," Dee Dee said, shaking her head.

"He was showboating, trying to impress you, instead of focusing on the job," Elontra said.

"Next thing you know, red lights are flashing and the alarm is blaring."

"How did you get out?" Elontra asked.

"Shit, we ran. But we got to the point where I kept going and Dominic stayed to cover me, and a cop came up behind him."

"You think he'll snitch?" Dee Dee asked.

"I don't think so," she said and thought that if he loved her as he said, he'd keep his mouth shut. All Jack could tell the police was her name. "But to be honest, I don't know."

"What about the cameras? Did his guy disable the cameras?" Dee Dee asked.

"He said that he bypassed the electronic security system and shut down all the security protocols. But I can't be sure of that either. When I got out and made it back to the van, the cops were putting Jack in the car."

"It's gonna be all right, Mika," Elontra said, but it was more of a hope than a promise.

"Yeah," Dee Dee concurred to reassure Shemika, but all three knew that this wasn't good and it was possible that either Dominic, Jack, or both were telling the police everything they knew about Shemika. Dominic knew her name and where she lived, and she had even told him what she did.

"I told him about us," Shemika said meekly.

"What?" Dee Dee exclaimed.

"I figured you did when you tried to get us to do the job with him," Elontra said.

"If he gives you up and the cops start looking at us—" Dee Dee began.

"Don't even go there, Dee Dee. But us lying low for a while wouldn't be a bad idea," Elontra said.

"What you wanna do?" Dee Dee asked.

"Go home, and let's get some stuff together and go somewhere for a week or two maybe," Elontra suggested.

"I think that's a good idea," Shemika said. "And I'm sorry for jamming us up like this."

"It's okay, Mika," Elontra said. "We got you."

"So where we gonna go to lie low?" Dee Dee asked.

Elontra took out her phone and searched for resorts near New York City and found Monmouth Beach Resort & Spa.

"It's in Monmouth Beach, New Jersey. It'll take us three hours to get there from the house."

"But we are going home first, right?" Dee Dee asked.

"Yeah," Elontra said, and she called the resort and made the reservations. "Okay, we're in. I got three rooms, and we can check in tonight."

"Good," Dee Dee said, driving faster.

Once they reached the house, the three went inside, packed a few things, and were back on the road, driving to Monmouth Beach, a beachside city in Monmouth County. It wasn't until they had checked in and were in their rooms that the ladies were able to relax.

Chapter Twenty-five

Overlooking a magnificent stretch of beach in Monmouth Beach sat the Monmouth Beach Resort & Spa, the only resort located directly on the beaches of the Jersey Shore. Elontra had reserved an oceanfront suite for each of them that each had a separate bedroom, living room, and large balcony.

It was just after seven in the morning, and Shemika was standing out on the balcony of her suite. She didn't get much sleep that night before. As one could expect, there was a lot on her mind: her continued freedom for one. Whether she liked it or not, her freedom wasn't in her hands. Her staying out of jail now depended on Dominic and Jack keeping their mouths shut about her. Since she couldn't be sure that Jack disabled them, there were also cameras and facial recognition that she had to worry about.

Shemika thought about Dominic. When she closed her eyes, she could see his face, could practically hear his voice. Just the thought of him made her happy and sad at the same time. She thought about the relationship that was developing between them. She thought that she was falling in love with him, and when he told her that he was in love with her, it took her breath away, and Shemika felt a rush of adrenaline and butterflies in her stomach. She wanted desperately to know what was going on with him. She wanted to call every police precinct until she found out where he was being held so she could go see him.

"Have you lost your fuckin' mind?" Dee Dee shouted when she said those words out loud. "They could have your picture and be waiting to arrest you on the spot!"

Although she wanted to, Shemika knew how bad an idea it would be for her to show up at the precinct to visit him. Even if they didn't have an image of her, she certainly fit the description. It would be like announcing that she was the tall black woman who got away that night.

It was all so overwhelming to her that she could barely think.

Shemika went back into the suite, closed the curtains, and stretched out across the bed. She tossed and turned for a while, and then she lay on her back, staring at the ceiling until her eyes finally shut and she fell asleep.

When there was a knock at the door, Shemika rolled over. As the knocking continued and got louder, she opened her eyes and glanced at the clock. "Two forty-five," she said and sat up.

"Mika! You in there?" Elontra said loudly through the door.

"Coming!"

Shemika got out of bed and opened the door. There stood Elontra and Dee Dee, and both had on bikinis.

"You been asleep all this time?" Dee Dee asked when they came into the room.

"I guess I needed it," Shemika said and lay back down on the bed. "I hadn't slept all night. I finally fell asleep sometime after seven this morning."

"We came by and knocked on your door on our way to the pool," Dee Dee said.

"I even tried calling your cell, but it's off," Elontra said.

"What are y'all getting ready to do now?" Shemika asked.

"We're going to change and then walk next door to Monmouth Village. The hotel concierge said that there are a lot of nice shops and places to eat," Elontra said.

"Have you eaten?" Dee Dee asked.

"No, I haven't eaten anything since yesterday," Shemika said. "And I'm getting a headache, so I need to eat something."

"Go on and get dressed, and we'll be back to pick you up, and then we'll go find something to eat," Dee Dee said on her way to the door.

When Elontra was ready, she knocked on Dee Dee's door, and they went to get Shemika. They ate at Ono Grindz Burgers and had made-from-scratch Hawaiian-fired burgers on Hawaiian sweet hamburger buns. Their next stop was The Shops at Monmouth Village, and they checked out a women's boutique called cXa by Jada, which had an assortment of clothing and accessories, and Maya & Chloe, a trendy women's apparel store. Once they finished shopping, they visited the Zora Art Gallery before heading back to the hotel.

"What now?" Shemika wanted to know.

"I don't know about you two, but I need a drink," Dee Dee said.

"The hotel concierge said that Kauai Lanai is the spot. It has a DJ from six to ten," Elontra said.

"Seems like you spent a lot of time talking to the concierge," Shemika noted as they walked to Kauai Lanai.

"He was cute," Dee Dee said.

"That's how you find out things. We might be here for a minute, and I wanted to know what's up."

"You really think we'll be here for a while?" Shemika asked.

"I don't know. I was just saying," Elontra said.

"Which brings up a good point. How do we know when it's cool to go home?" Dee Dee asked.

"Good question," Shemika said, and they both looked at Elontra.

"What y'all looking at me for?"

"Because it was you who suggested we come here," Dee Dee said.

"Well," Elontra said as they arrived at the bar, "I don't have an answer for that. But for the time being, let's just relax and enjoy ourselves."

"That's easier said than done," Shemika said and sat down at the bar.

"I know, Mika," Elontra said and sat next to her. She put her arm around Shemika. "But try to have some fun."

"I am, and I'm going to start by getting drunk off my ass," Shemika said.

"Well, you came to the right place," the bartender said, and he dropped a bar napkin in front of her. "What can I start you ladies off with?"

"I'm having an Aunt Roberta cocktail," Elontra said quickly.

"That the drink you were telling me about?" Shemika asked.

"Yup."

"I'll have one of those too," Shemika said.

"And for you, pretty lady?" the bartender asked Dee Dee.

Dee Dee looked over the drink menu. "I'm gonna try Death in the Afternoon."

"What's that?" Shemika asked.

"It's a cocktail created by Ernest Hemingway, and it's made with champagne and absinthe."

"Let's do it," Dee Dee said and handed him the menu.

"Coming up," the bartender said and went off to make their drinks as Elontra's phone rang.

She answered, "Hello, Pearson."

"I wanna see you."

Elontra laughed and got up. "I'm fine, how are you?" she questioned as she walked outside.

"I'm awesome. Excuse my lack of manners and my enthusiasm, but that's only because I wanna see you, Elontra."

"I'm in New Jersey for a minute."

"New Jersey? Fuck are you . . ." He paused and chuckled. "I mean, what are you doing in Jersey?"

"It's a long story, but you are welcome to come if you wanna see me."

"Where in Jersey are you?"

"Monmouth Beach. We're staying at the Monmouth Beach Resort & Spa."

"Oh, so you and your whole crew are down there. What, y'all taking a little vacation or something?"

"Yeah. Something like that," Elontra said. "But that's where I am if you wanna come to see me."

"Okay, me and CK gotta put in some work, but after that, I'm coming to you," Pearson said. "Because I really do need to see you, Elontra."

"You need to see me, huh? Well, I'll be here. But you should call before you come through. There ain't no telling where or what we're gonna get into tonight."

"I will."

"Okay, then. I'm gonna get back to my girls." She giggled. "Our plan is to get drunk off our asses. So I might be bombed out my mind when you get here."

"You go on, get back to your crew and have fun. I'll talk to you later."

"Goodbye, Pearson."

"See you soon, Elontra."

As announced, by the time Elontra, Shemika, and Dee Dee left Kauai Lanai, they were all drunk off their asses. They staggered back to the hotel laughing at damn near everything. Therefore, when Pearson called, Elontra was in no shape for company.

"I mean, you can come, but I'll probably be passed the fuck on out when you get here," Elontra giggled.

"'Cause she's fucked up!" Dee Dee yelled.

"She's right. I'm fucked up."

"Okay then," Pearson chuckled. "Why don't I just see you tomorrow?"

"Yes," she slurred. "That probably would be best."

"Probably would."

"I'm gonna go now 'cause I'm tired of holding the phone," Elontra said and ended the call.

"Bye, Elontra," Pearson said to nobody. "Damn. She hung up on me," he laughed and put his phone away.

"No fair!" Shemika shouted.

"What's not fair, Mika?" Elontra asked.

"I'm horny as fuck and my dick is locked up!" Shemika shouted, and then she started singing. "I wanna fuck somebody. I wanna feel the dick with somebody. Yeah, I wanna fuck somebody." Then she stopped walking and singing. "I would rather it be Dominic, but I just want some dick."

"Well, maybe you should have thought of that shit while we were at Kauai Lanai and those men were hitting on you," Dee Dee said.

Shemika shook her head. "Chopped meat! All of them were chopped meat. I want filet mignon!" *And that is Dominic.*

"I can't argue with you on that one," Elontra said as they staggered through the hotel lobby to the elevator.

"That bartender was kind of cute," Dee Dee said and pressed the button.

"That's 'cause you're into them white boys," Shemika said.

"Nah," Elontra said. "She said white boys don't do it for her."

"Well, they don't," Dee Dee said as the elevator doors opened, and the three got on.

They got off on their floor, and after they made plans to do the breakfast buffet at Til's Oceanfront Restaurant, they said good night and went to their separate rooms.

Later the next afternoon, Elontra was surprised to get a call from Pearson saying that he had just arrived in Monmouth Beach and would be at the hotel soon. She was surprised because she was too drunk the night before to remember talking to him.

"I did?"

"You did. You said that your plan was to get drunk off your ass."

She laughed. "I do remember saying that."

"And when I called back, you were fucked up and said that I could have come last night but you'd probably pass the fuck on out on me," Pearson reminded her.

"I did?" She laughed. "That doesn't even sound like me."

"You were drunk."

"Drunk off my ass apparently," Elontra said and laughed.

"Well, I'm in the parking lot."

Elontra told Pearson what room she was in, and he came up. When he arrived at the room, she opened the door wearing an Agua Bendita Verano Road Marine coverup over her Agua Bendita balconette bikini top and Eda low-rise bottom.

"Damn," he said. "You are so beautiful."

"Thank you," Elontra said, and once she put her room key in the beach bag she bought earlier that day, they left the room.

When Pearson said that he hadn't eaten all day, she suggested that they go eat at the Seaview Restaurant & Lounge in the hotel. Over seafood-stuffed fillet and blackened prime rib, Elontra finally got to ask the question she'd been dying to ask since she saw him and CK deal out that vicious beating the night she met him at Eastern Parkway Estates.

"So, Mr. Cautious, just what exactly do you do?"

"I'm a collector."

"A collector?"

Pearson sat back and chuckled. "I don't collect postal stamps or model cars or anything like that. When people owe the people I work for money, I collect it for them."

Elontra sat there for a second or two, gazing into his intense eyes. "A collector, huh?"

"Yes, beautiful Elontra, that is how I make my money," Pearson said and paused to think for a second. "I've never just up and told anybody like that before. I usually say that it's better if you don't know what I do, or I'll say something crazy."

Elontra leaned on the table. "Like what?"

"I'm a brain surgeon or a nuclear physicist." Pearson laughed, and he leaned forward. They looked into each other's eyes.

"Then why did you tell me?"

"I guess I wanted you to know."

"What do you do if they don't pay you?"

"I brutally explain to them the consequences of not paying."

"Yeah," she leaned back and chuckled. "I saw how that works."

"Does it bother you?"

"That you beat the shit out of people for a living? No, it doesn't bother me." She paused to decide if she was going to be honest with him. "Actually, it was kinda hot," she said, remembering how hot for him she was that night after watching him work.

When Elontra and Pearson left the restaurant, he wanted to head straight for her suite, but she had other ideas. It was Motown night at Kauai Lanai, and Elontra was excited about going. She'd grown up hearing her parents listen to all of the great Motown classics, and she had come to love them just as much as they did.

"That's when music was music. Singers sang in perfect harmony, and musicians played instruments," her father would always say.

When they arrived at Kauai Lanai, Dee Dee and Shemika were already there, and two black men were buying their drinks. They weren't staying at the hotel. They had made the hour's drive from Trenton because they'd found that Kauai Lanai was a great place to pick up vacationing drunk white women who had a touch of jungle fever. So imagine their excitement when they walked in and there sat Shemika and Dee Dee at the bar.

Although she was friendly and allowed the men to buy her drinks, Shemika missed Dominic so much that she didn't know what to do. Even though they were just getting started, being apart from him seemed like torture at times. But instead of letting herself be consumed by her sadness, she tried to keep a more positive mindset. So she was hanging out with her girlfriends. She was happy and grateful to have them, and Shemika tried to have a good time.

By the end of the evening, all four were tipsy and were singing the Marvin Gaye and Tammi Terrell classic "You're All I Need to Get By," and they all left the bar shortly thereafter.

Therefore, when Elontra and Pearson made it back to her suite, she was surprised to hear Shemika and Dee Dee talking and laughing on the balcony.

"What happened to the two guys you left with?" Elontra came out onto her balcony to ask.

"Wasn't nothing gonna happen with that," Shemika said because all she wanted was to be with Dominic. "At least wasn't nothing gonna happen with me," she laughed and looked at Dee Dee.

"I wasn't givin' up shit either." Dee Dee laughed. "Listen. One threw up on the beach right after we left the bar, and the other one had to take his drunk ass home," Dee Dee said.

Elontra laughed and went back into her suite, but once she and Pearson had sex and he passed out, Elontra was back on the balcony. "Come open the door and let me in."

Shemika opened the door to her suite, and Elontra joined them on the balcony. After laughing at Dee Dee's reenactment of what she called Mr. Hands and the Drunk, the conversation turned to whether Shemika was able to relax and enjoy herself.

"I am having fun," she laughed, but she really did miss Dominic and could think of little else. "I still wanna go home."

"So," Dee Dee began, "how long are we going to stay here?"

Once again, both ladies turned to Elontra.

"I don't know. We could leave in the morning if you want to."

"Yeah, we could, but we still wouldn't know what was going on, and that defeats the purpose of coming here to lie low," Shemika pointed out.

"We have no way of knowing whether Dominic and the other guy stood tall and didn't turn snitch. I hate snitches," Dee Dee said.

Elontra slumped in her chair. "I don't know what else to tell you."

Shemika picked up her bottle of water. "I say we give it a couple more days."

"I was thinking we stay the rest of the week," Elontra said. "But whatever's clever. You got any more water in the minibar?"

"Should be," Shemika said, and Elontra got up to go see.

"Bring me one too," Dee Dee said, and that was when she thought of a way she could help her friend.

Even though it was after two in the morning when she went to her suite, Dee Dee set her alarm for six a.m. Once she was showered and dressed, she hit the road and headed back to Long Island. After stopping to pick up something to eat, she made it to the house, went into her computer room, and powered up. For the next two hours, she tried in vain to get the information that Shemika needed.

"Fuck!" she shouted, disappointed in herself because she couldn't do it.

DeeDee had been so focused on reacquiring the skills that would help her crew with what they were doing that she'd let learning techniques that would help her now fall by the wayside. While she was sitting there chastising herself and pouting about it, it hit her.

"But I know somebody who can do it."

She backed away from the computer, got her phone, and made the call.

"Hey, Dee Dee," Kaiden answered excitedly, because even though white boys didn't do it for her, he thought that Dee Dee was amazing in every way and would not mind one bit if their relationship took a turn toward the physical. "What's up?"

"I need a huge favor."

"What's that?"

"I'd rather not say over the phone."

"Uh-oh, this sounds serious."

"It is. Can I come by so we can talk about it?"

"Sure. No problem," he said, excited that she was coming to his apartment. It didn't matter what she wanted to talk about. She was coming. "I'll text you my location."

"Thanks, Kaiden. I'll see you soon."

"Looking forward to it," he said, and Dee Dee could hear the enthusiasm in his voice. That was good because what she wanted him to do was a big ask.

When she got to Kaiden's Brooklyn apartment, Kaiden opened the door before she rang the bell. "I saw you coming," he said, pointing to the wide-screen split display that displayed the front and rear of his building, the lobby, and the hallway.

"Wow."

"I like to know who's coming. I got a lot of hardware here," he said as he reset the alarms.

"I see this," she said, looking impressed at all that he had. Her setup looked like child's play compared to his.

"So tell me what I can do for you."

"Can you hack the NYPD?"

"Wow, wasn't expecting that," Kaiden said. "Why do you want to hack the NYPD?"

"Can you do it?" Dee Dee asked without answering his question.

"Why do you want to hack the NYPD?" Kaiden asked again.

And once again, Dee Dee asked, "Can you do it?"

Kaiden looked at Dee Dee for a second or two. "Of course I can," he said, cracking his knuckles, and then he sat down and turned his baseball cap backward. "Have a seat." He pointed in her face. "Watch and learn, script kiddie," he said and got to work.

Dee Dee didn't appreciate being called a script kiddie, but that was what she was or she wouldn't be there begging for his help. She went and dragged a chair over and sat down next to him. She watched as his fingers moved quickly over the keyboard, and she tried to read the code he was dropping. Kaiden was fast, so it was hard for her to keep up.

"I'm in," he said and stood up. He extended his hand graciously toward his chair. "I don't need to know what you're doing."

"Thank you, Kaiden," she said and took his seat.

Now that she had access to the NYPD database, Dee Dee checked to see if there was a warrant for Shemika's arrest. Then she ran a search for Dominic Moore, and once she found his arrest record, she accessed the case file for the failed robbery. Once she had the information that she needed, she thanked Kaiden and was getting ready to leave.

"I don't know what you're into, but be careful, Dee Dee," Kaiden said as he walked her to the door.

"I will, I promise," she said and left the apartment and headed back to Jersey. On the way back to Monmouth Beach, Elontra called.

"Where are you? We came by to get you for breakfast, but you weren't there."

"In Brooklyn, about to get on the Verrazzano Bridge."

"What were you doing in Brooklyn?"

"I'll explain when I get there," Dee Dee promised.

"I'm in Mika's room. See you when you get here," Elontra said, and she ended the call.

"Where is she?" Shemika asked.

"Brooklyn, but she's on her way back here."

"What was she doing in Brooklyn?"

"She didn't say. Just that she was on the Verrazzano Bridge on her way back here. She said that she'll explain when she gets here."

It was a little after two in the afternoon when Dee Dee parked the 280ZX in the parking lot and made her way to Shemika's room. Elontra opened the door to let her in.

"Hey."

"How's Mika?"

"Still kinda down about everything," Elontra said. "She's out on the balcony."

"What I have to tell her should make her feel a lot better," Dee Dee said, and she followed Elontra out on the balcony.

"Where you been?" Shemika asked when she came outside.

Dee Dee sat down. "In Brooklyn, getting you what you need."

"What do I need?"

"You need to know if the cops are hunting you, right?"

"And?"

"There isn't a warrant for your arrest."

Shemika closed her eyes, and her head drifted back. "Yes!" she said triumphantly with her hands in the air.

"What about her boy?"

"He's not talking, and neither is the other one," Dee Dee announced, and they breathed a sigh of relief.

Shemika stood up. "Let's go home."

Chapter Twenty-six

After the mini vacation in Jersey, it was good to be home. Since Shemika didn't feel like cooking after the long drive, they ordered from Ephesus Mediterranean and Turkish Cuisine and had Adana kebab, karisik izgara, and beyti kebab delivered.

The following morning, Shemika was up early, and after she cooked breakfast, she started cleaning her house. That included tossing the leftovers that were in the refrigerator when they left town. Then she sat down and made a shopping list, and once she let her girls know where she was going, she headed for the supermarket. Shemika wandered around IGA, filling her cart with the items from her list, and then she paid for it and headed out of the store.

She had just reached her car when a black Yukon came down the aisle fast and came to a screeching stop in front of Shemika. The doors swung open, two men in masks got out, and one of them grabbed her, put a black bag over her head, and tried to get her into the Yukon.

"Help!" she screamed, dropping her purse and her car keys. "Help! Somebody, please help me!" Shemika struggled and screamed as they put her in the back of the Yukon and drove away.

"Shut her up!" one of the kidnappers shouted.

She was screaming, "Help me!" at the top of her lungs while trying to fight off her kidnappers until one put a gun to her head. Her eyes were open wide, and Shemika froze.

"You move or make another fuckin' sound and I'll put a bullet in your brain. Got that?"

Shemika nodded her head quickly as tears began streaming down her cheeks. The realization of her situation set in. She'd been kidnapped, and she did not know what would happen to her next. A million things bombarded her mind all at once.

Who are these people?

What do they want from me?

Are they going to kill me?

Are they going to rape me and then kill me?

"Ouch!" she shouted as one put plastic handcuffs around her wrists.

She couldn't tell how long they'd been driving, but it seemed like a long time before the Yukon came to a stop. Shemika heard the door open.

"Come on," one said, all but dragging her out of the Yukon. They were walking her so fast that she stumbled and fell. "Get up!" The man jerked her up.

"The lady said not to hurt her."

"I'm not gonna hurt her," he said and shoved Shemika in the back, and once again she stumbled to the ground. "It ain't my fault that she can't walk," he laughed. He jerked her up.

"Your funeral," the other said, shook his head, and kept walking.

Shemika could tell that she was now inside, and then they walked her down a flight of stairs before one said, "Stop." He grabbed her hands and cut the plastic handcuffs. Shemika heard a door open.

"Get in there," he said and shoved her.

Shemika heard the door close and lock before she pulled the black bag off her head. She was in a ten-by-ten room with no window and nothing to sit on. Thankful to still be alive and not getting gang-raped, Shemika leaned against the wall and slid down to the floor to wait for whatever this was about.

Shemika didn't know how long she'd been in that room, but it seemed like hours had passed before she heard the door open. A man with a ski mask came into the room.

"On your feet," he barked, and she stood up. "Let's go," he said and walked her back upstairs.

When Shemika got to the top of the stairs, her eyes opened in wide wonder at the fabulous surroundings. She was in somebody's mansion, that was certain. The man walked her to some double doors and knocked before opening the door and walking Shemika in. There, behind a Theodore Alexander mahogany and brass executive desk, sat Milica Ibrahimovic, the woman who contracted Dominic to do the job.

"Shemika Frazier. Mr. Moore's associate," Milica said, and Shemika nodded. "Would you care to tell me what happened?"

Shemika said nothing until the man put a gun to her head to motivate her. "Dominic accidentally tripped an alarm, and we had to get outta there."

"Most unfortunate."

"Yes, it was. Dominic and Jack got caught by the police."

"Yes, I am well aware of their status. As I said, most unfortunate." Milica paused. "You see, there is still the matter of Mr. Moore's fee. I paid Mr. Moore half of his fee in advance, and I don't have what I paid for," she said, and Shemika said nothing. Milica exhaled. "As I told Mr. Moore, I have no tolerance for failure, Ms. Frazier. Therefore, as his associate, you have three choices."

"Wait, what?"

"Return my money, get me what I paid for, or you and your friends Elontra Montgomery and Demeris Dennison will die. The choice, of course, is yours, but I strongly suggest that you choose wisely."

"I don't know what Dominic did with the money," Shemika said.

"Then you only have two choices."

"How much was his fee?" she asked, thinking that between her and her girls, they could just pay the money back.

"I paid Mr. Moore one hundred and fifty thousand dollars in advance."

"I don't have that much money."

"Then you will do the job, and you will get me what I paid for."

"I can't do the job," Shemika said.

"Then you want to die." Milica looked at the man. "Kill her."

"Wait!" Shemika shouted. She took a breath. "I'll do it. I'll get you what you want," she said rather than get shot.

"A wise decision. Bring me the item and I'll pay you the entire three hundred thousand dollars that I was going to pay Mr. Moore." Milica nodded, and the man handed Shemika a thumb drive and a burner phone. "After your botched attempt to obtain it, the item has been moved to a different location. All the information that you need is on that drive. That phone has one number saved. Call that number and leave a message if there is anything else you need to complete the job. Don't fail me again, Ms. Frazier." She looked at the man. "Take her away."

Shemika put the burner and thumb drive in her pocket and then quickly looked around at her surroundings.

"Let's go," he said, grabbing Shemika by the arm, and they left the office. He closed the door behind them and stopped. "Hands," he commanded, and Shemika held out her hands to be cuffed.

He put the black bag over her head once again and walked her out of the house and back to the Yukon. After another long ride, the Yukon stopped, and she heard a door open, and then her door opened.

"Give me your hands."

Shemika held out her hands, and he put her car keys in her hand and cut the handcuffs.

"Get out."

Shemika got out and pulled the black bag off her head in time to see the Yukon drive away. When she looked around, she saw that she was back at her car in the IGA parking lot.

Chapter Twenty-seven

It was dark when Shemika walked to her car and unlocked it. She had no idea what time it was, no idea how long she'd been held captive. When she got in the car, she saw that her purse was in the car. She quickly checked inside. Her identification, cell phone, and her money were all still there. Since they put her purse in the car, she wondered if her kidnappers had been nice enough to put her groceries in the trunk.

Shemika started the car and looked at the time. It was ten forty-five. That meant that she had been gone for almost twelve hours. Knowing that Elontra and Dee Dee had to be worried about her, she got her cell phone out of her purse to call them, but it was dead. As Shemika drove home, she couldn't stop her hands from shaking at times, and she broke down crying once or twice. It was hard to drive, but she made it home and gladly shut off the car.

Inside the house, Elontra and Dee Dee saw her car pull into the driveway. They watched from the window as she got out, checked the trunk of her car, shook her head, and then started for the house. Dee Dee jerked the door open as she reached for the handle.

"Where the fuck have you been all day?"

"I got kidnapped," she said as she walked into the house past Dee Dee.

She shut the door. "What?"

"You heard me. I got kidnapped," she said and plopped down on the couch.

"Who kidnapped you, Mika?" Elontra asked.

"Milica Ibrahimovic."

"Who the fuck is that?" Dee Dee wanted to know.

"She's the woman who contracted Dominic to do the job."

"Why did she kidnap you?" Elontra asked.

"Because she paid Dominic half of the money up-front, and she didn't get what she paid for."

"What did that have to do with you?" Dee Dee asked.

"I was with Dominic when he met with her about the job." She paused and looked at her friends. "He introduced me as his associate."

"Not good." Elontra dropped her head.

"What did she want?"

"She gave me three choices."

Dee Dee leaned forward. "What were they?"

"Return her money."

"How much was that?" Elontra asked.

"A hundred and fifty thousand dollars," Shemika said, and Elontra shook her head.

"What were the other two choices, Mi?"

"We could do the job and get her what she paid Dominic for."

"Or?"

"Or she'll kill us."

"Us?" Dee Dee questioned.

"She knows about you two. Elontra Montgomery and Demeris Dennison. She called you by name."

"What did you tell her?"

"I told her we'd do it," Shemika said to loud grumbles from Elontra and Dee Dee. "I didn't have a choice. She asked me for the money, and when I told her that I didn't have it, she was gonna kill me right then."

"So what do you have to do?" Dee Dee asked.

Shemika reached into her pocket. “I have everything we need to know to do the job on this thumb drive.” Dee Dee held out her hand, and Shemika handed her the drive. “And she gave me this phone if we need anything.”

“Let’s have a look.” Dee Dee got up, and Shemika followed her to the computer room.

Elontra was slow getting up from her seat but made it into the room in time to listen as Dee Dee read what was necessary to complete the job and reviewed the design specifications. Dee Dee sat back.

“These are pretty much the same security protocols that were in place at the previous location,” Dee Dee said. “Same amount of risk.”

“Plus a few other things that we didn’t have to deal with,” Shemika added excitedly. “Maybe we should just pay her back the money?”

“How much you got?” Dee Dee asked.

“No,” Elontra said definitely and firmly. “We are not doing that.”

“We’re not?” Shemika questioned.

“No, we’re not doing that. We are not going to give her our money. We’re doing the job.” Elontra leaned forward. “Listen, Dee Dee said this job has pretty much the same security protocols that were in place when you and Dominic tried to get it, right?”

Shemika nodded.

“Well, if he hadn’t been trying to show off for you, you and he would have gotten her the AI prototype, right?”

“True,” Shemika admitted.

“How much do we get if we get the prototype?”

“Three hundred thousand dollars.”

“Oh, yeah,” Elontra said, nodding her head and smiling. “We are definitely doing this job.”

“What you say, Dee Dee?” Shemika wanted to know. “Can you do it?” she asked because now it would have to be Dee Dee who had to hack the system and defeat all of the security protocols.

"For three hundred grand, I'll find a way to get it done for us."

"Three hundred thousand dollars might not be enough for us to retire on, but it is more than enough for us to stop for a while," Elontra said. "So what do you say, Mika? It's your call."

"What's it gonna be, Mi?" Dee Dee asked.

"Let's do it," Shemika said.

"Okay. Dee Dee, let's go through it again," Elontra said, and Shemika got up.

"I've got a bottle of Poet's Leap Riesling chilling. I'll be right back," she said and went to get the bottle. She stopped at the door and turned to face her friends. "Thank you."

"We got you, Mika," Elontra said.

"Yeah. What did you expect?" Dee Dee questioned, and Shemika left the room. "You really think we can pull this off?" Dee Dee asked Elontra.

"You sure you can do all that computer stuff?"

"I'll get it done."

"Then we can do this." Elontra sat back, nodding her head. "Mostly because we don't have a choice."

"True."

Chapter Twenty-eight

It was just after eight in the morning, and even though it was after three when she got in bed, Elontra was up and heading for the shower. The night before, she, Dee Dee, and Shemika were formulating a plan to get the AI prototype for Milica Ibrahimovic. When they were finished, she and Shemika called it a night, and Dee Dee said she'd be right back and went out.

Once she had showered, Elontra went and made herself a cup of coffee, sat down in the living room, and got started. It was sometime after ten when Shemika surfaced.

"Morning."

"Hey, Mika."

"What are you doing?"

"Going over the plans and the layout of the building for the job," she said without looking up from what she was doing.

"Have you eaten yet?"

Elontra looked up. "Did you cook?"

"I'll get breakfast started," Shemika said and went into the kitchen. She had fried chicken tenders the night before, so that morning they had chicken and waffles with blueberry syrup. After they ate, they got back to work.

"Once we're in and Dee Dee does her thing, that leads us to this point," Elontra said and pointed to a spot on the floor plan of the area leading to the vault. "This is a problem."

"That wasn't something that we had to deal with last time," Shemika said, "but we'll find a way to get around it." Shemika stood up. "You want another cup of coffee?"

"Please," Elontra said and handed Shemika her cup when she looked and saw that Dee Dee's car had pulled into the driveway. "Dee Dee's back!"

"Good," Shemika said on her way to the kitchen. "Now we can go over her parts of the job."

Shemika disappeared into the kitchen as the front door opened and Dee Dee came into the house.

"You're right. Like I said, we don't need to see each other anymore," an obviously annoyed Dee Dee said, taking the phone away from her ear, swiping end, and turning off her phone. "Hey."

"Hey."

"What you doing?"

"Waiting for you so we can go over your parts of the plan," Elontra said, and Dee Dee sat down.

"It's just a matter of me defeating their protocols and uploading the information to the system, and then we're in," Dee Dee said as Shemika came back into the living room. "Morning, Mi," she said and turned her attention back to Elontra.

Shemika handed Elontra her coffee and sat down.

"Thank you. Once we're in, we need a place to make the change."

Shemika pointed to a spot on the floor plan. "I was thinking this would be the best spot. What do you think?"

"I was thinking about changing in the locker room," Elontra said. "Seems like the obvious place."

"It does. But then I thought, what if somebody recognizes us and realizes that we're not supposed to be there?"

"She has a point," Dee Dee said. "Is there anything left to eat?"

"Your plate is in the microwave," Shemika said. "That's why I think this stairwell is the next best spot. Agreed?"

"Agreed," Elontra said, and Dee Dee got up.

"Agreed," she said on her way to the kitchen.

Once Dee Dee returned to the living room with the plate Shemika put away for her, they reviewed every aspect of the job until each was tired of talking about it. But there was still one sticking point.

"This guy." Elontra pointed.

After Dominic and Shemika's failed attempt to get the prototype, one additional layer of security was added to the mix. They had stationed a security guard outside the vault area to control access.

"We are going to need to get him off his post some kinda way. A distraction or something."

"I agree," Dee Dee said, "but whatever that distraction is, it needs to keep him away from the vault the entire time you're in there."

"How do we do that?" Shemika asked, and there was silence in the living room.

Elontra smiled.

"What?" Dee Dee asked.

"Not a distraction. Mika, call your girl and ask her—"

"She is not my girl!"

"Okay, call our current employer and ask her . . . No, call and tell her that we need the security schedule and their duty roster."

"On it," Shemika said and took out the burner to make the call. "What are you thinking?"

"That if we can't control him, replace him," Elontra said, and her girls smiled.

"We bring in our own man to replace theirs," Dee Dee said. "Brilliant!"

"Thank you." Elontra took a bow.

"Who did you have in mind?" Shemika asked.

"Pearson."

"You think he'll do it?" Dee Dee asked.

"I'll offer him ten grand to put on the uniform and stand there for a couple of hours." Elontra nodded. "Yeah, I think he'll do it."

"Sweet." Dee Dee stood up. "If we're about done here, I'm gonna go get in the shower."

"Okay," Shemika said, and she got up and started for her room.

"Before you go, Dee Dee, I got a question," Elontra said with as innocent a smile as she could muster on her face.

"What's that?" Dee Dee asked.

"Who don't you think you need to see anymore?" Elontra asked, and Shemika sat down.

"What's this now?" Shemika asked, and Dee Dee laughed a little.

"When missy here came in," Elontra said, grinning, "she was on the phone telling someone that maybe they didn't need to see each other anymore."

"Who were you talking to?" Shemika asked.

"You remember me telling you about the woman I met at Discount Electronics? Well, her name is Taylor. Anyway, when I get there, she says, 'We need to talk.'"

"Uh-oh," Shemika giggled.

"What did she wanna talk about, Dee?"

"She wants to know why the only time she hears from me is bedtime."

"Where have I heard that before?" Elontra asked, knowing that she was the one who asked it.

"I don't even remember what I said, but we went around and around about it. 'All we do is have sex. We never go anywhere or do anything.'" Dee Dee shook her head. "How do you tell somebody that you don't wanna do anything with them but have sex? So I ended up saying that we don't need to see each other anymore. She says, 'Maybe we don't.' I get up and say, 'I should go.' She says, 'No, stay, it's late and you've been drinking.' So I stay, we go to bed, she makes me scream, and I go to sleep. But in the morning, she's back on it, only now I'm using her for her sex because I never wanna go anywhere or do anything with her. I mean, if I wanna hang out with women, I got y'all," Dee Dee laughed.

"Well, there is something called men you could go out with," Shemika laughed.

"Right. And I would love to go out with men, but you got me living out here in white man land and I am a white man magnet. But white men don't interest me at all. And the black men I've met are all short and skinny, and you know me. I may be five two, but if a man ain't at least five ten with some weight on him, Dee Dee ain't interested."

"True, but like I said, a nut is a nut is a nut," Elontra giggled.

"That's what I got whiny-ass Taylor for," Dee Dee said, and they all laughed.

"But don't you miss dick?" Shemika wanted to know.

"Believe me, Taylor is like this insane ninja with a strap."

"That was more than I needed to know and a visual that I didn't need, Dee Dee, thank you," Elontra said and stood up.

"Where are you going?"

"To call Pearson," she said and went to her room.

When Pearson answered his phone, she told him that she had a favor she wanted to talk to him about, but not on the phone. He told Elontra that he was in Queens and that he could swing by and pick her up.

"I'll be there in thirty minutes," he said, and Elontra ended the call.

She went back into the living room. "Pearson will be here in thirty minutes."

Shemika and Dee Dee both smiled.

"Y'all don't mind entertaining him while I get ready, do you?"

"Don't worry. We got him," Dee Dee said.

"Take your time," Shemika said.

"Because I know I have questions for him," Dee Dee said.

"Tons," Shemika giggled as Elontra went to get ready.

She selected a chalk black Halston Analise one-shoulder minidress and a pair of Jimmy Choo crystal mesh pumps and got in the shower. When she was ready and came out of her room, Elontra could hear Pearson laughing.

"I got a friend who would love to meet you," he said.

"Is he a black man?" Dee Dee asked.

Pearson chuckled. "Yeah, he's a black man."

"How tall is he?" Dee Dee needed to know as Elontra came into the living room.

"About as tall as me. Six feet, I guess," Pearson said and stood up when he saw Elontra. "Hello."

"I didn't keep you waiting for long, did I?"

"Not at all." He cleared his throat. "You look incredible."

"Thank you. You ready to go?"

"Yes. It was good to see you ladies again," he said, moving toward the door.

"Good to see you too," Shemika said.

"I do wanna meet your friend," Dee Dee said.

"You talking about CK?" Elontra asked when they got to the door.

"Yeah, he likes a little short, sassy woman like her."

Elontra looked at Dee Dee. "You've seen CK before."

"I have?"

"That was Pearson and CK we saw that night at Eastern Parkway Estates," Elontra said and opened the door.

“What?” Dee Dee questioned, and then she thought about it. “Yeah, I wanna meet him!” she shouted to the closing door.

Once they were in Pearson’s car, he said that he was hungry and knew a spot where they had the best slices.

“I’m always down for good pizza,” she said, and they were on their way.

“So what was this favor you wanted to ask me?”

Elontra took a deep breath. “Might as well jump right in,” she said and told Pearson what they did, how they got involved with Milica Ibrahimovic, and then what they needed him to do.

Pearson laughed. “So let me get this straight. You and the other two cuties you run with are a robbing crew. And you rob banks?”

“And jewelry stores, but yeah,” Elontra admitted.

“And now, because of Dominic’s fuckup, you got yourselves hooked up with somebody who is forcing you to do a job that you need a man for. Is that right?”

“Right.”

Pearson shook his head. “‘I rob banks’ are the last words that I ever thought would pass over those pretty lips.”

“Will you do it?” Elontra asked as Pearson’s phone rang with a call from CK.

“I gotta take this.”

“I know you do.”

Pearson pressed talk. “What’s up, big boy?”

CK’s voice filled the car. “I know where Dre is.”

“Where?”

“His woman’s apartment. Where you at?”

“I’m in Massapequa with . . .” He glanced at Elontra. “I’m in Massapequa with Legs Diamond.”

“Legs Diamond?” Elontra silently questioned.

“Drop her off somewhere and come on.”

"No, we don't have time for me to drop her off." He glanced at Elontra and she nodded. "But I can be there in twenty minutes."

"Come on then."

Pearson ended the call and made a U-turn so he could meet CK.

"Legs Diamond?" Elontra questioned.

"That's what CK calls you. No matter how many times I tell him your name is Elontra, he still calls you Legs Diamond."

"Okay. Who is Legs Diamond anyway? Is that an actual person?" Elontra asked.

"Yeah," Pearson laughed as he sped through traffic. "He was a gangster in Philly in the old bootlegging days."

"So how did I get to be Legs Diamond?"

Pearson looked at Elontra's legs and shook his head as he drove. "I'm gonna take a big chance and say that it has something to do with your amazing legs. But you'd have to ask CK."

"Whatever." Elontra shook her head. "So will you help me out with this job?"

"Of course I will, Elontra. I'd do anything for you, but seriously, I am still tripping on you. A bank robber." He shook his head. "I just didn't see that one coming."

"Well, here I am, Elontra Montgomery, notorious bank robber."

When they got to Dre's girlfriend's apartment, Pearson saw CK leaning on a car, and he parked.

"Wait here. This shouldn't take long," Pearson said and got out of the car, putting his gloves on as he walked over to where CK was waiting. They talked and then went into the building together.

They had been in the building for about fifteen minutes or so when, all of a sudden, Elontra saw a man running out of the building. Then she saw CK and Pearson come running out after him. CK caught up and grabbed him by the collar, spun him around, and punched him in the face. He pushed him, and his momentum carried him right into Pearson. He punched him in the stomach, knocking the wind out of him, and he fell to his knees.

Elontra watched from the car as Pearson grabbed him by his shirt collar and slammed his head into a car door. When he collapsed to the ground, CK stomped him. Pearson pulled him up and slammed his head into the door again until the man was spitting blood. Pearson pulled him up from the ground and hit him with blow after blow until he went down again.

The beating was so brutal that Elontra wanted to look away, but she couldn't. She watched Pearson and CK stand over the man and stomp him. When he tried to cover his head to keep from getting stomped, Pearson started kicking him in the stomach. And then Pearson pulled him up and slammed him face-first into the hood of the car over and over again.

Then Elontra watched CK walk away, and Pearson let his beaten and bloodied body drop to the ground. They nodded at one another, and then Pearson got back in the car with her.

"You okay?" Pearson said as he started the car.

"Y'all beat the fuck outta muthafucka for real." Elontra shook her head. "I'm glad you're on my side."

She hung out with Pearson for the rest of the night. He took her to the club where he and his crew hung out, and CK introduced her as Legs Diamond.

"Notorious bank robber," Pearson added.

Chapter Twenty-nine

"Fuck!" a frustrated Dee Dee shouted.

With the date of the job fast approaching, Dee Dee was hard at work, trying her best to defeat all of the security protocols. To this point, her success had been mixed, and that wasn't good enough. It was part of her responsibility to get them into the building, and if she couldn't get it, they weren't going anywhere.

Dee Dee was able to get to a certain point, but when she tried to upload a file that was critical to the success of the operation, the message she got was: Access Denied.

"Fuck!"

She had tried to implement all of the suggestions that Kaiden had made: piggybacking on authorized connections, man in the middle attacks, nothing was working. Dee Dee slumped down in her chair and tried to think of something that she hadn't tried, but she had tried everything.

"Everything I know," Dee Dee said aloud, and that was when she made the decision to reach out for help. She pushed back from the console and got her cell phone.

"Hey, Dee Dee," Kaiden answered. "How's it going?"

"It's going all right, but I need your help. Can I come through?"

"Sure you can. I'll be here," Kaiden said.

"I'll see you in about an hour," Dee Dee promised, and she ended the call.

Once she got herself together, Dee Dee told Shemika and Elontra what was going on, what the problem was, and that she was going to Kaiden's apartment to see if he had any advice to offer on ways she could defeat it.

"Good luck. I guess I don't have to tell you how fucked we are if you can't do this," Elontra said as Dee Dee headed for the door.

"You don't."

"While you're over there, see if he can't help you out with your other problem," Shemika suggested.

Dee Dee stopped at the door. "What other problem?"

"Lack of penetration," Shemika laughed.

"Not my type. But I'm sure we'll all agree that him solving our access problem is a little more important than me getting some dick," Dee Dee said, and she left the house.

Elontra shook her head.

"What?" Shemika asked.

"Nothing."

"So I'm a little dick happy."

Elontra shook her head. "From the first time you got some."

On the drive to Kaiden's place, Dee Dee still tried to think of things she could have missed, reasons things went wrong, or what she could be doing wrong, and she continued to draw a blank. Although she didn't need the reminder because she was well aware of the situation, Elontra's reminder of how fucked they were if she couldn't get it done kept ringing in her ears.

When she arrived at Kaiden's apartment, he buzzed her in, and she walked to the unit wondering how she'd ask and if he'd do it. He was standing in the doorway smiling when she got there. Since that night that they met at Eastern Parkway Estates, and in the time that they had spent together since, Kaiden had become quite fond of Dee Dee. Of course, he wished the relationship would turn physical, but once she made it clear that wasn't happening, he had settled nicely into the dreaded friend zone.

"What's up, flydeedee?" he asked, calling her by her screen name.

"Something I need your help with, Cloudburst." When he closed the door, she stopped and turned toward him. Dee Dee took a breath. "I need to hack CBNP Holdings."

"Stop right there." Kaiden looked at Dee Dee for a second or two, and then he sat down. "First it was the NYPD database, and now you wanna get into CBNP's systems?" He shook his head. "No, Dee Dee, you need to tell me what is going on with you, and I mean everything, or I won't help you."

Dee Dee came and sat down next to him. "Where to start?"

"At the beginning. That's always a good place to start."

"A very dear friend of mine got involved with a man who was contracted to steal a prototype AI from one of CBNP's affiliates. The job went bad, and he and one of his associates were arrested." She paused and Kaiden nodded. "I needed to access the NYPD database to see if there was a warrant for her arrest."

"Shemika?"

"Yes."

"And the man she got involved with was Dominic?"

"Yes. But since his employer didn't get what she paid for, she is forcing Shemika to do the job, or she'll kill her, kill us."

"Who's 'us'?"

"Me and Elontra."

"Who is this woman?"

"Her name is Milica Ibrahimovic."

A panicked look washed over Kaiden's face. "What did you say?"

"Her name is Milica Ibrahimovic."

"Milica Ibrahimovic the arms dealer?" Kaiden asked excitedly.

"I don't know, I guess."

"Interpol has a Red Notice out on her."

"What's a Red Notice?"

"A Red Notice is a request to law enforcement worldwide to locate and provisionally arrest a person pending extradition."

"Oh," Dee Dee said, and that was when she realized that they were in deeper than any of them realized.

"You need to tell me everything, every detail, and don't leave anything out," Kaiden insisted, and Dee Dee told him the entire story from the beginning. "Wait, why would Dominic come to the three of you to fill out his crew?"

Dee Dee paused. "Because me, Mika, and Elontra are a robbing crew."

"You're a what?"

"A robbing crew. We rob banks, jewelry stores, that type of shit."

Kaiden shook his head. "This just keeps getting better and better." He paused. "So you all turn him down, and Shemika goes and does the job with him by herself."

"Right."

"Tell me everything you know about the AI prototype. Do you know what it's for or why Ibrahimovic wants to get her hands on it?"

"No clue. Just that she'll kill us if we don't get it." Dee Dee paused. "Will you help me?"

"Of course I will," Kaiden promised.

"Thank you." Dee Dee stood up. "I'm gonna get back to my girls, but I'll be back later tonight, and we can go over everything."

Kaiden stood up and walked Dee Dee out of the building to the car. "See you tonight," he said and closed her car door. He watched her drive away. "Fuck!" he said aloud and went back into the building. He locked the door, reengaged the alarms, and went to get a secure phone.

"Hello."

"We need to talk."

"Battery Park, one hour," she replied and ended the call.

An hour later, at the US Coast Guard World War II Memorial statue in Battery Park, Kaiden waited patiently for her to arrive. He stood up when he saw her coming.

"What you got?"

"Milica Ibrahimovic."

"The arms dealer?"

"You know any other?"

"What about her?"

"Apparently she is in the city, and she's using Demeris Dennison to steal an AI prototype."

"Demeris Dennison and Milica Ibrahimovic." Harper shook her head. "Flydeedee, this is the last place I expected you to show up."

"Then you really don't wanna know what she's been doing."

Harper shook her head. "What do you know about this prototype and why she wants it?"

"No idea."

"If Ibrahimovic wants it, it can't be good."

"What do you want me to do?

"Help her in any way you can. When's this going down?"

"Tomorrow."

"Okay," Harper said and thought for a second or two. "You do whatever you can to help her, and I'll begin to make some inquiries on my end. In the meantime, I need you to find out what Dee Dee knows about this AI prototype, what it's for, and why Milica Ibrahimovic wants it."

"Understood," Kaiden said and walked away from Harper.

When Dee Dee returned to the house, the equipment needed to print the cards, printer ribbon, ID card software, the camera, and cards that they requested from Milica Ibrahimovic had arrived along with the security schedule and their duty roster. Pearson was there as well, getting fitted with the uniform that he was going to wear the following day.

"You look nice," Elontra said because she had a thing for men in uniforms.

"I don't feel nice. I feel like a cop," he said as Dee Dee came into the house.

"How'd it go?" Shemika asked.

"He said he'd do it," Dee Dee replied. "I'm going back over there with the particulars, make sure we can get in and do what we need to do."

"Good deal." Elontra nodded. "All we need now is for tomorrow to come so we can get this behind us."

"Tomorrow can't come soon enough," Shemika said.

Chapter Thirty

"Okay, let's go over it one more time," Shemika said to a choir of grumbles.

"We've gone over it enough, Mika," Elontra said.

"Ad nauseam," Dee Dee added.

The day had arrived, and they were getting ready to do the job that evening. They had gone over the plan until each one could recite their part of the plan in their sleep. It was a simple plan when you got right down to it. All they had to do was pull it off and they'd be $300,000 richer, and they'd get to stay alive.

Their knowledge that Milica Ibrahimovic was a notorious arms dealer who was wanted by Interpol made her threat to kill them all the more real. But it didn't change anything.

"I just don't want anything to go wrong," Shemika said.

"It won't," Dee Dee assured her.

"We've come up with and planned for every contingency that we could think of. We're ready. Right?"

"Right," Dee Dee said enthusiastically, but to make Shemika feel more comfortable they went over it again.

Therefore, at three o'clock that afternoon, Pearson, dressed in a Continental security uniform, entered the CBNP Holdings building and went to present his ID card to the member of the security staff working that post.

The night before, Shemika used the camera to take pictures of each of them and then used the ID card software to print and then laminate the cards.

"What do you think?" she asked Dee Dee about the card that she made for her.

"Looks like a mug shot picture." She laughed. "But it looks good."

"Let's hope it's good enough to pass," Shemika said.

"It will be," Elontra said.

When Dee Dee returned to Kaiden's apartment, she went over the plan with him. She gave him $20,000 in cash, and then he got to work doing what Dee Dee couldn't. He was able to defeat the firewalls, access the security protocols, and upload personal profiles for each of them to access the CBNP Holdings building. Once they were in the building, the rest of Kaiden's job was to disable the cameras and eliminate any digital evidence of their presence.

Pearson handed security the card and waited to be passed through.

"You're clear. Have a good night," security said to Pearson.

"Thanks. You too."

Once he was out of sight, he took out the map he made for himself and then headed for the vault. When he arrived, there was another member of security seated outside of the vault, controlling access.

"Afternoon," he said, standing up and stretching. "Am I glad to see you."

"What's up?" Pearson said and swiped his ID card to take over the post.

"I just told you, I'm glad to see you. This has got to be the most boring post I've had since I've been working here. I mean, nobody came through, and nothing happened all day."

Pearson sat down. "Just the way I like it."

"Have a good night." He started walking away. "And stay awake." He pointed to the camera. "Big Brother is watching."

"Good night," Pearson said, glad that he pointed the camera out to him. He made a mental note not to look directly into it.

It was two hours later at the maintenance entrance that Elontra and Shemika approached the security station. They were dressed in All-American Cleaning Service uniforms. Shemika presented her ID and held her breath.

"You're clear. Go ahead," security said.

"Thanks."

When Elontra handed security her card, he ran the card through, and then he smiled at her. "I haven't seen you here before."

"It's my first night working here," Elontra said.

"I'm showing her the ropes," Shemika said.

"You're clear." He handed the card back to Elontra. "You're good to go."

"Have a good night," she said and walked away quickly with Shemika. "We're in."

"Okay. I'm going in," Dee Dee said and started for the front entrance, dressed conservatively in a gray mélange Totême wool-blend blazer, wide-leg trousers, Givenchy Voyou slingbacks, and a Bottega Veneta leather clutch. She handed her ID to security. He looked at the badge.

"Sonya Hampton," he said as he inserted the card into the reader. Dee Dee said nothing. "Have a good night, Ms. Hampton," he said, handing her back the card.

"Thank you," Dee Dee said and walked away. *Thank you, Kaiden,* she said to herself and proceeded to the office where she would do her part. "I'm in."

Now that they were all in the building, Elontra and Shemika made their way to the lower level to the boiler room. They needed a place to change out of their janitorial uniforms, and it was decided that there were too many cameras in the stairwell to risk the angles catching sight of them. There were fewer cameras on the lower level, and as long as they stayed close to the wall, the camera in the boiler room wouldn't detect them. Once they made it into the room, Elontra changed into a Balmain blanc knit cardigan suit while Shemika quickly came out of her coveralls to reveal the pink Akris punto belted crepe sable pants and short-sleeve striped pullover she had on.

"Ready?" Elontra asked and put on her badge.

"As I'll ever be," Shemika said, and they left the boiler room and headed for the vault.

Once she reached the twentieth floor, Dee Dee exited the elevator and walked down the hall to Sonya Hampton's office. She swiped the badge and went in. She sat down at the desk and then took the thumb drive from her clutch. Dee Dee inserted the drive and gained access to the system. She shut down all the security protocols that stood between Elontra, Shemika, and the vault area.

As quickly as they could, Elontra and Shemika got off the elevator and headed toward the vault. Pearson saw them coming and discreetly motioned for them to stop.

"Stand by. There's someone in the vault," he whispered.

Not knowing what to do because they hadn't planned for it, Shemika turned around and went the other way while Elontra kept walking toward the vault. She winked at Pearson as she passed. It was five minutes later when the two women came out of the vault. After spending a minute or two flirting with the new security guard, the women went away.

"All clear."

When Elontra and Shemika returned to the vault, they took out and presented their badges to gain access.

Please Enter Security Code:

"Code one Q, two A, seven, four B," Elontra said to the first of the biometric security protocols that had to be defeated.

Recognize Alison Wilkerson. Access Granted.

Shemika stepped up to the reader.

Please Enter Security Code:

"Code two C, three K, sixteen, six L."

Recognize Katherine Stevenson. Access Granted.

Meanwhile, in the security office, a member of the staff noticed something he thought was peculiar, and he called to inform his supervisor. "Excuse me, Lieutenant."

"What you got, son?"

"I have unauthorized access at terminal 245972."

"Whose office is that?"

He double-checked his list. "That office belongs to Sonya Hampton, sir. But according to her schedule, she's off tonight."

"I'll send someone around to check it out." He chuckled. "Probably one of the janitorial staff playing on the internet again," the lieutenant said and dispatched an officer to check it out.

Now that they had defeated the voice recognition system and had access to the vault, Shemika called Dee Dee. "We're in."

"I'm clearing the path for you now," Dee Dee said, and she deactivated the path. "The path is clear."

"We're on our way," Shemika said.

Elontra put her hand on Shemika's shoulder and was careful to follow in her footsteps until they reached the vault. They took out and put on the gloves that were cast with the handprint to get around the fingerprint recognition. They already had on the contact lens for the iris and retinal scans.

"You ready?" Elontra asked, and Shemika nodded.

At the same time, each one placed her hand on the gel pad and leaned toward the retinal imaging scanner.

Access Granted.

When the vault opened, Elontra quickly replaced the AI prototype drive with the one she'd brought along with her that Ibrahimovic had supplied. She handed the drive to Shemika, and she placed it in a small but secure metal box, and Elontra closed the vault.

"We got it," Shemika said.

"Leaving the vault now," Elontra said, and they made their way back along the path.

"I'm out of here. Meet you in the boiler room," Dee Dee said.

"We're out," Shemika said once they were out of the vault.

"Did you get it?" Pearson asked as Elontra passed him on her way to the elevator.

"We got it. Now come on," Elontra said, and Pearson followed her to the elevator. Shemika pressed the button, and they waited impatiently for it to come.

With the task completed, Dee Dee shut down the computer and left the office. As she walked down the hall, she heard the elevator stop on her floor.

"Oh, shit," she said and quickly ducked into the bathroom.

Dee Dee peeked out the door as the security guard passed. When she saw him round the corner, she came out and headed straight for the elevator. When the doors opened, she took it down to the lower level so she could exit the building with Elontra and Shemika dressed in janitorial uniforms. She made it to the boiler room and changed into the uniform. Once Dee Dee finished changing, she glanced at her watch.

"They should be here by now," she said aloud, and intending to meet them at the car, she came out of the boiler room and started for the exit.

"Hey!" a member of the security staff shouted, and Dee Dee froze.

She turned slowly. "Yes?"

"You're not authorized to be down here," he said, walking up to her quickly. "Let me see your badge."

Just then, the elevator doors opened. Elontra, Shemika, and Pearson stepped out and started down the hall. They saw the security guard and made eye contact with Dee Dee.

Not recognizing Pearson, the security guard asked, "Who are you?"

"I'm your boogeyman," Pearson said and punched the security guard in the face. When he hit him a second time, the guard went down.

"Damn, you hit hard," Shemika said.

"You two, go change," Pearson said. "We'll take care of him."

"Okay," Elontra said, and she and Shemika headed for the boiler room to change.

"Come on, Dee Dee. Help me get him out of the hall," Pearson said, and she helped drag the body into another room. Once they had secured him with his own handcuffs and used his tie to gag him, Dee Dee and Pearson met Elontra and Shemika in the hall, and they made their way to the exit. Security passed them through, and they were out of the building with the AI prototype.

Chapter Thirty-one

When they got back to the house, there was a celebration. Pearson had stopped at the liquor store and picked up five bottles of Moët & Chandon Imperial Brut champagne. He shook up a bottle and was about to pop the cork.

"Fuck you think you're doing?" Shemika said to stop him. "This is my house, not the locker room at the NBA Finals. You get champagne on my carpet, I'm sending the cleaning bill to you," she said, took her bottle to her lips, and went back to dancing to the music in her mind.

"Yes, ma'am," Pearson said and eased the cork out slowly so he didn't spill a drop. "We did it!" he shouted and turned up the bottle.

"We did it!" Dee Dee raised her bottle and shouted. She was sitting on the couch next to Kaiden. He had a bottle and was drinking along with them, but his mood wasn't as festive as the others.

Neither was Elontra's.

She was drinking straight out of the bottle as well, sipping champagne and raising her bottle each time it was appropriate. But her eyes were on the metal case that contained the AI prototype and the burner phone on the coffee table that Milica Ibrahimovic provided.

Elontra thought that the celebration was a little premature. Sure the job was a success, they got the prototype, and they got away clean, but the job wasn't over. Not until Milica Ibrahimovic had the drive in her possession and they had their money. Once they got paid and were safe, that was the time to celebrate, and not before.

"I wanna say again how much I appreciate what y'all did for me," Shemika said and raised her bottle. "To my girls. Always there for me, always having my back and my front."

Elontra raised her bottle. "To friendship."

"To unbreakable bonds," Dee Dee stood up to say. "Not even time and distance can break them."

"That's love." Pearson nodded and raised his bottle.

"I love you both," Shemika said and opened her arms. "Come on, y'all, bring it in!"

Dee Dee rushed into her arms as Elontra slowly got up and joined in.

"I have the very best friends in the world," Shemika said, and she drained the bottle. "Is there any left?"

"I think you've had enough to drink," Elontra said. "We still need to get paid."

Shemika held up her hand. "You're right. I gotta have a clear head to make the exchange."

"Right," Elontra said and went to sit down. She put down her bottle. "What's taking her so long to call anyway? I wanna get this over with."

"I called her and left a message that we got it," Shemika said and looked at her watch. "It's been over two hours."

"Why don't you call her again?" Dee Dee asked.

"No." Shemika shook her head and sat down on the loveseat next to Elontra. "She'll call. We just need to be patient."

Elontra patted her thigh. "You know that patience has never really been my thing. We did the job, got her what she wanted, and now it's time to get paid, and we never have to hear from her again."

"Let's hope that's the case," Dee Dee said.

"What's that supposed to mean?" Shemika asked.

"Only that we did the job. Did the fuck outta of it really," she said, and everybody nodded in agreement. "Next time she needs something stolen—"

"She calls her girl there," Elontra said, finishing Dee Dee's sentence and pointing at Shemika.

"I am not her girl. I don't know why you keep saying that," Shemika said excitedly. "She's just somebody we got to deal with. That's all. But I am not her girl."

Elontra laughed and held up her hands in surrender. "Okay, Mika, calm down." She paused and Shemika nodded. "But Dee Dee's right. Next time she needs something stolen in New York, we're her girls," she said, making a circle with her hand to include herself.

Shemika leaned close to Elontra. "For three hundred grand, is that a bad thing?" she asked quietly in her ear so Pearson and Kaiden wouldn't hear how much they were being paid for the job.

"No, Mika, it's not. We just need to get that money."

"Is that why you're sitting over there all frowned up?" Dee Dee asked.

She nodded. "I will feel a lot better when she has the drive and we have our money," Elontra said and drank the last of her champagne.

Two hours later the phone still hadn't rung. Kaiden had gone home, and Pearson had fallen asleep in a chair. That left Shemika, Elontra, and Dee Dee sitting around the coffee table staring at the box and the phone, willing it to ring. Minutes seemed to pass like hours.

Until the phone rang.

"About time," Elontra said and leaned forward in anticipation.

Shemika snatched it off of the coffee table. "Hello."

"There's a warehouse on Thirty-seventh Avenue in Long Island City. Be there in two hours and bring the drive," Milica Ibrahimovic said and hung up.

"What did she say?" Dee Dee asked.

"She wants to meet at a warehouse on Thirty-seventh Avenue in Long Island City in two hours."

Elontra stood up. "I think we should get there early and check it out."

"I agree," Dee Dee said, and she got up too.

Elontra shook Pearson. "Wake up. We're going."

"She called?"

"Yes. Now get up and come on," Elontra said, walking away. "We're meeting her at a warehouse on Thirty-seventh Avenue in Long Island City."

"Okay." Pearson stood up as Elontra went toward her room. "Where are you going?" he asked.

"To get ready," she said and disappeared into her room.

When she emerged from her room, Elontra was wearing a black floor-length Maje Grenchir leather trench coat with a belt and sleek slit pockets at the waist over her Dolce & Gabbana bustier strapless minidress.

"What are you dressed for?" Shemika asked.

"Trouble."

"You look like Trinity in *The Matrix,*" Dee Dee said on her way to the door.

Elontra slipped a gun into her coat pocket. "Trinity wished she looked this good on her best day," she said and followed her crew out of the house. "Y'all go ahead," she said as Dee Dee and Shemika made it to her car. "I'm gonna drive," she said and unlocked the Corvette.

"Good idea. We'll see you there," Dee Dee said, and she got in the car with Shemika.

Pearson got in the car with Elontra. "You think something's gonna go wrong, don't you?"

"I hope not. It's just a feeling, but I hope I'm wrong."

As Elontra drove off, Pearson took out his gun and checked it. "Trust your instincts, Legs Diamond. They will serve you well."

"Is that what you do? Live by your instincts?"

"Instinct and information have gotten me through situations for years. So trust yours. Like I said, they will serve you well."

It was a little over an hour later when Elontra turned onto Thirty-seventh Avenue in Long Island City and drove past the warehouse. She looked for Shemika and Dee Dee before she parked up the street where she could see both the door and the gated vehicle entrance. As soon as she turned off the car, her phone rang.

"You see anything?" Shemika asked as she and Dee Dee drove by the warehouse and drove around the block.

"No. It looks like the place is in darkness from here," Elontra reported.

"We're gonna circle back around and park."

When Dee Dee came back around the block, she parked across the street from the warehouse. Shemika got the box that contained the AI prototype.

"I'm gonna check it out."

"Let's go."

Shemika and Dee Dee got out of the car, crossed the street, and checked the door.

"Locked," she said. "What now?" she asked and checked the gate before returning to the car.

"I guess we wait," Dee Dee said on the way back to the car.

It was thirty minutes later when a midnight blue Ford Explorer pulled up outside the warehouse. One man got out to open the gate. The Explorer drove inside. He closed the gate, and then he went in the front door.

"I guess that's our cue. Let's go get this over with," Elontra said as she and Pearson got out of her car. They walked to the front door of the warehouse, where Dee Dee and Shemika were waiting.

"You two go ahead. We're gonna hang back," Elontra said, and Dee Dee nodded. "But we're right behind you."

"Ready?" Shemika asked.

"Let's go," Dee Dee said and grabbed the handle to go inside the warehouse.

"Is anybody here?" Shemika shouted as they reached an open space.

Once they rounded the corner, they saw two men standing by the Explorer. They had set up a table to make the exchange. "Over here!" one shouted back, and they approached the table.

As they got closer, Shemika saw a metal briefcase on the table. Elontra and Pearson entered the warehouse, but they kept their distance.

"Did you bring the item?"

Shemika held up the case that contained the AI prototype as she and Dee Dee walked cautiously toward the table. "Got it right here." She set the case down on the table.

"Open it," he demanded.

"You open yours first," Dee Dee insisted.

But when Shemika opened the case and the man saw that the thumb drive was in it, he reached for it.

Just then, Pearson saw a third man come out of the shadows.

"Gun!" Pearson shouted just as he began firing. Pearson returned his fire, and the man took cover. Pearson exchanged gunfire with the man. He ducked around the corner and returned fire.

As the shooting started, one of the men grabbed the case that contained the AI prototype, and the other began firing as he backed up to the Explorer. When Dee Dee grabbed the briefcase with the money, she and Shemika ran for cover.

Elontra pulled the MAC-10 from under her leather trench coat and began firing as Shemika and Dee Dee made it to cover. The man ran for the Explorer as the other kept firing. The third man came out from cover and fired at Pearson. He fired back and hit him with two shots in his chest. Once Dee Dee and Shemika made it to cover, Elontra reached into her pocket and took out the gun. She slid it to Dee Dee, and she began firing at the other man as he tried to make it to the Explorer.

When he made it to the Explorer, he got in, started it up, and drove off. The other man fired a couple of shots and then ran after the Explorer. Pearson aimed and fired, hitting the man in the back as he ran. As Elontra fired the MAC at the Explorer, it crashed through the metal gate and sped up the street.

"We gotta get outta here!" Shemika said, moving quickly toward the exit.

"Right behind you!" Dee Dee said and picked up the metal briefcase.

As they ran to the car, she couldn't help but notice how light the case felt. When they got in the car and Shemika drove away, Dee Dee opened the case.

"Empty!"

"What?"

"The fuckin' case is empty!"

Chapter Thirty-two

"The case is empty!"

"What do you mean it's empty?" Elontra asked.

"I mean the fuckin' case with the money is empty!" Dee Dee shouted as Shemika drove.

"Damn it. I knew something like this was going to happen. I'll talk to you at the house," Elontra said, and she ended her call with Dee Dee. She called Kaiden right away and asked him to meet her at her house.

"What's wrong?" Pearson asked.

"Ibrahimovic beat us. There was no money in the case."

"That's fucked up," he said, and there was not another word spoken by either one until they reached the house. As they pulled into the driveway, Elontra and Pearson watched Shemika and Dee Dee go into the house. "Elontra," he said before she got out, "I'm sorry."

"It's not your fault. You did what you were supposed to do. What's fucked up is that Ibrahimovic wasn't a woman of her word."

When Elontra got out of the car, she and Pearson went inside. Dee Dee disappeared into the kitchen, leaving Shemika alone in the living room.

"So she beat us," Elontra said as she came into the house with Pearson. He sat down on the couch.

"Yeah," an angry Shemika said. "I tried to call her, but it went straight to voicemail."

"And you have no idea where they took you that day, do you?"

"No. I was blindfolded the entire time. All I can tell you is that it was a mansion, and I think it took over an hour to get there."

Elontra sat down next to Shemika. "That's not much help."

"I'm calling her again," Shemika said and started to reach for the burner.

"Why?"

"Why what?"

"Why call her again? She knows she beat us. And even if she did answer, what's she gonna say? 'I'm sorry there was no money in the case'? 'It was all a big misunderstanding'?" Elontra paused. "No, Mika, she beat us. Simple and plain. She knows she beat us, and she's probably somewhere laughing at the three dumb black girls she beat right now."

Dejected, Shemika sat back. "I guess you're right."

"I know I am."

Just then, the kitchen door burst open, and Dee Dee came out with a bag of trail mix, a bag of Gummy Bears, and a twenty-four-ounce bottle of Mountain Dew.

"Oh, but we are getting our money back. You can trust and believe in that. If there's one thing flydeedee can do, it is hack a muthafucka's shit and take their fuckin' money," an angry Dee Dee said, passing through the living room on the way to her computer room. "Kaiden is on his way here now. When he gets here, send him back," Dee Dee said and closed the door.

Pearson stood up. "I'm gonna go."

"Wait a minute. I have something for you before you go," Elontra said, got up, and went to her room.

Pearson looked at Shemika. "I'm sorry that it didn't work out."

She posted a brave smile. "They tell me that's life. 'You're riding high in April, shot down in May.'"

"Yeah, but it ain't right."

"I guess that's why you do what you do." Elontra came out of her room with an envelope. "When people don't pay, you get that money." She handed it to Pearson.

"What's this?" he asked.

"Ten thousand dollars, as promised."

"I can't take this from you, Elontra."

"Why not? You earned it."

"Yeah, but you didn't get paid." He tried to hand her back the envelope, but Elontra wouldn't take it.

"You did your job. It's not your fault that the bitch has no honor."

"True." He held up the envelope. "You sure about this?"

"Yes, Pearson, I'm sure. It's your money."

"Take the money, Pearson," Shemika interjected. "She can afford it."

Pearson put the money in his pocket. "Thank you for being about your word."

Elontra walked Pearson to the door and kissed him on the cheek. "I'll call you later," she said, closing the door and thinking about honor and loyalty and what that really meant at a time like this.

Meanwhile, as Dee Dee got set to do what she used to do, and Elontra and Shemika sat around depressed because they got beat, somewhere in Bridgeport, Connecticut, the midnight blue Ford Explorer pulled into the long driveway of the mansion occupied by Milica Ibrahimovic.

What the driver didn't know was that he had been under helicopter surveillance from the time he left the warehouse. He had just parked the Explorer in front of the house and got out when he saw three black Chevy Suburbans come onto the property with their lights flashing. He started to reach for his gun, but when he saw the six armed men and women get out, he thought better of it.

"FBI!" one agent shouted.

The man laid his gun on the ground and put his hands up. The agent quickly searched him and found the box containing the AI prototype.

"You're under arrest," another agent said.

"Cuff him. You two, secure the perimeter. The rest of you, with me," he said and went inside the house along with four other agents. They spread out around the property and eventually made their way to the study.

When the agent swung open the double doors, Milica Ibrahimovic was seated behind the desk. She was startled by their sudden appearance and started to reach for the gun in her drawer but quickly thought better of it.

"Milica Ibrahimovic. I'm Special Agent Chad Esposito with the FBI. Would you mind coming with me? There are certain people with Interpol who would like to ask you some questions."

Milica Ibrahimovic stood up and put her hands behind her back.

"Cuff her and get her outta here," Esposito ordered. The agents cuffed and then walked her out of the house.

Not knowing that Milica Ibrahimovic had been taken into custody, back at the house, Kaiden arrived to help Dee Dee get the money that they were owed. Shemika let him in.

"Hello, Kaiden." She stepped aside to let him into the house.

"How are you doing, Shemika?"

"I've been better."

"So I heard."

"Hey, Kaiden. Dee Dee's waiting for you," Elontra said.

"Let me show you to her lair," Shemika giggled and led Kaiden to Dee Dee's computer room. She tapped on and then opened the door.

Dee Dee spun around in her chair. "Hey."

"I have Kaiden here just as you requested," Shemika said, smiling.

"Thank you, Mika."

"Can I get anything for you, Kaiden?" Shemika asked.

"No, thank you. I'm fine."

Shemika winked at Dee Dee. "See if you can't help her out with her problem," she said and backed out of the door.

DeeDee shook her head as Shemika closed the door behind her. "Thanks for coming. Have a seat," Dee Dee said and turned back to her console.

"No worries." He looked around for another chair, and since there wasn't one, he smiled and sat on the bed. "What can I do to help?" Kaiden asked, but he had a good idea what she wanted when she called and said that Ibrahimovic had double-crossed them.

"When you told me about Ibrahimovic and how she was some big-time arms dealer, I did a deep dive into her, trying to find out what I could about her, and—"

"And you're looking for her money, and you need my help finding it." He paused. "Am I right?"

"Yes." Dee Dee exhaled. "Can you help me?"

Kaiden smiled at Dee Dee and stood up. "Of course I'll help you. I'd do anything for you."

"Thank you."

He turned his baseball cap backward. Dee Dee got up as he cracked his knuckles and sat down. "Watch and learn, script kiddie," he said and got to work.

Dee Dee went and got a chair from the dining room and dragged it into the room. She sat down next to Kaiden. Once again, she watched as his fingers moved quickly over the keyboard.

"How many words a minute do you type?"

"I don't know. A hundred maybe. Now be quiet," he said and kept typing.

It didn't take Dee Dee long to realize that Kaiden wasn't randomly searching for Ibrahimovic's money. He knew exactly where he was going and was soon bypassing the firewalls and defeating the security protocols at the Union Bank of Switzerland. After a while, Kaiden stopped and looked at Dee Dee.

"It's only got one hundred and ninety three thousand in the account, but—"

"I'm taking it." Dee Dee motioned for him to get up.

"Sure you wanna do this?" Kaiden asked, smiling as he got up.

"Move," she said and sat down.

While she was waiting for Kaiden to arrive, Dee Dee had opened an account at DMS Bank & Trust, the second-oldest bank established in the Cayman Islands. Once she had transferred the money out of Ibrahimovic's account and into her account, Dee Dee logged out and sat back.

"Got you, bitch." She turned to Kaiden. "Thank you."

"No problem. Sorry it wasn't the entire three hundred."

"That's all right," she said, and he followed her out of the room as Dee Dee went to tell her girls.

"You think she'll know that it was us who took her money?" Shemika wanted to know.

"Nope. Flydeedee leaves no traces behind." She winked at Kaiden.

He glanced at his watch. "She probably won't even notice. I'm sure she has much more important things to worry about."

Dee Dee turned to Kaiden. "Thank you again. I really appreciate it."

"I do too," Elontra said.

"You're welcome. I'm gonna shove off," Kaiden said and started for the door.

"I'll walk you out," Dee Dee said, and she followed him to the door.

Once they were outside, Dee Dee had a question. "You already knew about the account with Ibrahimovic's money, didn't you?"

"I did. When you called and said that something went wrong with the exchange, I kinda figured that Ibrahimovic stiffed you on the money." He leaned against his car. Dee Dee leaned next to him. "I did a little checking on her myself, so I knew that she wasn't above sticking people, so I went on and did a deep dive of my own, and I found where she hides her money. After that, it was easy peasy, grits is greasy."

Dee Dee laughed. "Thank you, Kaiden."

He pushed off the car and opened the door. "No problem. I'd do just about anything to help you, Dee Dee. I hope you know that."

"I do, Kaiden. And thank you again. We couldn't have done any of this without you," Dee Dee said as Kaiden got in his car.

When Kaiden drove away, Dee Dee waved goodbye to him and then turned toward the house. Elontra and Shemika were watching from the window. She gave them the finger and then came into the house.

Chapter Thirty-three

Now that they had gotten paid and felt like they were safe from Milica Ibrahimovic, it was really time to celebrate. They had heard about a new club called Gotham that had just opened and were going to go there. However, when Pearson told them that one of Shemika's favorite rappers, Key Lowe, was appearing at Atravessa, they decided to go there instead.

"Even though we robbed the place?" Dee Dee asked as she and Shemika arrived at the club.

Pearson, who was already there with Elontra, had added their names to the guest list, and they were escorted to the VIP room upon their arrival.

"It does feel a little funny being here," Shemika said to Dee Dee.

"I noticed that there were twice as many cops outside when we came in," Dee Dee replied.

"You noticed that too?" Shemika laughed as Elontra sat down at the table next to her.

"Noticed what? I'm so nosy."

Shemika leaned close to her. "That there are more cops outside."

"You think that's for us?" Elontra questioned, laughing.

The show was amazing, Key Lowe put on an excellent performance. As for Shemika and Dee Dee, they had a great time. They danced, and the men were buying drinks for them like it was free. It wasn't long after the show ended before Elontra and Pearson disappeared for the night.

By the time Shemika was ready to go, Dee Dee had met and given her number to two men, both of whom were over six feet tall, and as was her preference, they both had some meat on their bones. Shemika met somebody, too, and she was interested in him, but Dominic was still on her mind, so she got his number and said good night.

"I just might call you," she said, knowing that she wouldn't, patted his cheek, and left him standing there like the exceptional temptress she was.

When they got back to the house, they talked for a while about their evening. Since Key Lowe had packed the house, each joked about robbing Atravessa again before Shemika said good night to Dee Dee and she headed off to bed.

"Good night, Mi." Dee Dee went to her room and was about to break out the purple party mix, but then she thought that Taylor would be a better option, so she called her instead.

"Can I come by?"

When Taylor angrily said, "Come on," Dee Dee left the house so Taylor could make her shake and scream.

In the morning when Shemika emerged from her room, the house was empty and in silence. She had a bit of a headache from all of the drinking she'd done the night before, and since there was nobody home, she decided to eat out instead of cooking. She went to The Ridiculous Bagel and ordered the Ridiculous Burrito with three eggs over easy, sautéed mushrooms, onions, and home fries. "And could I get that with cheddar instead of American cheese, please?"

"You sure can."

Elontra was up early that morning as well. She had an appointment at CV Nail and Spa, where she planned to pamper herself with CV's signature facial, a thirty-minute massage, a paraffin manicure, and a milk honey pedicure. She also had her legs waxed and got a Brazilian wax.

Dee Dee got pampered as well that morning. After Taylor made her shake and scream, she cooked breakfast for her and served it to Dee Dee in bed. While she ate bacon and eggs and sipped coffee, Taylor apologized for pressuring her.

"I really don't want to stop seeing you," she said, and she promised to be more understanding that Dee Dee wasn't ready for the type of relationship Taylor wanted. "Maybe we can try again?"

"I'm not ready to stop seeing you either. But let's take it slow," Dee Dee said because it didn't make sense to cut her loose until she found a suitable replacement.

And after Taylor treated her to a pulse-pounding orgasm in the shower, Dee Dee went home, and she was surprised to find that nobody was home. She looked in the kitchen, and then she called Shemika's cell.

"Hello."

"Hey, Mika."

"Hey."

"I just got home and nobody's here. Where you at?"

"I'm at The Ridiculous Bagel. You want me to order you something?"

"Yeah, you know what I like. I'll be up there in a few."

"See you when you get here."

Dee Dee ended her call and left the house. When she went outside and turned around after locking the door, she saw a black Chevrolet Express work van parked in front of the house that wasn't there when she came in. As she got closer, the double doors of the van swung open. Two masked men jumped out and grabbed Dee Dee. One quickly covered her mouth with a handkerchief soaked in chloroform, and she was unconscious seconds later.

After pampering herself, Elontra was feeling amazing when she came out of CV Nail and Spa. She walked to her car, thinking about calling Pearson but knowing that he said that he had to make a run with CK. She had just about reached her car when a black Chevrolet Express work van pulled up alongside her.

Suddenly, the double doors of the van swung open, and two masked men jumped out. One grabbed her, and as it was with Dee Dee, the other covered her mouth with a chloroform-soaked handkerchief and put Elontra in the van unconscious.

At The Ridiculous Bagel, Shemika had finished her Ridiculous Burrito, and Dee Dee still hadn't arrived. She had called her when the food arrived and again when the server refilled her coffee. She got no answer to either call and simply assumed that Dee Dee had changed her mind about coming to join her. She got Dee Dee's food to-go and paid the check. Shemika left there, taking out her cell phone as she walked.

"Hey, Dee, what happened to you? Anyway, I got your food to-go, and I'm on my way home," she said and was about to hang up the phone when the black Chevrolet Express work van pulled up alongside of her and the double doors swung open. Two masked men jumped out.

"Not again," she said as one grabbed her and covered her mouth with chloroform. They put her in the van, and she heard the doors close before she was unconscious.

When Shemika opened her eyes, she found herself stretched out on the floor and in a small room with no windows. As it was the last time she was taken against her will, Shemika didn't know how long she'd been in that room, and it was a while before she heard the door open and a man came into the room.

"On your feet," he commanded.

Shemika got up and walked out of the room.

"Walk."

As he walked alongside her, two things stood out right away. She wasn't masked, and the man walking beside her wasn't wearing one either. She was wondering if that meant that they planned to kill her when the man stopped and opened a door.

"Get in there," he said and gave her a little shove in the back so she stumbled into the room.

"Mika," Elontra said, and she bounced up and hugged Shemika. "Are you all right?"

"I'm all right," Shemika said as the door closed, and she looked around the room. The table, chairs, and big mirror on the wall caused her to assume that they were in some type of interrogation room.

"Where'd they take you?"

"I was having breakfast at The Ridiculous Bagel."

"They got me at the nail salon. I guess Milica Ibrahimovic knows we stole her money."

"I think so."

"You hear from Dee Dee?"

Shemika nodded and sat down at the table. "I think they got her, too. She was supposed to meet me at The Ridiculous Bagel, but she never made it."

"I hope she's all right," Elontra said and sat at the table next to Shemika.

In another part of the building, Dee Dee opened her eyes, lifted her head from the table, and looked around. She knew from experience that she was in an interrogation room. She got up, walked to the mirror, and banged on the glass.

"I'm awake now. So let's get to it," she said and banged on the mirror again.

A few seconds later the door opened, and a man walked in. "Let's go," he said, and he escorted Dee Dee down a long hallway and up a flight of stairs before stopping at a room and opening the door. "In you go," he said and shoved her into the room, laughing as he closed the door.

"Muthafucka," she said as she stumbled into the room.

"Dee Dee!" Elontra and Shemika shouted, glad to see her and that, for the time being, she was safe. They got up from the table and rushed to hug her.

"You all right?" Shemika asked.

"I'm okay. What's going on?"

"We think Mika's girl—"

"She is not my girl!"

"We think Milica Ibrahimovic knows that we took her money and now she wants it back," Elontra said as they sat down at the table.

"And that is where you'd be wrong, Elontra," a female voice came through the speakers in the room.

"I know that voice," Dee Dee said and tried to remember where she knew it from.

"Demeris Dennison, Elontra Montgomery, and Shemika Frazier. You ladies are in a lot of trouble," the voice said, and seconds later the door opened.

The woman walked into the interrogation room, and now Dee Dee was sure that she knew exactly who the woman was, and she wasn't glad to see her.

"Hello, Dee Dee."

"You know her?" Elontra asked.

Dee Dee nodded her head. "This is FBI Special Agent Cassandra Harper—"

"FBI Special Agent in Charge now." The agent took a slight bow.

"The FBI agent who arrested me."

"That's right, ladies." Harper sat down at the table. "I'm Special Agent in Charge Harper with the FBI, and I want to welcome you to the Dog Team. This is my unit." She paused and looked around the interrogation room and at the three unimpressed faces before her. "You see, I believed that the best qualified people to catch criminals are other criminals. Therefore, this team is comprised entirely of former criminals I've caught over the years, arrested, and flipped to become productive members of this team."

Harper got up and stood in front of Dee Dee. "I don't know if you know this, but in her day, your friend here was one of the best hackers I've ever had the pleasure of pursuing," Harper said as she began walking around the table. "In fact, if it weren't for one of her partners getting greedy and going back to the slot machine one time too many, I would have never caught her." She was circling, taunting in her tone. "She was so good that I was sure—I mean, I might have gone so far as to bet my career—that as soon as she got out, she would go right back to doing what she did because she was so damn good at it. I knew your skills weren't up to par," Harper said, and tapped on the mirror, "so we gave you plenty of help." The door to the interrogation room opened, and Makaiden Hellström walked in.

He didn't go on the run after he famously managed to hack into the United States Pentagon's network. Special Agent Harper caught Kaiden and flipped him to her cause.

"Kaiden?" a shocked Dee Dee questioned because she couldn't believe what she was seeing. She instantly felt betrayed.

"Hi, Dee Dee," he said meekly and sat at the table across from her, barely able to make eye contact with her.

Harper continued, "Anything you needed to know to get back in the game I made available to you." She pointed at Kaiden. "You had a wealth of knowledge and information at your disposal."

Harper stopped in front of Dee Dee and put her hands on the table.

"And what did you do with that wealth of knowledge and information you had at your disposal?" She pointed at Elontra and Shemika. "You start robbing banks with Lucy and Ethel here."

It was then that Harper's phone rang, and she looked at the display. "Excuse me, I have to take this." She started to walk away. "But don't go anywhere. This is just starting to get good."

When she left the interrogation room, Dee Dee looked at Kaiden. "FBI agent, huh?"

"Yeah," he said and dropped his head a little.

"So I was just an assignment to you, huh?"

"At first. I mean, it started out that way. It's just like Harper said. I was assigned to help you get back in the game."

"To set me up."

"Yes." He leaned forward. "But you were . . . you were you, and I began really enjoying you and spending time with you, and I think you know it became more than that," Kaiden said as Harper came back into the room.

"Sorry about that. Now where was I? Oh, yeah." She raised one finger in the air. "You, flydeedee, one of the best hackers I've ever gone after, you start robbing banks with Lucy and Ethel there." Harper shook her head and resumed circling the table. "What a waste of talent." She stopped in front of Shemika. "And then you go and get yourself involved with Milica Ibrahimovic. We have the prototype by the way. And Ibrahimovic." She glanced at her watch. "Right about now she's on her way to Europe, where Interpol agents are waiting to take her into custody." She smiled. "Thank you three very much for your assistance in taking her into custody."

"You're welcome," Shemika said.

Harper resumed her walk. "So where does that leave us? Bank robbery is a federal crime, punishable by up to twenty years in prison." She stopped in front of Dee Dee. "Add on federal wire fraud charges and you're looking at a lot of time, Dee Dee." Harper got the chair and dragged it next to Dee Dee. "But there is an alternative." She sat down.

"What's that?"

"Come work for me," she said, and Kaiden smiled and nodded. "I can show you the world that changed while you were inside, give you access to the latest technology, and we forget all about this bank robbery business." She paused. "Now normally I'd say take your time and think about it, but the bank robbery suits are in the hallway waiting to take the three of you into custody and charge you." Harper stood up. "So what's it gonna be: thirty years Fed time, or come and work for me?"

"What about them?" Dee Dee asked, pointing at Elontra and Shemika.

"I was getting to that. Elontra Montgomery and Shemika Frazier. You two are apparently pretty resourceful. Neither of you has a job. Ms. Frazier has never had a job. And yet you live in a four-bedroom house with a pool in the suburbs. I can use that type of resourcefulness. So I make the two of you the same offer. You come and work for me, or I let the bank robbery suits take you. What's it gonna be? Thirty years or work for me?"

"Hard pass," Dee Dee said. Elontra and Shemika nodded in agreement.

"Yeah," Elontra said and took Dee Dee's hand in solidarity.

Shemika took Elontra's hand. "Me too. I pass."

Both Harper and Kaiden looked shocked. He got up, walked toward the door, and opened it. He nodded sadly at Dee Dee and moved on. Harper observed the determined looks on their faces and exhaled.

"In that case," she said and walked toward the door, "you're free to go."

"What?" Dee Dee questioned.

"You're free to go. What I meant when I said that you three were resourceful is that other than an alleged vague statement that may or may not have been made to Agent

Hellström, the bureau has no actual evidence that you three were involved in any bank robbery. So you're free to go."

Dee Dee, Shemika, and Elontra looked at each other and stood up.

"But before you go, let me offer you a bit of advice. The bank robbery suits may not be in the hallway waiting to take you into custody and charge you." Harper raised her right hand to testify. "But trust me when I say the bureau is watching. You had a good run, but now it's over. Capisce?" Harper paused as another man came into the room. "Agent Mendes will take you home."

Dee Dee, Shemika, and Elontra started toward the door.

"And, Dee Dee, you need to understand that I am looking for flydeedee to make a comeback and go back to doing what she was great at, so behave yourself."

"I will. You will never hear from her again, Special Agent in Charge Harper," Dee Dee said as she walked past the agent. Shemika and Elontra followed her out.

"That was close," Elontra said softly as Agent Mendes escorted them out of the building.

"Too close," Dee Dee said. "I just knew we were going to jail for sure," she whispered on the way to the car.

"But we're not, so let's go home and try not to do this shit ever again," Shemika said.

Elontra took her hand. "Yeah."

Dee Dee took Elontra's hand. "We're done. End of story."

Coming soon

Coming for the Queen

Zari

Preview

She was born Queen Nefertiti Bosman, the second child of Richard and Tamera Bosman. Her brother, King Idris Bosman, was twelve years older than his baby sister. Her father, who was known on the streets as King Richard the First, had ruthlessly controlled a huge chunk of the Atlanta drug market for years. And when his son was old enough to understand, he began teaching him the business, and King quickly became just as ruthless as his father, if not more so.

However, when Queen was born, the doting father insisted that his precious baby girl would have no involvement whatsoever in his business. Therefore, she had a completely different upbringing from her brother. By the time she was born, there was no more battling for territory. They were on top and living the glamorous life. King and his family lived in a seven-bedroom house on two acres of land with a maid in Alpharetta, a city in northern Fulton County, part of the metro Atlanta area.

Tamera saw to it that Queen attended the best private schools and participated in a variety of after-school activities. She attended church regularly with her mother. Queen even spent a few years singing in the choir. She was a very social young lady with many friends, and when it came time to date, Queen was very popular with the boys.

Tamera made sure that her daughter had the best of everything, and although young Queen knew how her father and brother made their money, and her mother taught her what she needed to know to survive in that family, she was shielded from any involvement in their business.

That ended on her sixteenth birthday.

To celebrate her coming of age, her parents took her to Ray's at Killer Creek, a restaurant that featured the finest cuts of meat, the freshest seafood, and award-winning wines. Her brother, King, was late as usual for family functions, and King Richard got tired of waiting.

"One day that boy will learn the value of time." He picked up his glass. "Look at our beautiful baby girl. Not a girl anymore. You're becoming an amazing young woman."

"Thank you, Daddy."

"And that's all because of you."

"I can't take all the credit," she said modestly, but it was the truth.

"But you should because it all belongs to you," he said to Tamera just before two masked gunmen rushed into the restaurant with automatic weapons and began firing. King Richard grabbed his baby girl, and they hit the floor as the seemly endless onslaught of bullets rained over their heads. When the shooting finally stopped, King Richard looked at his daughter.

"You all right?" he said, pulling out his weapon.

"I'm okay."

He bounced to his feet and was about to rush to the door and go after the gunmen when he heard a gut-wrenching scream.

"No! Mommy, no!"

King Richard turned to see his lovely wife Tamera lying in a pool of her own blood.

"Oh, my God, no," King Richard said, and he dropped to his knees.

"Mommy!" Queen screamed while she cradled her mother in her arms. "Mommy!" she kept screaming.

"Get an ambulance!"

While someone called the first responders, King Richard held his wife and his daughter. Shortly thereafter, King arrived at the restaurant and saw his family.

"Oh, no."

When the ambulance arrived, the first responders did all they could, but they weren't able to save her. Tamera Bosman was laid to rest a week later.

During that time, Queen never said a word to her father. She blamed him for her mother's murder, and that silence between them lasted for five years. During those years, she attended and graduated from Howard University in Washington D.C., one of the most prestigious HBCUs in the country.

The next time she saw her father was on the day that Queen graduated. Naturally, she hadn't told him about nor did she invite him to the event, but King did. She was polite when she saw him after the ceremony, and the very proud father congratulated his daughter.

Therefore, she didn't object too strongly when he said, "I made dinner reservations," and began walking to the limo as if the past six years hadn't existed. Like time had healed the wound left by the loss of her mother.

It hadn't.

King and Queen looked at one another. "For me, please?" he said.

"Only for you, big brother. Only for you," she said, and he put his arm around her.

"I am so proud of you."

King Richard stopped when he noticed they weren't right behind him. "Y'all coming?" Despite his usual bravado, he knew the possibility did exist that she wasn't coming.

"Yeah, Pop, we're coming," King said, and they started for the limo.

The conversation over dinner focused on Queen and what she had accomplished being the first college graduate in their family.

"This is what you're mother and I always wanted for you." He got uncharacteristically misty. "She would be so proud of you."

"Thank you, Daddy," Queen said because she wanted to be polite. However, it made her mad, and what she wanted to say was something like, "I know she would have been proud of me. But she's not here to tell me because my mother took a bullet for you."

King took her hand. "I'm proud of you too, Queen." He kissed her hand.

"Thank you, King."

The polite conversation continued over dessert and cocktails, so when the limousine dropped off her father and brother at their hotel, Queen went in with them to chat in the lobby. That conversation, as all conversations between father and son did, quickly devolved into a conversation about the family business. As she sat listening, Queen remembered that she and her mother used to be privy to their conversations, and her mother would often offer her perspective. At times, her perspective was welcome, at times it wasn't, but it was always respected. However, it reminded her of her loss, so when her father began speaking about her returning to Atlanta and taking her place running the family's legitimate businesses now that she had graduated, Queen stood up and politely said good night.

"I told you not to bring it up," she heard King say as she walked away.

The following morning, she saw them to the airport, but she told them that she wasn't coming back to Atlanta. Her plan was to stay in D.C. and use the connections she'd made over the past four years to land a position on some congressional staff.

It was two years later that Queen received a call from her brother.

"Pop has liver cancer. The tumor is too large to be removed safely. The doctor says that he's got maybe a year with treatment, six months without treatment."

"I'm sorry."

"Come home, Queen."

"No."

"Why not?"

"I have a life here."

"I know I'm asking a lot, but I need you. So I'm asking. Come home, Queen," King requested, and when she refused and once again mentioned something about her future and working on a congressional staff, King had a question.

"How's that working out for you?"

In the past two years, Queen had had plenty of second and third interviews, but to that point, no one had hired her.

"Come home. I need my sister."

"Only for you, King."

Although he had treatment, five months later King Richard Jemore Bosman was laid to rest next to his wife Tamera in a grand ceremony. By that time, Queen had assumed her position at her brother's side. She was King's advisor. In that capacity, she dealt a lot with Bernard Golden, whom King called his hand. As the hand to King, Bernard was an advisor and managed the day to day running of their drug enterprise, dispensing discipline on King's behalf. In that role, he often found himself at odds with Queen, and the result was an adversarial and contentious relationship. It didn't matter to King because their sometimes wildly opposing viewpoints served him well.

It happened one night when Serena—the estranged wife of Milo Hawkins, one of their men—came to Ipanema, the nightclub their family owned, operated, and laundered their money through. She was beaten and wearing torn and bloody clothes. When King saw her, he demanded to know who did it.

"Milo did it, King. But please, don't kill him. It was my fault for not doin' what he say."

King had her rushed to the hospital, but Serena Hawkins died three days later of injuries sustained in the beating. After her funeral, King was walking to the limo with his men, and Bernard asked an angry King what he wanted done with Milo.

"Kill him," King replied.

Bernard turned to his best man, Branson Myers. "You heard the man."

Milo Hawkins was dead that same night. Three days later the police arrested Branson Myers for his murder. Facing twenty years in prison for voluntary manslaughter, Myers gave the prosecution what they wanted and agreed to testify that the murder was committed on the order of King Idris Bosman.

After a lengthy trial, he was found guilty of conspiracy to commit murder, which was punishable by not less than one year and no more than ten years of imprisonment. On the eve of his sentencing, King asked Queen and Bernard to join him to announce who would succeed him while he was in prison.

"They're going to sentence me to ten years in the morning—" he began.

"You don't know that," Queen said, still hoping for the best.

"Yes, I do, Queen." He took her hand. "Maybe not ten years. But it's just a matter of how much time the judge gives me. But I am going to prison for a long time." What he said next surprised both Queen and Bernard and would set the tone for their future. "And I need you to step up and run things while I'm gone."

Queen looked at Bernard and observed how his facial expression changed from shock to disappointment to anger. And then he turned and looked at Queen. She knew in that second that his anger was directed at her. King saw it too, and later that evening, he warned her that she would need to watch Bernard.

"Like my life depended on it."

As expected, the following morning, King was sentenced to ten years for conspiracy to commit murder and was remanded to the Georgia Diagnostic & Classification Prison in Jackson, Georgia.

It was two days later when Bernard made his move.

That evening, Queen was to attend a party at Ipanema for an album release party for Salomé Warner, a national recording artist who was signed to the record label that her father had invested in early on and she was now part owner of. Once she was dressed, Queen asked her bodyguard to bring the car around to the front of her Lithonia home.

"Yes, ma'am."

She was walking out the door when he started the car, and it exploded. The bomb blast knocked Queen off her feet. She lay there, watching her car burn, knowing that the bomb was intended for her, and she knew without having to be told that Bernard Golden was responsible for the attempt on her life. She vowed revenge. It was the following day that she got the footage from the security company clearly showing Bailey Reed, one of Bernard's loyal soldiers, planting the bomb.

"Find out where Bernard is," she ordered and was told that night both Bailey Reed and Bernard would be at a strip club called Passion.

Armed with a 9 mm, Queen entered Passion and moved quickly to the table where Reed and Bernard were being entertained by three of the club's finest. Queen walked up to the table.

"Queen," Bernard said as she raised her weapon and shot Bailey Reed twice in the head before she turned the gun at Bernard and fired.

Like the coward she'd always known him to be, Bernard ran toward the rear of Passion as Queen fired at him. One of her shots hit him in the shoulder as he ran and made it out the back door.

"Find him, but don't kill him," Queen said to her new bodyguard, Torin Peterson.

The effort to find Bernard was complicated by people within her organization taking sides. Some were loyal to Bernard and thought King made a mistake passing him over in favor of Queen, and some remained loyal to her.

However, it was a week later when Torin came into the room and whispered in Queen's ear. "We caught Wolf and Ziggy," he informed her. They were two more of Bernard's top people.

"Where are they?"

"Tied up in the storage room at Ipanema."

When Queen arrived, three of Wolf's men were dead. Wolf was on his knees with a gun pointed at his head, and Ziggy was tied to a chair and taking a beating from King's longtime enforcer, Quentin Rivers. Shaqkena Lincoln, who most people simply called Assassin, was there as well.

Queen watched as Rivers pummeled Ziggy with hard punches from his gloved hands and asked him questions that he refused to answer.

"Where's Bernard?" he asked repeatedly, and Ziggy said nothing.

"This is getting us nowhere."

Queen uncrossed her legs, stood up, and ran her hands down her body to smooth out the front of her Markarian Nicolette metallic floral midi dress. Then she pulled the gun out from her Valentino Garavani Rockstud grainy calfskin leather clutch and walked up to him.

Queen put the barrel to his temple. "You will tell me what I want to know. And you are going to tell me now."

"Fuck you, bitch."

"No, fuck you," she said and pulled the trigger. She walked over to Wolf. "Get him on his feet," Queen ordered.

When Rivers and Torin jerked him up and tied him to a chair, she put the gun to his head.

"Now do you want to tell me what I want to know and stay alive, or do you want to be dead like Ziggy?"

"He's hiding at Aurora Barlowe's house."

"You should have told me that when I asked you the first time," Queen said, raising the weapon, and she shot Wolf twice in the head. She kicked Wolf's body out of the chair. "We're done here."

"Yeah, Queen," Shaqkena said, looking back at the two bodies on the floor. "We most certainly are done here."

Queen looked at her dress and noticed that there was blood on it. "Take me home, Torin. I got blood on my dress."